HER LAST DAY

OTHER TITLES BY
T.R. RAGAN

FAITH McMANN TRILOGY

Wrath
Furious
Outrage

LIZZY GARDNER SERIES

Abducted
Dead Weight
A Dark Mind
Obsessed
Almost Dead
Evil Never Dies

WRITING AS THERESA RAGAN

Return of the Rose
A Knight in Central Park
Taming Mad Max
Finding Kate Huntley
Having My Baby
An Offer He Can't Refuse
Here Comes the Bride
I Will Wait for You: A Novella
Dead Man Running

HER LAST DAY

A
JESSIE COLE
THRILLER

T.R. RAGAN

THOMAS & MERCER

Text copyright © 2017 Theresa Ragan

Published by Thomas & Mercer, Seattle

www.apub.com

Amazon, the Amazon logo, and Thomas & Mercer are trademarks of Amazon.com, Inc., or its affiliates.

ISBN-13: 9781542046060
ISBN-10: 1542046068

Cover design by Damon Freeman

Printed in the United States of America

To all the nurturing, hardworking, tolerant, creative, and courageous women in the world who know the value of listening but who aren't afraid to speak up when their voices need to be heard.
When things get tough, you get tougher.
This is for you.

PROLOGUE

Ten Years Ago

He awoke to the smell of burned flesh. The acrid fumes filled his lungs. The crackling roar of fire was deafening, the smoke thick.

He was trapped within the passenger seat of a car, hanging upside down, a mangled piece of plastic and metal pressed against his stomach. He couldn't see the bottom part of his legs, but he felt a fiery heat around his feet and ankles.

The car teetered back and forth, precariously, as if at any moment it might roll into the black abyss he saw through the broken windshield. Every muscle tensed. He had no idea how steep the fall would be if the vehicle lost its bearings.

His lungs burned.

He coughed, tried to breathe, then jerked backward when an arm fell limply through the flames and landed on the middle console. Charred fingers, skin melting from bone.

The driver was engulfed in flames.

They were both going to die if he didn't find a way out.

Trying to move his legs felt like wasted effort. They were pinned tight and wouldn't budge. He reached for the buckle, touched searing-hot metal, and let out a shattering scream. Excruciating pain ripped through his body, sending jolts of electricity pulsing through his veins. Yanking his hand back, he watched blisters immediately form on his fingertips as flames licked at his pants from beneath the crushed console.

He held his breath and began desperately banging his elbow against the glass, again and again. The window finally cracked, then shattered.

Throat and lungs parched, he leaned that way, gasping for breath.

Thick plumes of smoke escaped through the jagged hole he'd made and then disappeared into a dark, starless night.

The smell was haunting, the pain intense.

He was running out of time.

Again he grabbed for the buckle. He had no choice. He shouted obscenities through gritted teeth as his fingers clasped tightly to both sides of the metal, his thumb pushing the "Release" button. This time when he smelled burned flesh, he knew it was his.

Click.

He dropped, headfirst, to the ceiling. His right leg came loose, while the other remained pinned above him. Flames were everywhere now, red-hot tongues licking every part of him as he clutched the window frame spiked with shards of glass. Numb with pain, he held tight, every muscle straining as he used his freed leg to push off and yank his other leg free.

Scrambling, he pulled his way through the shattered window and out of the burning death trap. Broken glass ripped through his clothes and cut into flesh as he dragged himself from the wreckage. The pain shooting through his body was nothing compared to the blistering heat. No sooner had he pulled himself free than he was rolling downhill, past a boulder, arms thrashing, fingers grasping for a hold of grass and thorny weeds. Bam! He slammed into the trunk of a tree, his head jolting back with so much force he thought he might have broken his neck.

Seconds passed before he lifted his head, relieved to be away from the smoky wreckage at the top of the hill. He looked the other way. Had he rolled another five feet down the slope, he would have disappeared off a steep embankment and into a gully.

He lay still on grass and dirt, drinking in fresh, cool air as he stared back at the flames that still hissed and popped, sending sparks into the air.

The smell of gas made him think of the driver. Was it too late for the driver to escape?

On his belly, he clawed at the dirt, making his way back up the hill.

With only one good leg, he made it just a few feet before an explosion left his ears ringing. The car burst into flames, sending debris into the sky. He ducked at the sight of metal coming at him. A car door flew past and nearly took off the top of his skull.

A loud, prolonged squeak coming from the wreckage prompted him to lift his head in time to watch the burning metal slowly tilt his way.

Shit!

A hulk of burning rubber and metal came crashing down the hill after him. Putting his weight into his knees, he lunged for the nearest boulder, plastered his body flat into dirt and grass, and waited for the flaming mass to sweep him to his death.

The earth rumbled beneath him. The air was hot, the smell haunting. A whoosh of movement stirred the air above as the mass swept overhead. Another explosion erupted, creating a wall of heat behind him. He pried his face from the dirt and looked down at the wreckage now wrapped around the tree he'd left only moments ago. Whoever had been inside the car could not have survived.

He used his forearms to push himself over so that he was lying on his back, staring up at a dark sky. The kaleidoscope of pain arising from cuts and bruises, broken bones, and blistering skin stopped him from moving again.

Just as well.

He needed to shut his eyes, if only for a moment, before he attempted to claw his way back up the hill. It felt good to close his eyes, even peaceful despite the fire burning a few feet away—a blaze that now sounded like the crackling flames you might hear coming from a fire pit at a campground.

He wondered about the driver then. Was it a he or she? And why didn't he know? Where had they been going? Each question brought another, but he drew a blank when it came to the answers.

The thing that worried him most, though, had nothing to do with the driver and everything to do with himself.

Dizzy and short of breath, he realized he had no memory of where he'd come from. He didn't know if he was single or married. No recollection of any children, friends, or family.

Who was he?

ONE

Jessie Cole, private investigator, had been detained inside a small room at the Sacramento Police Department for thirty minutes now as Detective Aaron Roth lectured her. Another police officer stood in the corner.

She zeroed in on Detective Roth's mouth as he talked. It was a habit she couldn't seem to break. In grammar school she'd had a friend who was deaf. Twice a week Jessie had attended speech-reading class with her, not only for fun but because they were inseparable. She also knew American Sign Language (ASL). In eighth grade her friend had moved away, but Jessie never lost her ability to read lips or sign.

In his midforties, Aaron Roth was five foot eleven and had a cleanly shaved head and a thick mustache. As he rambled on—lecturing, reading her rights—she thought about the first time she'd met the detective ten years ago. The eagerness she remembered seeing in his eyes appeared to have been replaced with annoyance and resentment.

"Did you hear a word I just said?" he asked.

"Yes."

His brows drew together. "And?"

Although his mustache covered half his upper lip, she could still see that his lips were pale. Redness in color was said to indicate better cardiorespiratory fitness but also meant a higher estrogen level. She couldn't remember where she'd read that useless tidbit, but it had something to do with being able to distinguish male from female based solely on the lips. She glanced at the clock. "I need to go, Detective. I was supposed to pick up my niece ten minutes ago."

"Oh," he said, angling his head just so. "You have to go? Well, that's too bad." He jabbed a finger in the air. "You're a piece of work. You shot someone. And not for the first time. You're not going anywhere."

A shiver of anxiety crawled up her spine. "I did nothing wrong," she said, stiffening. "I understand the laws regarding use of deadly force. I was defending myself and others against a forcible and atrocious crime."

"And yet after everything you went through a few years ago, you shot the man anyhow."

"My life was in imminent danger." She tapped a finger on the table for emphasis. "I saved 'innocent bystanders from unavoidable danger of death.'"

The detective frowned. Clearly he was not impressed by the fact she'd memorized parts of the California laws concerning self-defense.

"There were people everywhere," she said, surprised by the desperation in her voice.

Sitting straight and tall, arms crossed, he nodded. "We're in the process of collecting evidence and talking to witnesses."

"You might be interested in watching this." She reached inside her backpack, pulled out a black box attached to a thin strap of Velcro, and placed it on the table between them.

Roth eyed it warily. "What is it?"

"It's the smallest, lightest GoPro on the market. Easy one-button control and waterproof."

Roth glanced at the other police officer in the room.

The big guy shrugged.

"Are you trying to tell me you taped the incident?" Roth asked her.

"That's exactly what I did," Jessie said. "Since all the hullabaloo the last time I was forced to use my weapon, I've been recording my daily activities whenever I'm working a case."

The detective lifted a brow. "Shooting and killing another person is against the law."

Her stomach roiled. "Is he dead?"

"Critical condition."

She tried not to let him see her relief. "This was a simple case of self-defense. He fired at me first. Twice. In a public place."

The door came open.

It was Andriana Iudice, Jessie's good friend and lawyer. Thank God.

Andriana's vibrant reddish hair, rows of tightly spun ringlets, had been pushed away from her face with bobby pins that matched her funky platform shoes adorned with giant sunflowers. Her face and neck were a splotchy red from the heat, which had reached 102 degrees before Jessie had been shoved into the back seat of a police cruiser and brought to the station.

Andriana placed her soft leather briefcase on the table and pulled out a chair next to Jessie. After she was seated, she said, "You didn't tell them anything, did you?"

"She's been here for thirty minutes," Detective Roth said matter-of-factly. "What do you think?"

Andriana asked the detective for a moment alone with her client. His exhale came out sounding like a groan as he pushed himself to his feet and left the room, the second officer on his heels.

Jessie's hands shook as she watched the two men leave. She did her best to hold herself together, but the truth was she was a wreck. She'd shot a man, possibly killed him. It had all happened so fast. Instinct hadn't been the only reason she'd pulled her weapon and fired. Less than ten feet away, children had been playing when Koontz pulled out his gun and shot at her.

"What happened in the park?" Andriana asked as soon as the door clicked shut.

Jessie took a breath. "I was hired by a woman, Adelind Rain, to watch Parker Koontz, a man she believes has been stalking her for months."

"Is it true? Has he been stalking her?"

"Yes. I've been watching him for over a week, and every afternoon he leaves his office to make his way to the bank where Adelind's employed. He stands on the street corner and waits for her to go to lunch. I've never seen him approach her, but he never takes his gaze off her. After work he goes home to change his clothes, eat, whatever. Around nine p.m. he's back at Adelind's house peering through the windows."

"So he hasn't actually threatened her in any way?"

"No. He hasn't touched her or left any goodies at her door, if that's what you mean. I've got a few pictures of him near the window, but the high bushes have made it difficult to get a clear picture. But she's scared and I don't blame her. She wants to get a restraining order, but she needs proof he's dangerous."

"What does he do for a living?"

"He's an attorney at Roche and Koontz downtown."

"Interesting."

"Today I followed him through Capitol Park. After he walked through the rose garden, he stopped and turned my way. Before I could figure out what he was up to, he pulled out a gun and fired two shots at me."

"Was anyone else hurt?"

"Not that I'm aware of. It was lunchtime. People were screaming and running. It was total chaos. When he lifted his gun for the third time, I shot him before he could fire."

"Did you kill him?"

"He was still alive when they wheeled him away on the stretcher. According to Roth, he's in critical condition." Jessie's shook her head in disbelief. "I might have killed him."

"You did what you had to," Andriana told her.

The door came open, which concluded their conversation.

Detective Roth and the other officer stepped inside. "Looks like we're going to have to lock her up," Roth said.

Andriana shot to her feet. "On what grounds?"

"We have a witness who has stated that you were the initial aggressor. The DA's office needs more time before they agree to your release. Besides," Roth said to Andriana, "Jessie wasn't at home. It was broad daylight, and she wasn't exactly protecting her family, now was she?"

Jessie's heart dropped to her stomach.

"She doesn't have a reckless disregard for human life," Andriana shot back, "and she was defending others."

"Blanks," Roth said matter-of-factly. "Koontz was shooting blanks."

The blood rushed from Jessie's face.

Detective Roth signaled for the officer to cuff her and take her away.

"Is that really necessary?" Andriana asked.

Roth ignored her.

Jessie had been butting heads with Detective Roth for years, but she never thought he'd stoop this low. Jessie reached for her bag, but Roth ordered her to leave her things. They would take inventory of her belongings, and everything would be returned if and when she was released.

"You can't do this," Jessie appealed to Roth as she was cuffed. "I was protecting every person in that park today." She turned back to face Andriana. "I told Olivia I would pick her up today. She'll be worried." That was an understatement. Her niece, Olivia, had been four years old when her mother disappeared and Jessie became her guardian. Since then, Olivia worried about everything and everyone.

"I'll get her for you, Jess," a male voice said.

All eyes landed on the detective standing at the door.

Colin Grayson.

She and Colin had a past—a sordid past that began with long nights of conversation followed by steamy sex—and ended three months later with a surprise visit from his wife.

Colin's dark hair had grown, and his hair swept over one eye. He wore jeans and a T-shirt, which told her he was working undercover. His disheveled, rugged look only added to his appeal. Jessie had met him ten years ago—the same day she'd met Detective Roth. Colin had been a rookie cop at the time her sister went missing. He was the guy assigned to listen to her story and fill out a missing person's report. Not only did he turn out to be a good listener, he'd been extremely supportive, a shoulder to cry on.

Colin had been up front with her, telling her he was separated from his wife and in the process of getting divorce, but when his wife showed up on her doorstep to let Colin know she was pregnant, they were both blindsided.

For the next week or so, she and Colin talked and cried until finally they both agreed it was best if Colin went back to his wife and tried to make it work. They lasted five years before calling it quits for good.

As fate would have it, nine months ago Jessie ran into Colin at a local grocery store, and once again they became fast friends—platonic friends this time, friends without benefits—until six weeks ago when Colin told her he was falling in love with her and wanted to take their friendship to the next level. He thought it was time they started dating. But Jessie wasn't ready for anything more, and she hadn't seen him since.

"Time to go," Roth told Jessie, yanking her back into the harsh reality that she would be spending some time behind bars.

She looked at Colin. "Are you sure you don't mind picking up Olivia?"

"It's not a problem."

"What if they keep me for more than a few hours?" she asked as she was escorted out the door.

Colin looked at Roth. "How's it looking?"

"Could be hours. Could be days," Roth said. "You know how these things work."

"Oh, come on," Andriana cut in.

"If they keep me overnight," Jessie told Colin, "could you—"

"I'll make sure Olivia's taken care of," he said.

Two

He pushed the dresser to his right, then leaned over and pulled open the wooden hatch. A hot wave of stench crept out of the dark space below. He turned away and coughed before he grabbed his backpack and slipped his arms through the shoulder straps. He then made his way down the stairs and into the underground room his father had built beneath their house before he was born.

The room was a one-thousand-square-foot space consisting of two jail cells made of crude metal bars and another enclosed cell with a slot in the middle of the door that made it easy to feed his prisoner without opening the door.

He waved his hands around to get the air circulating before lighting the oil lamps hanging from metal hooks on the wall. The space had been reinforced with concrete, which had created condensation. It was dank and damp, and the walls were covered with mildew. A large crack ran through the back wall and across a section of cement flooring. At times he wondered if these walls would cave in and the living space above might collapse on top of him. If his father had been smart, he would have used another inch or two of concrete and thicker rebar.

Too late now.

He opened the metal door. The man inside had a long, scraggly gray beard. He'd named him Dog. At the moment, Dog was crouched in the corner of the small space muttering to himself. In the cell next to Dog was Garrett Ramsey, a thirty-five-year-old man who looked closer to fifty. Garrett was rolled into a tight ball on the hard ground and appeared to be sleeping. As he did for all the animals on the farm, he kept the ground littered with straw.

He walked past Garrett's cell and made his way to the stool in front of the third cell and took a seat. He removed his backpack, retrieved a tin can of sardines and a water bottle from his bag, and placed it all on the floor next to his feet. "Are you thirsty?"

She nodded.

He picked up the bottled water, slid his arm through the metal slats, and placed it inside her cell.

She licked her lips, but apparently her wariness of him overrode all else.

Next he pulled a pen and notebook from his bag. "What's your name?"

He already knew it was Erin Hayes. When he'd found her on the side of the road with a flat tire, she'd accepted a ride, which he'd found surprising. Getting someone inside the car was usually the most difficult part. After drugging her and bringing her to the farmhouse, he'd looked through her purse. Her ID had provided her name and address. A search through social media had done the rest. But he would ask her questions anyhow because conducting interviews was half the fun. He thought of it as the beginning of the end.

When he realized she hadn't answered him, he looked up from his notebook. "Are you having a hard time finding your voice?"

Another nod of her head.

The drugs were probably still wearing off. "I'll give you a few more minutes, but that's all, okay?"

He'd stripped her of her clothes before tossing her in the cell. She was sitting in the corner on a pile of straw. Every time he met her gaze, she looked away. He didn't like that.

"Before I begin the questioning, it's probably a good idea if I lay down a few ground rules. To start, I insist you call me 'Sir' at all times. If I ask you a question and you don't answer right away, I consider that to be rude, and you would have to be disciplined. Punishment is not negotiable and comes in many forms." He sighed as he thought about what to say next. "To give you an idea of what I'm talking about, should you make me angry, I might decide to electrocute you. Have you ever been electrocuted?"

She shook her head, the fear in her eyes making his heart beat faster.

"I could find the pliers and yank out one of your teeth instead. It all depends on my mood." He chuckled as he remembered the woman named Jill who'd been forced to eat soup he'd made out of vile things he'd collected. "I could make you consume large quantities of something hideously distasteful." He lifted an eyebrow. "There has been a time or two where I've allowed a prisoner to pick their own poison, so to speak. See? You just never know."

He stared at her, unblinking.

When she saw him staring, she averted her gaze again.

"No. No. No. Look at me. Never look away when I'm talking to you. I hate that."

She did as he said.

"Okay," he said. "What's your name?"

"Erin."

Good for her. She was off to a good start.

"In what city do you live?"

"Elk Grove."

"What is the name of your best friend?"

"Amber."

"How old are you?"

"Eighteen."

"Do you have a boyfriend?"

"Yes."

Every time she answered a question, he tossed a sardine her way, sometimes smacking her in the face or arm. She didn't bother eating them as he wrote her answers down.

She answered every question until he asked, "What are you most afraid of?"

That was when she broke down and started to cry.

Damn. For some ridiculous reason, he'd thought she would be different from the others. Maybe it was because she'd seemed so comfortable with jumping into the passenger seat of his car and carrying on a conversation with a complete stranger. He riffled through his backpack and pulled out his Taser.

"Snakes," she said when she saw what he had in his possession. "And you. I'm afraid of you."

He made a sad face. "Too late."

He dug into his pants pocket for a key, walked over to Garrett's cell, and unlocked the door. Garrett hadn't been eating much lately, and his ribs were beginning to show.

For the most part he took the clothes from his prisoners so they couldn't hide anything in their pockets or use the fabric to hang themselves. Plus, he liked to demean them and make them feel vulnerable.

Hovering over Garrett, trying to see if he was breathing, he kicked him in the shin. When that failed to get him moving, he wondered if Garrett was dead. That would be a shame. The man had lasted longer than most. He'd been there for months, and his survival instincts were strong. When he leaned over to check his pulse, Garrett's eyes opened. "Kill me. Please. I'm ready to die."

"Don't be so dramatic. Get up. I have someone I want you to meet." Garrett's readiness to die upset him. What made so many of his victims want to give up so easily? He'd endured far worse torture than this. And in the end, it had made him stronger.

Garrett pushed himself up from the ground, his arms shaky, his legs wobbling. The Taser kept his captor in line as he nudged him out the door.

Erin didn't move a muscle when he unlocked her door and shoved Garrett inside. Once the door to the cell was secure, he sat back down on his stool and watched them, hoping they would interact on their own.

Garrett was usually a social being. He was a professor at Davis. His wife had been one of his students. They had adored each other. But then after only four weeks in captivity, Garrett had misbehaved by drowning her in the bucket of water he'd placed in the cell so they could wash up. He'd said he only wanted to put her out of her misery. Couldn't bear to see her hurt. Garrett had ruined all his fun, and he'd paid dearly for his mistake.

"My name is Garrett Ramsey," his prisoner told the girl as he crawled toward her. "Do whatever he tells you to do or—"

"Stay away from me!" She jumped to her feet, her palms covering her small breasts as she kicked her legs to keep Garrett from coming any closer.

He watched them both, wondering what would happen next. But patience was a virtue, and a trait he did not possess. "Kiss her!"

Erin's back was up against the cement wall. "Stay away from me!"

Garrett looked over at him.

"You know what to do."

Garrett crawled back to the cell door, pulled himself to his feet, and waited for his master to hand him a weapon. He knew the drill.

He slid the Taser into Garrett's hand. "Her name is Erin. I want you to Taser her, and then I want you to kiss her while she writhes on the ground. Make it a good one, Garrett. Pretend it's your wife you're kissing."

Garrett had been beaten and abused for so long, he no longer questioned his master's authority.

Garrett held up the Taser, flipped the switch, and jabbed her in the shoulder.

Erin screamed. Arms flailing, she dropped to the ground. One quick jolt was all it took. As she thrashed around on the floor, Garrett crawled on top of her and brought her mouth to his.

A thump and a howl coming from the other cell made him groan. He walked over to Dog's cell and banged a fist against the door. "Knock it off in there."

More wailing sounded, forcing him to pull out his keys. Before he had a chance to step inside, his phone buzzed, reminding him it was time to feed the animals. Garrett and Erin forgotten, he relocked Dog's cell, then walked back to where he'd been sitting on the stool and began gathering his things. A flash of movement caught his eyes. He looked up, surprised to see Erin standing so close.

Her arm shot out through the space between the bars.

Zap.

The metal tongs pricked the side of his neck. The pain was surprisingly shocking, sending him to the floor. On his side, teeth clenched, he saw her reach for his bag and then struggle to pull it into her cell. There was nothing he could do but watch her dump its contents onto the ground, her fingers clawing through his things.

As Garrett cowered in the corner, the palms of his hands clutching both sides of his head, the girl continued her search, determined to find something that wasn't there.

He'd been right about her. She was feisty and brave. And he couldn't wait to discipline her.

THREE

As Colin walked to his car, he inwardly scolded himself for volunteering his services.

His reasoning was twofold.

Number one, he was busy working the Heartless Killer case. The serial killer had been leaving a trail of fear throughout the city of Sacramento for six years now. Every morning before school, parents warned their children to be aware of their surroundings and never go anywhere alone. Even the wariest residents were unnerved.

The FBI profiler who had been brought in to help said the Heartless Killer was a smart, single white male, a loner between the age of twenty-nine and thirty-six who came from a troubled family and had most likely suffered significant abuse. The list went on.

Traits of many serial killers.

Nothing new.

Based on his findings, Colin would add that this particular single white male killer was fearless. He went into people's homes and took victims from public places in broad daylight without being detected. That was *not* something a lot of serial killers did. When it came to his victims, the killer didn't seem to care about gender or age. He wasn't a sexual predator, but like most serial killers, he enjoyed power and control.

Twelve months ago, the last time the killer had struck, every detective in investigations had been pulled in to work the case. Whenever that happened, they worked twelve-hour shifts until the leads dried up, which was where they were right now. Although he'd gotten six hours of sleep last night, the longest in a while, Colin was surviving on fumes.

The second reason he shouldn't be running after Olivia was because he'd vowed to stay away from Jessie after he'd made the mistake of suggesting they turn things up a notch and start dating. Jessie had not hesitated to tell him she wasn't ready to be anything more than friends.

He knew dating a cop wasn't easy, since cops tended to be inquisitive, worked long hours, and always had a target on their backs, but Jessie came with her own set of difficulties. She was a complicated woman who could be stubborn and much too serious.

And yet, despite it all, he loved her.

She was compassionate to a fault. She was patient and understanding, and his daughter, Piper, adored her. Jessie was everything he wanted in a relationship. And yet the moment she'd told him she wasn't ready for anything more, he'd walked out of her life. He'd thought it would be easier for both of them, but now he knew better. He missed her.

He used his key fob to hit the "Unlock" button from a few feet away. Then he pulled out his cell phone and called Olivia. No answer.

As he pulled out of the parking lot, his phone rang. It was his sister, Emma. He hit the "Talk" button on the console. "Hey, sis. What's going on?"

"Where are you?"

"On my way to pick up Olivia from school."

"Olivia Cole? I thought you and Jessie were finished."

"It's a long story."

"I bet."

He said nothing. Merely waited for her to state the reason for her call.

"Kimberly is getting married," she finally blurted.

"Interesting."

"Why is that?"

"I saw her two days ago when I was picking up Piper, and she didn't say a word. But good for her. I hope she and Nate are very happy."

"His name is Niles."

"And you called me to tell me this, why?"

"Because she asked me to be her maid of honor."

The news shouldn't have surprised him or bothered him in any way, but it did. It didn't matter that he and Kimberly had been divorced longer than they'd been married. His ex-wife had a way of making sure he always knew what she was up to, always finding a way to update him with every detail of her life, making sure he knew she was doing just fine without him. Asking his sister to be in her wedding would only help her cause. It wasn't enough that his nine-year-old daughter rattled off a long list of Nate's glowing attributes every time Colin had her for the weekend. "I didn't know the two of you were that close," Colin said. "Isn't Nate the guy she met at Starbucks?"

"His name is Niles, but what's your point?"

"They've known each other for what, a couple of months?"

"Two years this Friday."

Wow. Time really did fly. The truth was he didn't like Nate. There was something about the guy that hit every nerve. He didn't like the idea of Nate being a father figure to Piper.

"Are you still there?"

"Yeah, still here."

"So, do you mind?"

Before he could figure out what Emma was talking about, his phone buzzed. "I've got another call coming in. Sorry. Gotta go."

"Call me later," she said.

"Will do." He picked up the incoming call from Levi Hooper, forensics, and said, "Detective Grayson."

"More bad news," Levi said. "Blood and hair samples from the homicide in Citrus Heights came back. We have nothing to tie this murder to the Heartless Killer."

While Colin let that sink in, Levi asked, "What's next?"

"Briefing first thing tomorrow morning."

"Okay, I'll make sure everyone's there. See you then."

Colin drove up to the curb in front of C. K. McClatchy High School, climbed out of the car, and took a look around. Then he called Olivia's number for the second time. Still no answer.

A few kids lingered here and there, mostly stragglers waiting to be picked up. Inside the front office, there was an elderly woman wrapping things up for the day. The school day had ended twenty-five minutes ago, and she hadn't seen Olivia. Colin figured Olivia had either gotten a ride home or had decided to walk.

But since he was at the school, he made the rounds and checked the library, the cafeteria, and the football field before he headed back to his car.

By the time he merged onto Freeport Boulevard, he was concerned. Where the hell was Olivia, and why wasn't she answering her phone? Olivia was fourteen, responsible for a kid her age, but that wasn't making him feel better.

And what about Jessie? He didn't like the idea of her being locked up. Although she was proud of her by-the-book methodology of investigative work, she had a tendency to act too quickly, seldom taking enough time to think things through. She'd looked pale sitting in the holding room. She'd looked hollow-cheeked, too, as if she hadn't been eating enough or getting much sleep. Seeing her worn down like that made his heart ache.

Jessie. He'd fallen in love with her the moment he'd laid eyes on her ten years ago. And then his soon-to-be ex-wife showed up, and that was it. Jessie told him to get out of her life and go back to his wife, where he belonged. So that was what he did. Five months later Piper was born. He loved his daughter, and for that reason he'd done everything he could to make it work, but the next five years had been just that . . . work. No laughter, no playful banter, no long conversations about dreams and goals.

His thoughts were cut off when he spotted a group of people huddled together. As he slowed, he got a glimpse of a very familiar fourteen-year-old girl sitting on the sidewalk with five or six people hovering around her.

Olivia.

His heart raced as he pulled to the side of the road, jumped out of his vehicle, and ran toward her. Why was she on the ground? The thought that she might have been injured made his insides turn. He cut between the people, relieved to see that Olivia was okay. It was the dog in her arms that was injured. "Olivia," he called.

She looked at him. She'd been crying. Mascara she wasn't allowed to wear streamed down both sides of her face. "It was a hit-and-run," she said, her voice shaky. "I think he's dying."

Colin looked at the people standing around. "Does anyone know who the dog belongs to?"

"There's no collar," a woman said.

Colin kneeled down for a better look. The dog was medium size, part bulldog or maybe boxer. There wasn't a lot of blood, but it didn't look good. The animal's breathing was shallow, its ribs well defined, which told him the dog had been living on the streets for a while.

"We have to save him," Olivia said.

Colin exhaled, told her not to move, and then jogged back to his car, where he grabbed a blanket from the trunk and spread it across the back seat. He hurried back to Olivia and scooped the dog out of her arms. Once she and the dog were situated, Colin drove to the closest veterinary hospital.

After the dog was taken to a back room to be examined, Colin made a few phone calls. Olivia sat in the lobby, her foot tapping nervously against the floor. More than an hour later, the veterinarian, a tall woman wearing green scrubs, walked toward them. Her expression was somber, making it difficult to read the situation. "Could I talk to you alone for a minute?" she asked Colin.

He looked at Olivia. She'd been through a lot in her young life. He'd spent enough time with her to know she was a straight shooter, and she appreciated that quality in others. No reason to keep anything from her. "Go ahead," he said. "You can talk to both of us."

"The good news is he's been stabilized."

"And the bad?"

"He has a broken leg that will require surgery."

Ah. Now he understood why she'd wanted to talk to him in private. Surgery wasn't cheap, and most teenagers, like Olivia, didn't make decisions based on money. It was all about emotions in cases like this.

The doctor tipped her chin. "Laura will go over the details with you." She gestured toward the woman behind the counter.

After she walked away, Colin said, "I'll be right back. I'm going to go talk to Laura."

"You're going to tell them to do the surgery, right?" Olivia asked.

"I need to get some additional information first, okay?"

"I have nearly two hundred dollars in my savings account," she told him. "If you drive me to the bank, I can get it out for you."

"Why don't you wait outside? I'll be right there."

Ten minutes later Colin found Olivia sitting on the curb next to his car. "Get in," he said. "I'm taking you home."

She pushed herself to her feet. "Are they going to put him down? If they are, I want to be there with him when they do."

"He's being rolled into surgery as we speak."

"Seriously?"

He nodded.

She smiled as big as he'd ever seen, then ran over to him and wrapped her long, skinny arms around his waist and squeezed as hard as she could.

He'd missed the kid. "Okay, okay," he told her. "Don't get too excited. We'll have to put an ad in the paper and make sure he doesn't belong to someone, and then there's the matter of your aunt Jessie."

"Jessie won't mind. She's going to love Higgins."

"Higgins?"

"That's his name," Olivia said. "I always knew if I ever got a dog, I would name him or her Higgins. Have you seen the movie *Benji*? Adorable dog who always shows up in the nick of time to save the day?"

"I have a vague recollection. But what does any of that have to do with Higgins?"

"The dog who played the part of Benji," Olivia relayed as they both climbed into the car, "was actually a shelter dog named Higgins."

"Interesting." He buckled his seat belt and made sure she did the same.

"Do you think Higgins will make it?"

He paused to think about it. "Yeah, I do. He looked like a fighter. Tough times make for tough people . . . and dogs."

Four

It was a quarter past five when Ben Morrison left his workplace, a ten-thousand-square-foot cement-gray building that housed the *Sacramento Tribune*. He'd been working as a crime reporter there for twenty years, the first ten of which he had no recollection of, owing to a car accident that had left him with retrograde amnesia.

After the accident he'd had no memory of his sister or his deceased parents. But something beautiful *had* come from the tragedy. He'd fallen in love with and married the nurse who'd helped put him back together again. At his wife's insistence, he'd tried to reconnect with his sister over the years, but she and her husband had moved to Florida, and his phone calls went unanswered.

Today was another hot one. The air was thick and dry, sucking the moisture out of every living thing and making it a chore to breathe. It had been a long day, and he was eager to get home. As he approached his 1978 Ford Club Wagon, he heard a distant call for help and stopped to look around and listen.

There it was again. Was somebody in trouble?

He ran to the edge of the parking lot, where pavement merged with soil that sloped downward into a wooded area covered with brittle leaves.

Although he couldn't see any smoke, he could feel it burning his throat. He heard the crackle and snap of a fire, but he couldn't see anything unusual. His heart rate accelerated. "Is someone out there?"

No answer.

"Ben! Is there a problem?"

He turned to see his coworker Gavin Whitney rushing to his side. "What's going on?"

"Do you smell smoke?" Ben asked.

Gavin took a couple of sniffs. "No. I don't smell anything." He wiped his brow. "It's hot as hell out here, though. I bet we could fry an egg on the asphalt about now." He planted a hand on his hip. "If this heat wave lasts too much longer, people are going to start dropping like flies."

When Ben didn't respond, he added, "More people die from a heat wave than lightning, tornadoes, hurricanes, or floods."

Ben had a difficult time listening to anything but the hiss of the fire as it moved closer.

"I've gotta get going," Gavin said. "Are you sure you're okay?"

He wanted to grab Gavin's shoulders and shake him. Couldn't he hear the fire or smell the acrid smoke? When Ben looked back at Gavin, he imagined himself reaching into his briefcase for a hunting knife and plunging the blade into Gavin's chest.

It seemed real, and it all happened fast.

The look on Gavin's face when he realized he'd been stabbed made Ben wonder what exactly Gavin was experiencing. What did it feel like to be stabbed in the chest? Was there pain? Or did shock override all else? Definitely the latter, Ben thought as he watched Gavin stumble backward, leaving a trail of blood as he went.

Gavin's eyes widened as he looked at the knife protruding from his body. There was no sign of pain on his face, only a shuddering shock wave of surprise.

Ben's pulse rate spiked, and he blinked to clear his vision.

Suddenly Gavin was smiling and waving. "I'll see you tomorrow," he said in a cheerful voice. "Tell the family hello for me, will you? We've got to get the boys together again one of these days."

It took a second for Ben's foggy brain to clear. Gavin was fine. There was no knife protruding from his coworker's chest. No blood anywhere.

Ben looked down at the briefcase still clutched within his fingers. He no longer heard screams for help or the crackle of fire.

He sniffed the air. It was smoke-free.

Relief mixed with apprehension consumed him as he made his way to his car. Injuries from long ago made it feel as if his left leg were made of solid steel, heavy and awkward.

The knife in Gavin's chest, the blood, the screams . . . this wasn't the first gruesome scene he'd conjured over the past few months, but this one had certainly lasted the longest.

Breathe in. Breathe out.

That was what his therapist would tell him to do if he were still seeing her. Although he didn't like what had just transpired, he wasn't too worried. In his line of work, he'd seen it all. It wasn't the gory thoughts that concerned him, but the disorientation and lack of emotion that accompanied these random imaginings.

He unlocked the van and used the roll handle to pull himself in behind the wheel. Sweat trickled down both sides of his face as the engine roared to life. He drove out of the parking lot and merged onto Capitol Avenue. Forty minutes later, after stopping at the store to pick up a gallon of milk, he walked into the two-story house where he had lived for the past nine years with his wife and two kids. It was a quaint Cape Cod–style home at the end of a cul-de-sac in Citrus Heights. He set the milk on the wooden bench in the entryway and then headed for his bedroom upstairs so he could change his clothes.

"Ben, is that you?"

He made an about-face, grabbed the milk from the bench, and walked into the kitchen instead. His wife stood in front of the stove, making stir-fry. He gave Melony a peck on the cheek. She worked full-time as a trauma nurse at Mercy General, took care of the household and two children, and yet she always had a smile for him.

"Ben," she said when she noticed his shirt was soaked through, "you need to get rid of that old van and get something with air-conditioning. This is ridiculous."

"You know we can't afford a new car right now. Abigail is going to need braces soon, and we need to fix the fence out back." He sighed. "I'm going to go upstairs and change, and I'll be as good as new."

"Is your leg bothering you?" she asked, always perceptive.

"I'm fine."

When he returned, both Abigail and Sean were in the kitchen helping Melony set the table for dinner. Sean would be eight soon, and his face still lit up every evening when Ben arrived home from work. "Dad!" he said. "Can we ride bikes around the lake this weekend? We could skip rocks like last time."

"No," Abigail said in a tone that made her sound sixteen instead of nine. "Mom and Dad promised they would both come to my soccer game."

Sean frowned. "Soccer is boring."

"That's enough," Melony cut in. "Get the napkins, Sean."

Ben inwardly smiled. Every so often his coworkers asked him to join them for a beer after work, but he rarely said yes. He preferred to be home with his wife and kids. His nickname at the office was "Family Man," which suited him just fine.

After dinner and homework were finished for the night, Melony put the kids to bed while Ben washed the dishes and then made his way to the family room to wind down and watch a little television. He settled into his favorite recliner. As he clicked through the channels, the image of a young woman flashed across the screen.

He sat up for a better look.

His breath caught in his chest. Dark hair, mesmerizing green eyes, and a full mouth. He knew that face. Not once since his accident had he felt such an intense feeling of recognition. To this day he had no idea why he'd been in a stolen car with Vernon Doherty, a man with a long list of traffic offenses, including two DUIs.

According to the show's host, she had been twenty when she went missing ten years ago. He hit "Pause" so he could read the description of tonight's *Cold Case TV*. This particular episode had originally aired three years ago and was titled "The Runaway Sister."

He hit "Play" and listened closely as the host interviewed the missing woman's older sister, Jessie Cole.

Melony entered the room, and he raised his hand to stop her from speaking. She crossed her arms and waited him out. When it was over, he hit "Pause" again. "Sophie Cole," he said. "Does that name ring any bells?"

"No. Why?"

"I think I used to know her. There's something familiar about her."

"It's a cold case," Melony reminded him. "Was she from the area?"

He nodded. "Sacramento."

"Well, that explains it. You probably did a story on her at the time."

"I don't know." He rubbed the back of his neck. "I've been seeing things lately, Mel."

She took a seat next to him and rested a hand on his back. "What do you mean?"

"Today as I walked to my car after work, I smelled smoke and I heard screams rising above a crackling fire. When Gavin Whitney appeared and asked me if I was okay, I saw a knife plunged deep into his chest."

He looked squarely into Mel's eyes. "I saw every detail of Gavin's face when it happened. The shock. The horror. There was blood everywhere. It was as real to me as you sitting next to me right now."

Ben couldn't bring himself to tell her he was the one who had stabbed Gavin, mostly because the images had worried him—made him feel odd, confused—as if a part of him had actually enjoyed watching his coworker suffer. *No*, he quickly decided. It wasn't enjoyment he'd felt, but curiosity mixed with fascination.

"But there was no knife," Melony stated. "Gavin was fine, right? Is that what you're telling me?"

"Yes. Gavin is fine. There was no knife in his chest, no fire—no one was screaming. But I saw it all plain as day." He looked away, feeling suddenly exhausted, the end of the day hitting him hard.

"Your doctor told you this might happen," Melony said. "Do you remember? She said at any given time you might start to see things, disturbing images that could shock you, including flashbacks from the accident. The sound of the fire. The screams. It all makes sense."

Ben said nothing. She had no idea about all the random images he'd been seeing, or how often. Gruesome scenes of murder and mayhem, dead bodies, lifeless eyes, too much blood, always blood.

"Ben," she tried again, "you've been a crime reporter for twenty years. That coupled with the head injury has surely messed with your brain. It's a wonder you haven't been having flashbacks for years."

There was a short pause before she added, "I've seen what head traumas can do to people. It's obvious to me why you might be having these dark thoughts, but you should talk to Lori Mitchell and see what she says."

He nodded. She was right.

The kids called for Mom from upstairs. She pushed herself to her feet.

"I'll be right up," Ben told her.

After she kissed his forehead, then left the room, he thought of Sophie Cole. He knew her. He'd met her. But where? He rushed to grab pen and paper and then rewound to the part where they provided a hotline number in case anyone knew anything about what happened to her. He jotted down, "Jessie Cole, sister to Sophie, private investigator living in the Sacramento area."

And then he got an idea.

FIVE

Erin walked slowly around the inside perimeter of the cell, her fingers trailing across rebar and then the rough cement wall as she searched for a way out. She couldn't stop shivering.

She forced herself to sit back down and think for a minute. Instinct insisted she stay calm. The oil lamps had been turned off, but Erin could still see shadows and hear the crunching of straw whenever Garrett moved.

"You have to kill me," he said. "The boss is angry, and that means he'll be back."

"I won't kill you, so stop asking. We need to save the battery power and use the Taser on that monster when he returns."

"You don't have to use the Taser on me. You're young, and you haven't been here long, so you're still strong. Wrap your fingers around my throat, and press your thumbs against my trachea. If I struggle, don't let go."

He crawled close enough to her that she could see the whites of his eyes. "I'm begging you," he said. "Please. I can't do this any longer."

"I won't do it."

"You don't have to use your hands. I'll lay flat, and you can use your knee to do the job."

Erin ignored him as she went through the backpack for the third time, making sure she hadn't missed any secret compartments. So far she'd found a few bottles of water, a granola bar, a pen and paper, a quarter, a nickel, and two pennies.

She heard slurping. Garrett was munching on a sardine. *Gross.* She tossed the backpack away from her. "There's nothing in there."

Garrett scrambled across the floor and began his own search through the bag. His body was skeletal, his skin almost as white as the paper in the notebook she'd found. She squinted and held the notebook inches from her face as she tried to read the madman's writing. The first person listed in capital letters was ANNA WOOD. Under "Description" he'd written: dark hair, blue eyes, round face. Twenty-six years old, five foot five, with buck teeth and a large forehead. In the margins were drawings with arrows and labels pointing out freckles, moles, and unusually long toes.

Disgusted, Erin turned the page. The next five pages described all the things the sicko had done to Anna Wood, complete with dates and times. She'd died fourteen months ago, right here in the same cell where Erin was being kept.

Her stomach churned.

There were more victims, too. More than a dozen. Men, women, children. He seemed to have no preference as to race, gender, or age. He liked to exploit their worst fears and then torture them to see their reactions.

Erin closed her eyes and thought about her parents and siblings. She'd always hated being the middle of six children, but now it seemed so petty. She was one of the lucky ones. Her parents loved her. They doted on every one of their six kids. She missed her brothers and sisters, and if she ever saw them again, she'd never think a bad thought about any of them for as long as she lived.

A sharp noise came from the third cell in the underground room, making her jump. It sounded like a barking dog. She couldn't see inside because that cell was enclosed, the walls made of cement instead of rebar. Whoever was inside *was* barking. Every third or fourth bark sounded like the howl of a wolf. "What is that?"

"That's just Dog. Get used to it."

"Is it human?"

"It's an old man. If you stick around long enough, I'm sure you'll get a chance to meet him."

"The guy who has us. Do you know his name?"

"Sir, Master, Boss—take your pick."

Erin watched Garrett for a minute. He was working hard to rip the backpack to pieces. She wondered what he was doing but didn't ask. "How long have you been here?"

"Too long," he muttered. After a long pause, he said, "Three months and three days."

Chills raced up her arms.

"For the first twenty-eight days, I was here with my wife."

Hope blossomed. "Did she get away? Where is she?"

"No," he said. "She's gone."

Erin's shoulders sagged. She wasn't sure she wanted to know what had happened to his wife, but she found herself asking, "How did he manage to get two of you?"

"We were enjoying a picnic in a remote area. There was a stream and wildlife, a beautiful day. And then this guy comes along, out of the blue, and starts chatting about something. I don't remember what exactly. My wife, a stranger to no one, began conversing with him. Like her, he had majored in social work. Or so he said. I grew bored and took a short walk to the edge of the stream. Less than five minutes later I returned, and they were both gone. Everything else was still there—the blanket, the basket, the food. Panicked, I think I ran back to the stream and called out her name. Hell, maybe I ran in circles. I don't remember. Next thing I know, I'm being Tasered. While I was on the ground, he poured something into my mouth. A clear liquid. No taste. I don't recall anything after that. I woke up here."

"And what about your wife?" she asked, unable to let it go.

"You don't want to know."

"He killed her?"

"I did."

It wasn't fear that had her stomach in knots, but surprise. It was clear that Garrett had loved his wife. She watched him and waited, unwilling to press him further.

Garrett remained focused on ripping the backpack into pieces, but it wasn't long before he continued with his story. "I had to kill her," he said. "He kept insisting that my wife do things to me that she could never do. And every single time she refused, she was punished for her disobedience, as he likes to call it. On the seventh day, she asked me to put her out of her misery. She wanted to die rather than suffer another day. On the twenty-eighth day, I did as she asked."

Garrett was crying now, his shoulders shaking in despair.

"I'm sorry," Erin whispered.

"I'm only sorry it took me so long."

Erin thought about how many people had perished down here, and for the first time since she'd awoken in this dreadful place, she wondered if she would die here, too.

Six

While Olivia sat at the kitchen table doing homework, Colin made some calls and worked on what he needed to go over with his team in the morning. Frustrations in the department were at an all-time high. Now that all leads had been exhausted, he realized it might be time to have one of the retired detectives look over the case files to see if they could find anything that might have been missed.

He also considered getting the media involved, have them do a story on the case and ask for help from the community to see if they could spark someone's memory. Someone out there knew something. Either he wasn't willing to come forward, or he had no idea about the importance of what he'd seen.

Too many guys in the department had worked long hours, missing out on family events—and for what?

The Heartless Killer had been hanging around for too long.

He needed to be stopped.

And yet it wasn't going to be easy to find a killer whose MO kept changing. The Heartless Killer was no Jack the Ripper. He didn't go after only prostitutes or strangle every victim. Many of his crimes appeared to be premeditated and well planned, which would slate him as an organized killer. And yet he was probably also charming and possibly attractive, since he was able to approach his prey and then lure them away. Only two of the victims had been left at the scenes of the crime. The majority of them were taken somewhere to be tortured and abused for months before he disposed of their bodies. More frustrating, as in most serial-killer cases, the probability that there were victims they had yet to discover was high.

Although the Heartless Killer's MO was not well defined, his signature was. Torture and mutilation had occurred with every victim connected to him thus far. As far as Colin could tell, the Heartless Killer's fantasies had developed over the years. The first two bodies connected to the killer had been dumped, as if the killer was in a hurry or afraid he might be seen. But his confidence had grown, and he'd begun to stage his victims, propping the corpse against a tree or a wagon wheel in the middle of a pumpkin patch. He often removed the heart and placed it on or near the body. This staging was most likely done to shock authorities and show them he was all-powerful and in control.

"I'm not stupid, you know," Olivia said from the kitchen, pulling him from his thoughts.

Baffled, Colin caught her gaze through the doorway. "I never said you were."

"Then why don't you tell me what's going on with Jessie? She usually texts if she can't pick me up from school. And she *always* calls when she's going to be late. But it's almost nine, and she never called."

"Speaking of which, why didn't you answer my calls earlier?"

"I have a new number." She picked up her phone and pushed some buttons. "There. I sent you a text. Now you have my new number." She was still giving him the same sort of look Piper often gave him.

"What is it?" he asked.

"You still haven't answered my question. Where's Jessie?"

Colin scratched the side of his neck.

"And why were you the one who picked me up today?"

"Why—is that a problem?"

She shrugged. "I don't mind. It's just that Andriana or Bella's mom are usually the people who pick me up when Jessie can't." She sighed. "I thought you were done with Jessie dragging her feet when it came to the two of you."

"Is that what Jessie told you?"

"No, that's what Andriana said when I asked why I hadn't seen you lately."

That sounded like Andriana. Colin could tell by the tone of her voice that Olivia was upset with him. "I never should have disappeared from your life without talking to you first. I'm sorry."

"I don't care about that."

He knew it wasn't true. He could see the hurt in her eyes. But he let it go for now.

"So where is she?" Olivia asked again.

He had hoped there might be an off chance that Jessie would be released before nightfall. But it wasn't looking good. *Time to come clean.* "Jessie was working a case today when the man she was following fired a shot at her, forcing her to shoot back."

Olivia jumped to her feet. "Was Jessie hit?"

"No."

"Are you sure?"

"Positive."

"Okay." She sank slowly back into her seat. "Is the man dead?"

"He's in critical condition."

"That's not good—is it?"

"No. It's not good."

"How much trouble is she in? Is she in jail?"

"Yes, she's in jail. Andriana was there when I left. The two of them will get it all straightened out, and Jessie will be home in no time."

He didn't like the worry he saw scrawled across Olivia's young face. She was a good kid and had a big heart. Before he could say anything more to ease her mind, his cell buzzed. He picked up the call, listened for a minute, said thanks, and disconnected.

Olivia was on her feet again. "Was that about Higgins?"

He nodded. "He's doing better than expected. We can pick him up in the morning."

"Thank goodness!"

"Yeah," he said. "Thank goodness." Now he needed to figure out how he was going to come up with the money to pay for the surgery, which was going to cost him more than they had originally quoted. After he got that problem settled, he would need to figure out how to break the news to Jessie that she was now the proud owner of an injured dog she didn't have time for.

SEVEN

Jessie was jolted awake by a bloodcurdling scream.

It took her a second to remember she'd slept in jail. The cot was lopsided, and the place smelled of vomit that someone had tried to cover up with bleach. Detective Roth had been kind enough to make sure she was put in her own holding cell, far enough away from the shit disturbers to get a few hours of sleep.

She sat up and pushed tangled hair out of her face. This wasn't the first time she'd been thrown in jail, but it was the first time she'd ever spent the night there. There were no windows, and she had no idea what time it was. She wondered about Olivia. Was she okay? Had Colin made sure she'd gotten something to eat? Did he take her to school?

Feeling dizzy, Jessie lowered her head close to her knees and took deep breaths. She'd never done well in small enclosures, and the strong smell of disinfectant wasn't helping.

A few minutes later, footfalls sounded. Down the corridor she saw a guard coming her way. Following close behind was Andriana. *Thank God.* Keys rattled, and the iron door slid open.

"How are you doing?" Andriana asked.

"Never been better," Jessie said. She looked at the guard and waited for him to cuff her, but that didn't happen.

"Bail has been posted," the guard said. "You can collect your things at the front desk."

Jessie looked at Andriana. "They set bail?"

"Come on," she said. "Let's get your things, and I'll take you home. We'll talk on the way."

Their footsteps echoed off the walls as they walked down a long corridor leading to the front of the building. Through a maze of cubicles, she could see a group of patrol officers taking roll call before their shifts. The moment Jessie stepped outside, she took giant gulps of air, filling her lungs. One night inside the six-by-eight cell had felt like twenty. It was morning, but it was already warm. The heat wave was expected to last another day or two. In an hour the air would be stifling hot.

Side by side, she and Andriana walked across the parking lot. "What's the deal with bail? Why wasn't I notified?"

"You were lucky to get bail. We have a problem."

Jessie stopped in her tracks. "Let's start with who bailed me out?"

"Your father did."

"Seriously? How?"

"He pledged his property."

"How would he even know what had happened? And why would he do that?"

"Because I asked him to."

Jessie scratched her forehead. "That's insane."

"I'm not just your lawyer—I'm your friend. Nobody had enough money for a cash bail, and unfortunately it took the bail-bond agent two minutes to see that you had exactly zero assets. The only way he could help you was if someone could post a property bond. The agent will keep a stiff fee. If you don't show up for your court appearance, your dad loses everything."

Arms crossed, Jessie looked the other way. She hardly ever spoke to her dad. After her mother ran off years ago, her father had started drinking. Too many DUIs later, he'd spent eighteen months in prison. It was a downhill spiral from there. Her younger sister got pregnant, and Jessie knew she had to get her sister and niece away from Dad. Sophie's disappearance didn't help his drinking problem. Whenever Jessie paid him a visit, he'd swear he'd given up drinking, but he was only lying to himself. She did her best to stay away from him.

"Come on," Andriana said, walking ahead. "Get in the car. Your dad is the least of your worries. We need to talk."

Jessie climbed into Andriana's black Prius and buckled herself in. "I'm listening. What's going on?"

"It's about Parker Koontz."

Jessie didn't like the worry lining Andriana's voice, especially since her lawyer wasn't a worrier by nature. "What about him?"

"Koontz is a criminal defense lawyer—"

"And?"

"And his partner is saying Koontz had been carrying a gun because he was afraid for his life. For the past week a woman was stalking him. A woman who fits your description."

"You've got to be kidding me."

"This is not a joke."

Jessie unclenched her jaw. "What else?"

"His partner, David Roche, wants justice. He wants *you* behind bars. His firm has clout. He knows people. And at this point, it's your word against his."

Jessie was tired, and her neck hurt from sleeping on the flimsy cot. "This is bullshit. You know that, right?" Jessie started searching through her purse. "I don't have my gun or the GoPro. I need to go back inside."

"The police are keeping your gun for now. I have the GoPro. I'll upload the video and then give it back to you." Andriana backed out of the parking space and merged onto the main road. "We have a little less than four weeks to prepare for court."

Jessie frowned. "You know I can't afford to pay you. I'll have to let the court roll the dice, appoint me an attorney, and call it a day."

"Don't be silly. We'll barter."

Jessie stared out the window and watched the other cars go by in a blur. "I have nothing you could possibly want."

"You can babysit my kid once a month."

"For the next ten years?"

"Yeah," Andriana said with a smile. "That would work."

Twenty minutes later, Andriana dropped Jessie off on Nineteenth Street in front of the old purple house in Midtown she rented. Surprised to find the front door unlocked, she walked inside. For the next few seconds, she stood on the landing and listened to the noises floating down from above. The house was small. There was no downstairs per se, only a straight-and-narrow set of wooden stairs leading up to the living area above, which consisted of two bedrooms, a kitchen, and a family room.

She made her way quietly up the stairs until she saw the back of Olivia's head. She was sitting on the couch, watching TV. "What's going on here?"

Olivia shot to her feet. "You're home!"

Jessie made her way to the TV and turned it off. "Yes, I'm home. And so are you. You should be in school." Out of the corner of her eye, Jessie saw something move. Lying on a blanket near the large-paned window overlooking the street was a dog with a cast on its back leg. She looked at Olivia and raised both hands in the air. "Seriously? Do you really think this is what I need right now?"

"No," Olivia said, "but what was I supposed to do? Nobody was there to pick me up, so I started walking home. And then *bam*!" Olivia waved a hand toward the dog. "That poor animal flew through the air. The car that hit him just kept right on going. It was horrible." Olivia's eyes watered. "Was I supposed to leave him in the middle of the road to die?"

"No. Of course not." Jessie raked a hand through her unkempt hair.

Colin stepped out from the kitchen. He was drying his hands on a dish towel. "The dog's name is Higgins," he told her.

Jessie sighed.

"Higgins needed surgery, so we weren't able to pick him up from the vet until this morning."

Olivia snuck off to her room, leaving Jessie alone to deal with Colin and the dog. Jessie decided to start with the dog. When she bent down close, a low growl erupted from the animal's chest. He lifted his head high enough for her to see a curled lip and sharp teeth. Jessie pushed herself upright and took a step back.

"First time he's growled at anyone," Colin told her. "He must not like you."

"Story of my life."

"Oh, that can't be true," he said, his tone patronizing. "I like you."

She crossed her arms over her chest.

"The problem is, I like you too much. It's been that way since the first time I ever saw you."

"And yet you didn't bother to call me after your divorce was final."

He looked baffled. "Is that what this is all about? That's why you've been pushing me away?"

She shook her head, wishing she hadn't said anything. "It's complicated."

"Try me."

"This isn't a good time." She lifted her hands in frustration. "I shot a man, Colin. He could die."

"Yeah. You've had a rough night. We'll talk about this some other time."

"Thanks," she said. "For everything. Even the dog."

He kneeled at the dog's side and stroked the animal's midsection as he looked up at her. "So, we're friends again?"

"We always were." She cared about Colin more than he knew, but she was hurt that he hadn't contacted her after his divorce. And hurt again when she'd told him she wasn't ready to date only to watch him walk out of her life. "So, what's the deal with Higgins?" she asked, changing the subject. "He's so thin. Is he going to make it?"

"No telling how long he was roaming the streets before he was hit. He's drugged up right now, but once he wakes up, he'll need to move around. The cast will protect his injured leg."

"How much do I owe you?"

"Never mind."

"No. You've got enough problems. How much?"

"Nada. It's bad enough you're the one who's going to have to take care of him." He looked up at her. "What's the deal with the Koontz guy? Did they drop the charges against you?"

She shook her head. "It turns out Koontz spent the past week telling his partner at his law firm that he was being stalked by a woman who looks like me. Apparently he was afraid for his life and made sure everyone knew about it."

Colin gave the dog one more stroke across the ribs before he stood. "What was the deal with this guy? I mean, why were you following him?"

"My client needed proof he was stalking her so she could get a restraining order."

Colin rubbed his chin. "And Koontz is an attorney?"

She nodded. "I knew that when I took the case, but it gets worse. According to Andriana, his partner is upset, and he wants justice. Her words, not mine."

"If Koontz knew you were following him, why didn't he confront you instead of pulling out a gun?"

"Good question," Jessie said. "The whole thing makes no sense." She paused, thinking. "To want me dead, he must have been extremely worried about others finding out about his extracurricular activities. Assuming he'd done his homework," she continued, "he would have known I was a private investigator with a license to carry. He would have known what happened three years ago."

"Don't go there," Colin said. "You were protecting a police officer. You did the right thing."

Jessie had been doing surveillance on a man whose wife suspected he was cheating on her. Her plan had been to follow the husband and report back to his wife. But a fight had broken out inside the house. Neighbors heard the commotion and called the police. An officer arrived within minutes, and as he walked toward the house, Jessie saw the husband approaching the officer from behind, gun aimed and ready to fire. Jessie got out of the car, told him to stop or she would shoot. He fired and missed. She fired and hit her target. He died instantly. The scene still haunted her, but it hadn't stopped her from pulling out her gun and firing in a public park.

She paced the room. "Why would Koontz shoot blanks? It makes no sense."

"Maybe he didn't know the gun was loaded with blanks. Either that or he was suicidal."

It was quiet for a moment while they thought about different scenarios of what might have happened.

"How much time do you have before your court appearance?"

"Less than a month."

"Sounds like we have our work cut out for us."

"I can't ask you to help me, especially when you're so entrenched in finding the Heartless Killer."

"You need to dig deeper into Parker Koontz's life. The woman who hired you can't be the first woman he's harassed. Maybe you should have a chat with his partner."

"That's a good idea."

Jessie met his gaze. "I'm sorry, you know, about everything. I didn't mean to push you away. You surprised me. That's all."

"Nothing to be sorry about. One of these days you're going to wake up and realize you can't live without me. Let's just hope it's not too late when that happens."

His phone buzzed, breaking into her thoughts. After reading his text, he said, "I've got to go," then grabbed his things from the coffee table and started down the stairs to the front door.

"Colin," Jessie called, worried she might not see him again.

He turned back to look at her and waited.

"Thanks for being there for me," she told him. "It means a lot."

"Sure. I'll call you later. You know—to check on Higgins."

"Thanks."

There was nothing wrong with Colin Grayson, she thought as he walked away. It was all her. She was confused. He'd broken her heart before, and the thought of allowing him in again only for him to realize she wasn't the one scared her to death.

The sound of the door opening and closing brought her back to the moment. Colin was gone. And she had work to do.

EIGHT

Erin awoke to the sound of chattering teeth. It took her a second to realize she was the one making the noise. She wondered how long she'd dozed off for. She was freezing, and it was pitch-dark.

As her gaze darted around the cell, she rubbed the chill from her arms. "Garrett?"

No answer.

Pushing herself to her feet, she hoped her eyes would adjust to the dark. No such luck. She held both arms straight and stiff in front of her like a mummy in an old black-and-white movie and walked slowly across the small space. A few seconds passed before her hand came into contact with something cold and fleshy. She yanked her arm back. "Garrett," she said again. "Is that you?"

Still no answer.

She swallowed as she reached out again and forced herself to touch whatever it was in front of her. It was definitely a human form, bony, skeletal. She held back a cry. Standing on the tips of her toes, she felt the cloth around his neck, and realized then what he'd been doing with the backpack. He'd spent hours ripping it to shreds. She'd thought he'd wanted to ruin something that belonged to the man upstairs. But she'd been wrong. Garrett had seen the backpack as his chance out of here once and for all. He'd made a rope and noose to hang himself with.

She held his wrist, felt for a pulse, but there was none.

Her stomach tightened as a sharp pain gripped her heart and squeezed.

Garrett was dead. And now she was alone with a dead man.

Her heart raced as she grabbed hold of the bars and shook them. "Let me out! I want out!"

Unable to stop the tears from coming, she crawled back to where she'd been sitting before, got down on all fours, and felt around for the pile of things she'd collected. Her mind raced as she pulled the pen apart and then hid the coins under a pile of straw.

Calm down, she told herself. *You need to think. Think. Think.*

She'd already eaten the granola bar and now wished she'd saved half of it for later. She would ration the water. Before she had time to plan beyond that, the door at the top of the stairs creaked open, shedding a thick stream of light across the room.

She could see Garrett now. His face was swollen and black, and he seemed to be looking right at her. She clutched her stomach as she looked away.

Footsteps sounded, prompting her to reach out and grab the Taser. Her hands shook as she held it in front of her, her thumb ready to flip the switch when the time came.

A match ignited. The oil lamps were lit, providing a soft glow.

"Oh, would you look at that," he said, walking toward Garrett so he could take a closer look.

Don't judge a book by its cover was the first thing that had gone through Erin's mind when she'd awoken in the cell yesterday. She guessed her captor to be in his early thirties. He was clean-cut and newly shaved, just as he'd been when he'd offered her a ride. He was well spoken, too, and he had a nice smile. Nothing about him had set off alarms.

But now she knew better.

From outside the cell, he was touching Garrett, poking and prodding. Was he making sure he was dead? Or was he having fun with him even in death? The thought horrified her.

Although Garrett wasn't facing him, he reached through the bars, put a finger to Garrett's lips, and wagged his finger back and forth, making a hollow popping sound emit from Garrett's mouth.

She held her breath.

He pulled his hand back through the bars, never taking his gaze from hers—a cold, hard stare. If there was a devil, he was it. "Such a shame," he said. "I was going to attach electrodes to his testicles and shock him."

Erin stiffened as she stared back at him, unblinking.

He pressed his face up close to the bars. "You would have loved it."

Hoping to provoke him, she growled at him. "You're a monster. A bloody monster."

He frowned.

Come and get me, asshole. She needed to piss him off enough to get him to come inside so she could Taser him and then make a run for it. There was no way he was getting his weapon back without a fight.

"I like you," he said. "You have spirit."

"You are a disgusting pig."

He smiled.

She couldn't get over the fact that he looked like a regular guy. His light-colored hair was cut close around his ears. His bangs swept across a high forehead. Just a regular-looking guy. Had she seen him on the street, she never would have given him a second look. He could have been a professor or a grocery clerk. Nothing about him stood out.

"I can make you do anything I want." He smiled. *"Anything."*

"Fuck you."

"Oooh. A nasty girl with a foul mouth." He made a slurping noise and then said, "Intoxicating."

She recalled Garrett telling her to do whatever the freak told her to do because otherwise he would get angry. And there was no telling what he would do if he was angry.

Well, she wanted to find out. Better to anger him quickly, she thought, and possibly catch him off guard. Besides, the nine-volt battery in the Taser wouldn't last forever.

"Are you the Heartless Killer?" she asked.

"What if I am?"

She shrugged as if it didn't make a difference one way or another. But it did matter. If he was the Heartless Killer, then that would mean he would never let her go, especially now that she could identify him.

"Everyone is talking about you," she said after a short pause. It was true. Parents had been worrying and lecturing their kids about the serial killer on the loose for years now. Mostly they said to stay alert, never walk home alone, and, of course, don't talk to strangers. Until she'd been brought here, though, it had been white noise. The man standing before her had been like an old folks' tale or the bogeyman under the bed. A bad guy nobody ever thought much about until another body was found. She remembered a friend telling her that the killer chose his victims at random, taking multiple victims before disappearing for months. They called him the Heartless Killer, but she had no idea why.

"Have you watched the news lately or read the paper?" she asked when he didn't respond. He just stood there staring at her, creeping her out, which meant he was winning. "I've read about the things your whore of a mother did to you," she lied. "No wonder you're a little messed up in the head."

His jaw twitched. That was a good sign. She needed him to lose control and hopefully enter her cell, where she would have the upper hand.

"You need to shut that dirty mouth of yours," he told her, "or I'll make you eat crow. Literally."

Erin had never personally read one word about him. She had no clue what police investigators were saying, since she'd never cared one way or another.

She cared now.

The good news was she'd obviously triggered his anger, so she stuck with it. "I read that your slut of a mother forced you to take showers with her so you could soap her up real good and make her moan with pleasure."

He reached into his back pocket and pulled out a key.

Come on. Come on. Her gaze kept landing on Garrett. She hoped the weirdo didn't leave him hanging there. No one should have to die like that. Tortured for months in a cold, dank cell in some creepy man's basement.

Focus, she reminded herself as he unlocked the door. "You don't even know who your father is, do you? Is it the postman? Or maybe it's your next-door neighbor."

The door clanged open. He stepped inside. Smiling now, he ignored her verbal jabs as he approached. Two feet away from her, he stopped and stared. And then, without warning, he lunged, baring his teeth and curling his hands into claws as he came at her.

She'd expected as much and jumped to the side.

He jerked to the right. She moved to the left.

He went left. She went right.

His eyes were bright. It took her a second to realize he was in his element, toying with her, having fun. The second he stepped close enough, she jumped forward and jabbed the prongs into his chest. She held tight, giving him a good long jolt.

He cried out as he fell to the ground, his arms and legs flailing.

She had no choice but to hop over him, and when she did he grabbed hold of her ankle and yanked her to the ground. The Taser flew from her hands, breaking into pieces.

He was laughing, his body no longer twitching. How could that be?

She kicked and screamed, then reached around for his face and jammed her thumb into his eye.

He cursed and let go.

She jumped to her feet and scrambled through the cell door. She got as far as the bottom step before he grabbed her leg and she fell. Her chin hit the stair, sending a searing pain through her skull.

"Nice try," he said as he dragged her back to the cell. "You obviously know nothing about me. Because if you did, you would know I used to dream of being a Boy Scout someday. The Boy Scouts of America is one of the largest scouting organizations in the US. *Be prepared!*" He laughed. "*Always* be in a state of readiness in mind and body to do your *duty!*"

Once they were inside the cell again, he released his hold on one of her legs so he could lift his shirt and reveal another layer of fabric.

"It's polyester," he said. "A special fabric neutralizes any stun-gun jolt. Works every time. Prisoner has my Taser and thinks he has the upper hand." He laughed as if that was the funniest thing ever.

Her heart raced. He was insane. She realized that this might be her last chance to get free. Before he reached for her leg again, she drew it back and slammed her foot into his shin.

He cried out and stumbled backward, but he wasn't kidding when he'd said he was prepared. Before she could get past him, he pulled a small canister from his waistband and sprayed her in the face.

Her eyes burned. The pain was intense.

He pushed her to the ground.

Get out of here, she told herself. *Get out now!* On hands and knees, she scurried back to where she'd left her pile of makeshift weapons. The granola wrapper crunched beneath her fingers.

Again his long, cold fingers grasped her ankles before he dragged her from the cell.

No. No. No! She reached out blindly in front of her, arms stretching, fingers searching. The pen. Where was the pen? Her hand passed over the coins.

"It's time for you to take a time-out in the box."

NINE

Jessie's first stop after leaving Olivia home with the dog was her dad's house in East Sacramento off Riverside Boulevard. It was the house where she and Sophie had been raised. With its unstable foundation, cracked walkways, and neglected grounds, she was surprised the property had been accepted as a pledge toward bail. She knocked on the door, three hard raps.

Her dad used to be a carpenter, but after he'd started drinking, he couldn't be trusted to show up on time. Now he worked as a handyman. Ethan Cole's Handyman Services. She was about to get her hopes up when she heard lumbering footfalls approaching from inside.

The door came open.

"Hi, Dad."

He tightened the sash on his robe. Although his thick salt-and-pepper hair was all over the place and he needed a shave, for a fifty-nine-year-old drunk, he was in pretty good shape. Clearly he wasn't expecting visitors.

"Can I come inside?"

"Yeah, um, sure, of course."

She stepped past him, walked down the hallway and into the family room. Empty beer cans littered the coffee table, and clear plastic cups used as ashtrays were filled to the brim. When she opened a window to air the place out, she saw the old swing set out back, where she and her sister used to play when they were little girls. It was rusty now and had one broken swing that dangled from a chain.

She went to the kitchen next and dug through drawers and cabinets until she found a garbage bag. As she walked around the family room, tossing empty cans and plastic cups into the bag, she held up an empty can of beer and said, "Looks like you've been busy."

"Did you come here to lecture me?"

"No. I guess not." She set the can back on the table and the bag on the floor next to her feet. He might have his own handyman business, but he didn't look very handy at the moment. "Don't you work anymore?"

"I don't appreciate your tone."

She anchored her hair behind her ears. He was right. She hadn't come all this way to make him feel like shit. "You shouldn't have pledged your property, Dad. This house is all you've got."

"I've got you and Olivia."

"Not if you continue to drink yourself into an early grave."

"A few beers are all I had."

"Give me a break, Dad. It smells like Bourbon Street in here. There's an empty bottle of whiskey sitting on the TV stand. Never mind that it's noon and you look as if you just dragged yourself out of bed."

"Why do you do this to me?"

"What am I doing to you, Dad?"

"I try to do something good, and you come over here pointing accusing fingers at me. I had a few friends over last night. That's all."

All he did was lie. "I never should have come."

"Why did you?" he asked as he followed her to the door.

"To say thank you. It was a dumb idea."

"This is all your mother's fault, you know. She always wanted to turn you girls against me, and she did exactly that when she left us all here to rot."

"Jesus, Dad." Jessie turned toward him before opening the door. "Mom left a zillion years ago. Get over it. Thousands of men have been fucked over by their wives and vice versa. That's life, Dad. When are you going to get that? *You*," she said with an admonishing finger, "are the only one who can choose to change your life for the better. Friends and family have offered you help. I have offered you help, but for whatever reason, you just want to sit in your stupid recliner, guzzle booze, and sulk. I refuse to watch you continue to ruin your life because one selfish woman decided to up and leave."

His eyes watered, but she felt no sympathy. She'd seen it before. "You've already wasted too many years. It's time for you to realize you deserve better and then make some changes." She opened the door and stepped outside.

"How did you do it?" he asked.

She looked at him. "Do what?"

"How did you stop thinking about her?"

She knew he meant Mom. "It was easy. Two months after she left, I read about a plane crash that killed everyone on the flight. I told myself she was on that plane. I even picked out which seat she'd been sitting in when it went down."

Jessie didn't wait for a response. She just walked off. No goodbye. No hug. No friendly wave. Just like always.

———

It was after one o'clock when Jessie arrived at the bank dripping with sweat. She should have taken her car instead of hopping on her bike.

Adelind Rain, the woman who had hired her to follow Parker Koontz, was a bank teller. The moment Jessie walked through the door, Adelind saw her and gestured for her to have a seat. Fifteen minutes later, Adelind approached and asked her if it was okay if they talked outside. The young woman was taller than Jessie remembered. Her light-colored hair was pinned back in a sleek and fashionable topknot. Everything about her was striking.

Jessie followed her out the double doors and to the right, where a couple of benches had been placed for workers to take a break. Traffic was thick this time of day. Across the street were apartment buildings, a coffee shop, and a Mexican restaurant. Another bank employee stubbed out a cigarette in the dirt circling a tree and headed back inside.

"I only have a few minutes," Adelind told her. "What's going on?" She looked around worriedly. "Is he here?"

"I take it you haven't seen the news."

Adelind pulled a face. "It's too depressing."

"Parker Koontz is at the hospital. He's in critical condition."

Her mouth dropped open. "How?"

Jessie pointed across the way. "He stood at that street corner yesterday waiting for you to appear. I knew you had taken the day off, but he didn't. When he left, I was following him through Capitol Park when suddenly he turned and fired two shots at me. I fired back. Hit him in the chest."

"Oh no. I'm so sorry. Are you okay?"

"I'm fine. He was shooting blanks."

"Why?"

"I have no idea. But his partner at the law firm is upset. Apparently Koontz had been telling him he was the one being stalked and harassed."

"That bastard."

Jessie nodded. "The woman he's been describing looks a lot like me."

"That's crazy."

"I'll have to make a court appearance in a few weeks, and I'll need your help to prove he's been stalking you and others. The first time we talked, you hinted about not being the only woman Koontz has been harassing. I need a name."

Adelind said nothing.

"My ass is on the line here," Jessie said, wondering why she would hesitate.

"Fiona Hampton is the other woman who was stalked by Koontz. She works at the coffee shop on the corner of Sixteenth and N."

"Are you two friends?"

"No. About a month ago, I was waiting in line for my coffee order when Fiona asked me if I knew the man in the suit sitting at the table outside. Although I had never seen him before that day, it was Parker Koontz. She said he was a pervert and that he'd stalked her for weeks before finally disappearing." Adelind took a breath. "Fiona said that wasn't the first time she'd seen him follow me to the coffee shop. I was surprised, but I wasn't too worried. I went outside to confront him, but he rushed off before I could talk to him. Sure enough, after that day, I saw him everywhere. It didn't matter where I went—to the grocery store, to work, to a bar to meet a friend, he would show up. That's when I knew I had to do something to stop him."

"Did you ever try to confront him after that first time?"

She nodded. "More than once. He was always far enough away to run off before I could catch up to him. I called the police a couple of times, hoping they could question him, but he always disappeared before they showed up."

"So he never approached you or tried to have a conversation with you?"

"Never. But there is more to the story that I haven't told you. Only because I thought I was being paranoid. As of last night, though, I knew it wasn't my imagination. Someone has been in my house when I'm gone."

"Did you call the police?"

She shook her head. "I'm not sure I have enough proof."

"How do you know someone has been inside your home?"

"Lots of little things," Adelind said. "A brand-new carton of milk, opened and half-gone by the time I got home from work. The smell of my perfume in the garage. A dirty glass left in the sink. And pictures on the wall that had been reorganized. I was really starting to think I might be going crazy. But then I decided to conduct a test. I placed my workout clothes neatly on my bed. When I came home, they'd been moved, everything back where they belong."

Jessie whistled through her teeth.

Someone exited the bank. "Adelind," the woman called. "Jerry is looking for you."

Adelind stood. "Jerry's my manager. I've got to go. I'll call you later."

Jessie watched her take brisk steps back into the air-conditioned bank. About to get up and go, Jessie had a weird feeling she was being watched. She examined the cars parked at the curb: A Jeep with fancy hubcaps. Silver Acura with a dent in the driver's door. Beat-up Nissan truck without a bumper or a license plate. And so on and so on. Every vehicle was empty. Her gaze drifted to the luxury apartments. Eight stories high. Some of the windows were covered with blinds or curtains. Some open and some closed. Her gaze roamed over the apartments until she spotted a shadowy figure. Her skin prickled. Someone was standing at the window in the center apartment on the sixth floor. If she'd had her backpack with her, she would have pulled out her binoculars to get a better look.

But this wasn't her day. She didn't have her backpack, camera, or anything else of any use, so she stood and walked away without so much as a backward glance.

TEN

"Not now. I'm busy," Ian Savage said without looking up.

Ben Morrison ignored his boss and took a seat in front of Ian's rough wood desk, which he'd made from a fallen oak tree. Tall and reed thin, the man was nearing seventy. In a crowd, or anywhere for that matter, you couldn't miss his abundance of silver hair. Old woodsy cologne came off him in waves, which always made Ben think the old man had more than one gargantuan bottle of the stuff hidden away at home.

"This will only take a minute," Ben told him.

Ian continued to search through files and papers stacked in front of him, ignoring Ben completely. He was always misplacing something, always grumpy and seemingly discombobulated.

"I want to do a serial story. Just enough words every week to keep readers wanting more."

Ian's reply came out sounding like a grunt, which motivated Ben to continue. "I want to investigate the disappearance of a young woman who went missing ten years ago," Ben said. "But first some backstory. Two sisters are abandoned by their mother. Father takes to drinking. Teenage daughter gets pregnant. After one DUI too many, Dad goes to jail. Older sister drops out of school to try to help her younger sister with baby. Younger sister goes out one night and never returns. Ten years later, she's still missing."

"Just like more than half a million other missing people in the United States," Ian muttered as he placed all the papers and files back into one tall stack and started his search again.

"No," Ben said. "This is different."

"How?"

"We're the number two rated paper in Sacramento."

"Thanks for the reminder."

"*CSI* and *Cold Case TV* are two of the most popular shows right now," Ben continued. "The Cole sisters were born and raised right here in Sacramento. Sophie Cole disappeared and was never heard from again. Her older sister, Jessie Cole, never returned to school to get her degree. Do you want to know why?"

"No."

"Because she never stopped looking for her sister. For the first two years, she worked closely with the police. Then she became a private investigator. Ten years after her sister disappeared, she's still a PI. She works out of an office not too far from here."

Ben knew Ian well enough to know he was interested because he kept glancing his way before pretending to examine the same piece of paper. He was curious but determined as always to play hardball.

"Yesterday," Ben told him, "Jessie Cole was following Parker Koontz through Capitol Park. Koontz fired off two shots, and Cole fired back. Koontz is in critical condition."

Ian looked up. "That's the woman you're talking about, huh?"

Ben nodded. "Koontz is a criminal defense attorney. From what I've read about him, he's well respected in the community."

"So, what exactly are you selling here?"

"This would be *Cold Case TV* on paper and all over social media. This will be a story about a family, two sisters born and raised right here in Sacramento. One's missing. The other won't stop looking."

"How are you going to find the time for this project?" Ian asked. "Maybe you could help Gavin out with the Heartless Killer case."

Ben raised his hands, palms up. "The last thing we need around here is another dead-in-the-water story about a serial killer who's been given the wrong nickname."

"What's wrong with the Heartless Killer?" Ian wanted to know. "One of his victims was stabbed in the heart, wrapped in Christmas lights, and left under the tree for her family to find. Another victim, also stabbed in the heart, with a screwdriver I might add, was placed in the middle of a pumpkin patch, right where all the little kindergarteners could find the body. And the most recent victim they found had her heart ripped out of her chest. I would call that heartless."

Ben grunted. "Human nature demands that everything be given a label. The Heartless Killer has been around for seven years—"

"Six," Ian cut in.

"Okay, six. His original victims had bite marks; another had her eyelids removed. What about the guy with dead insects stuffed inside his nostrils, and—" Pain sliced through Ben's skull, like a lightning bolt striking his brain. He grabbed both sides of his head and squeezed his eyes shut. In his mind's eye, he saw a woman's naked body stretched out in a field of tall green grass. If not for the thin red line across her throat and her bloodless face, he would have thought she was alive.

"Hey," Ian said, worried, "are you okay?"

Ben opened his eyes, pinched the bridge of his nose, and said, "Damn migraine." He shook off the image. "The point is the killer could have been given any random nickname, so why bother? How about the Phantom, since some say he doesn't exist at all? Four years ago the woman who escaped before he could drag her into the woods told detectives the man sang 'Hound Dog,' so why didn't they call him Elvis?"

Ian nodded. "See? You could help put another spin on this whole thing."

"The public is tired of the same old thing. They want to be entertained."

Before Ian could say another word, Ben swiped a hand through the air as if to erase all this nonsensical talk before continuing on with his original reason for entering Ian's office. "Back to the Sophie Cole case. My focus will be on the missing sister and my own investigation into finding out what happened to her. The media attention surrounding the shooting in the park will merely be icing on the cake, pulling readers in, making them eager to know more."

Ian narrowed his eyes. "People will get to know Jessie Cole through your eyes." He waggled a crooked finger at Ben. "If you do this right, everyone will want to know what happened to Jessie Cole's sister."

"That's right." Ben shrugged. "What do we have to lose?"

Ian smiled. Not something he did often. "You should take a look in the mirror right now, because you look a lot like the Ben Morrison I interviewed twenty years ago."

"Yeah? How so?"

"Determined, passionate . . . two of the reasons why I hired you on the spot."

Ben used to wonder a lot about *that* Ben Morrison, the man he used to be but could no longer remember. He pushed himself to his feet and went to the door.

"Where are you going?" Ian asked.

"You're busy, and I need to get started if I'm going to have the first thousand words on your desk by Monday."

"Did you hear me say yes? Did those words ever come out of my mouth?"

"I didn't hear you say no," Ben said as he made his exit.

ELEVEN

Fatigue was setting in by the time Jessie arrived at the building on Nineteenth Street where she rented a two-hundred-square-foot space for $400 a month. It was the smallest office in the building, but the only one that had a window facing the street. The best part was that it was only a block and a half away from where she lived.

She blew at a light coating of dust on the stainless steel sign on the door that read: JESSIE COLE DETECTIVE AGENCY. She unlocked the door and stepped inside. The first thing she'd done after finding the place was paint the walls light gray and install white crown molding, making it look up-to-date and professional. Her desk, a sturdy piece of wood with four steel legs, faced the door. The window overlooking the street was to her right and provided a lot of natural light. A row of filing cabinets against the wall took up most of the space. The nicest piece of furniture was her client chair. She'd found it on a street corner with a sign that said, TAKE ME. So she had. It was a polyester blend fabric with no stains and only one small tear underneath the seat cover that nobody could see unless they turned the chair upside down.

She had a vent in her office but no thermostat to control the air-flow. Although it was hotter than hell outside, it was freezing inside. She grabbed a sweater from the hook behind the door, then settled into her mesh swivel chair behind her desk, pulled out her cell phone, and went through her messages.

Before the unfortunate event in the park, business had been picking up. Although her clients varied, including the occasional husbands or wives who paid her to keep a close eye on their spouses, she preferred to focus on cold cases and missing persons. Jessie had started her PI business serving subpoenas and doing subcontracting work for companies that wanted proof that an employee wasn't injured and shouldn't be collecting workman's compensation. Ever since she'd located fifteen-year-old Tonya Grimm, though, a girl who had been missing for two weeks, hiding out at a friend's house to avoid her parents' constant bickering, the public tended to think finding people was her expertise.

The first message on her phone was from an angry woman who called Jessie a killer. Her stomach tightened. She thought of the man lying in the hospital and wondered if she deserved this woman's ire. She'd done everything by the book. She'd pulled out her weapon to defend herself and others. She had a license to carry, and she never worked a case thinking she'd have to do anyone harm. She hit "Delete." The second message was also from a woman, but she'd called to congratulate Jessie for taking down one more douchebag in the world. Jessie sighed. The last three callers were interested in hiring her to do investigative work.

By the time she'd returned calls, answered new ones, paid bills, and sent out invoices for services rendered, she had a couple of potential new clients. She looked at the clock, surprised that it was already four. She wanted to talk to Parker Koontz's partner, David Roche, but she decided to put that off until tomorrow. As she readied to leave, her cell rang. She picked up the call as she headed out the door.

"Is this Jessie Cole?"

"May I ask who's calling?"

"Ben Morrison, crime reporter with the *Sacramento Tribune*. I was hoping you had some time to talk."

She'd known the press would call sooner or later. Parker Koontz was well known, an established lawyer in the area. If she ignored the press, they usually became more determined. Better to deal with it now and get it over with. "I have a few minutes right now."

"I'd prefer to meet in person. Would tomorrow work?"

Jessie sighed. "Does this have to do with Parker Koontz?"

"I'm calling about your sister, Sophie."

He had her attention. She walked back into her office and took a seat.

"I happened to watch an old episode of *Cold Case TV* the other night when they aired your story," he told her. "At the end of the show, they mentioned that there have been few leads and that Sophie has yet to be found."

"That's correct."

"I'm calling because I'm interested in doing a story about you and your family. I would also like to conduct my own investigation on your sister's disappearance."

"Why would you want to do that?"

"Well, you were born and raised here in Sacramento. Our readers enjoy hearing about locals. And the public is also fascinated with cold cases."

"I see."

She was about to turn down his offer when he said, "There's also a possibility that I knew your sister."

A chill raced up her spine.

If he'd known Sophie, his name would have come up at some point in the past decade, wouldn't it? After her sister had disappeared, she'd done everything possible to get the media involved, but there was always something more interesting going on in the world, and the police received hardly any tips. Since Jessie had been taking care of Olivia during the day and working nights, she didn't know who Sophie hung out with other than a woman named Juliette. And Juliette had told her that Sophie was a loner and had few friends.

She still didn't know the identity of Olivia's father. There were only two men Jessie had talked to in the past ten years who admitted to having spent time with Sophie. One of those men told Jessie outright that her sister liked sex, plain and simple. He said she would hang out at one bar or another, looking for someone to show her a good time. And it never took her long to find what she was looking for. The other guy she'd talked to hinted at the same thing. Both fellows agreed to take a lie-detector test and have blood drawn. Neither ended up being Olivia's father, and both were telling the truth about not having seen Sophie in the weeks leading up to her disappearance.

"Are you there?" Ben asked.

His voice gave her a jolt. "I'm here." Her mind swirled with speculation. "Can you tell me where you met my sister?"

"It's complicated."

If he knew anything at all about Sophie, then she needed to meet with him.

Jessie looked at her calendar. "How about tomorrow at ten o'clock in my office?" She gave him the address.

"I'll see you then."

She hung up the phone and turned on her computer. She typed his name into the search bar and hit "Return." The name *Ben Morrison* popped up in a long list of search items.

She clicked on the first link.

Just like he'd told her, he worked for the *Sacramento Tribune*. His bio talked about him being a family man who'd been married for nine and a half years. He and his wife had two children—a boy and a girl. Apparently he'd been in a horrific car accident near Blue Canyon, past Colfax.

Wow, Jessie thought. Six months after his accident, he married the nurse he'd met at the hospital where he'd been recovering. *Interesting.*

She read on. He'd escaped the burning vehicle but suffered severe head trauma along with third-degree burns on more than half of his body. He was eventually diagnosed with retrograde amnesia, which prevented him from accessing memories prior to the crash. But he'd said he might have known Sophie. Did that mean his memories were returning?

She clicked on images of Ben Morrison.

He was a big man, broad-shouldered and tall, at least three inches over the six-foot mark. He had a square jaw and hooded eyes. He would be hard to miss in a crowd and easy to recognize tomorrow when he came to visit. Something about him, though, gave her goose bumps. Maybe it was the hawkish stare or the fact that he wasn't smiling in any of the pictures. Whatever it was, she told herself she would have to be cautious.

Did she really want a stranger's help?

Yes, she wanted answers. Yes, she wanted to know where her sister was. But the idea of having her family's story dragged through the mud and left wide-open for public scrutiny when Olivia was starting high school didn't sit well with her.

Damn. She never should have agreed to meet with the man.

She thought about calling him back, then changed her mind. If Ben Morrison knew anything about her sister's disappearance—anything at all—then she needed to know what it was. Not a day went by that she didn't wonder whether her sister was dead or alive.

TWELVE

Colin stood on the side of a frontage road that ran parallel to Highway 80. This morning's briefing concerning the Heartless Killer case had been short. A career criminal apprehension team (CCAT) would continue to work surveillance and talk to witnesses from past crime scenes connected to the killer in hopes of coming across a new lead.

Unlike mass murderers, whose rage often erupted in one catastrophic act of vengeance, serial killers did whatever they could to escape detection. Even with the advancement of investigative techniques, there was only so much forensics could accomplish. Unless the killer was betrayed by an accomplice, identified by a relative, or grew overly confident and, in turn, increasingly careless, he could go on killing for years to come. It had been documented that about 20 percent of all serial killers were never brought to justice for their crimes.

It was times like this that Colin felt for every detective who'd worked the case and would never get back time missed with loved ones.

Six years. Thirteen victims—that they knew of—and one frustrating dead end after another. He'd known what he was getting into when he'd become a police officer and then an investigator. He knew about the potential dangers, the long and irregular hours, and the stress that came with such a position. But chasing after a killer who'd been plucking victims from the street for years on end made him feel powerless.

Shortly after the briefing, Colin had gotten word of a missing girl from Elk Grove, a city in Sacramento County south of the state capital. As he stood there now, he watched the tow truck drive off with Erin Hayes's Subaru attached to the flatbed. The girl had been missing for forty-eight hours. Her car would be taken to the lab, where they would check for fingerprints, traces of blood, and hair and fibers.

There wasn't much traffic in the area. No witnesses so far. Footprints outside the driver's door appeared to belong to Erin. They would know more later.

Levi Hooper with the forensics unit finished talking to the photographer, then headed Colin's way. "No trace evidence as far as I can see with the naked eye."

"If those are Erin's footprints," Colin said, following the path with a pointed finger, "which is likely, she never walked to the back of the car to check out the flat tire, and she didn't walk along the side of the road, either." He pointed at the distinct prints in the dirt. "The shoe prints disappear onto pavement, which tells me someone showed up and gave her a ride immediately after she got the flat."

"Agreed. Nothing here has been disturbed. No signs of a struggle. No personal belongings left behind."

"The question we need answered," Colin said, "was someone following her, or was it happenstance?"

For a moment the two men stood there quietly.

Colin's stomach turned at the thought of a young girl being out there somewhere needing their help.

"I better get to the lab," Levi said after a while.

"I'm going to head over to Elk Grove to talk to the girl's family," Colin said. "I'll catch up with you later."

First thing the next morning, Jessie headed for the offices of Roche and Koontz. It was easier for her to walk than drive. As she passed by the rose garden in Capitol Park, every muscle tensed. Feeling weirdly out of breath, she stopped and looked around. Her heart pounded inside her chest, and her breath caught in her throat as she was brought back to the moment she'd shot Parker Koontz.

What was wrong with her?

It wasn't just the Koontz incident that was bothering her. It was everything, and it all hit her at once. She walked to a nearby bench and took a seat.

What was she doing with her life? Thirty-four years old, and yet she still didn't have her shit together. After Mom left, she'd done everything she could to try to keep her family together. But Dad had been unable to bear living without the woman whose only excuse for leaving was that she couldn't handle the pressure of raising two daughters. After Dad started drinking, Jessie found out her sixteen-year-old sister was pregnant. It had been up to Jessie to pull everyone together, but she'd failed at every turn. First her father. Then Sophie.

Jessie used a sleeve to wipe her eyes. Olivia didn't stand a chance.

For most of her life, she'd felt as if she were riding a nonstop Ferris wheel that she couldn't get off. A few years after her sister had disappeared, she'd decided to become a PI in hopes of helping other people find their loved ones as she continued her search for Sophie. But looking around now, at the city, the place she'd lived her entire life, she realized she couldn't save the world.

Hell, she might not even be able to save herself.

Her foot bounced as she watched passersby and listened to the sound of birds between the honk of a horn and the roar of a car's engine. She could sit there all day, she realized, doing nothing but simply being. But she didn't have the luxury of time.

Forcing herself to her feet, she drew in a breath and continued on down Twenty-First Street. If she could hold it together long enough, she might be able to keep her ass out of jail.

By the time she walked through the front door of the office of Koontz and Roche, she was feeling better, stronger. The front lobby was made up of rich mahogany furniture and crystal wall sconces. The woman behind the desk looked up and asked if she had an appointment.

Jessie knew that getting to talk to David Roche was a long shot, but she had nothing to lose. "I don't have an appointment, but my name is Jessie Cole. It's important that I talk to David Roche."

The woman appeared to recognize the name. She reached for the phone, hit a button, and told the person on the end of the line that Jessie Cole was here. After she hung up, she stood and gestured toward the double doors directly behind her. "Mr. Roche has a full schedule, but he said he has a few minutes before his next meeting. Come this way."

Jessie followed her into a large office with floor-to-ceiling windows behind a massive desk covered with neatly stacked papers. The woman disappeared, and the man behind the desk came to his feet and walked around the desk to offer his hand.

His handshake was firm.

A tall man, his arrogance appeared to be woven into the fine fabric of his fitted suit. His dark hair was slicked back, his nails well manicured, and his smile phony.

Before coming, Jessie had done enough research to know he was married with two children. A former prosecutor with more than twenty years of experience in criminal and business law, his website touted a "Superb 10/10 rating." Andriana's opinion of David Roche was less than stellar. She'd run into him in court more than a few times, and she'd told Jessie he was a snake in the grass who was more worried about his pocketbook than fighting for a client's rights.

Roche pulled out a chair and gestured for her to have a seat, which she did. While he made his way back to the chair behind his desk, she noticed all the awards and diplomas hanging on the wall.

As soon as he was situated, he propped his elbows on the rich mahogany in front of him and made a steeple with his fingers. "I must admit I'm surprised to see you here. You do realize the man you shot and put in the hospital is my partner?"

"I do."

"Well, then, you should know you've made things difficult around here. My workload was already heavy, but without Parker here to evaluate cases, file motions, and help our clients with their legal needs, our law firm, thanks to you, is quite frankly fucked."

His crassness didn't bother her. She thought it telling that he worried more about his workload than the fact that his partner was in a coma, struggling for his life. She lifted her chin. "I'm sorry you've been put out, but I had no choice but to defend myself after your partner decided to pull out a gun and fire at me. For that reason alone, I think it was rash of you to press criminal charges."

"If you know anything about the law, you'd know it's up to the prosecutor to press charges, not me."

"I believe it was your name on the document filed with the police department."

"True, but—"

"And the prosecutor in charge, your good friend Nicholas Levine, attended law school with you, is that right?"

The lines in his forehead deepened. "A mere coincidence, I can assure you."

The tone of his voice was heavy with annoyance as he continued on with a rambling lecture. "Individuals do not press charges, nor do police," he told her. "Only a municipal, state, or federal attorney can decide to charge someone with a crime. Prosecutors are the ones who make the decisions based on evidence provided by people and police."

Jessie enjoyed watching him lose his cool. "What can you tell me about your partner's extracurricular activities?" she asked, figuring she had nothing to lose and everything to gain if he answered her questions and gave her some insight.

He leaned back in his chair, his fingers entwined, his smile strained. "I am married with two small children. I don't have time to keep track of what Parker does or does not do in his free time."

"So, you know nothing about the young woman he was allegedly stalking?"

"That's a serious accusation. I hope you have proof."

"Yes, thank you. I believe there is video footage."

His face paled.

"I was wearing a video device while doing surveillance. It should come in handy when I see your prosecutor friend in court."

He glanced at his watch. "I've already given you more time than you deserve, but I'll tell you this, Ms. Cole. Parker Koontz is an outstanding citizen and has spent every year I've known him volunteering his time for numerous charities and events, including the Special Olympics. Parker started a program to befriend the elderly at local homes for people without relatives or friends. I could go on, but as I said earlier, I am busy. If you do your homework, Detective, you'll discover that Parker Koontz is well respected in the community, and you'd be hard-pressed to find too many people who would have anything bad to say about him."

His gaze was piercing, but Jessie refused to look away. "I have done my homework," she said, "and Parker Koontz may be an outstanding citizen, but he's also a Peeping Tom and a stalker, and I aim to prove it."

He surprised her by asking, "Do you have any idea why Parker was carrying a weapon?"

"I heard he thought he was being followed. But why carry a gun loaded with blanks if he truly felt he was in danger?"

"Carrying a gun loaded with blanks sounds like something Parker would do. You might not be aware that Parker had been attacked before."

"No. I didn't know," she said, wondering if Roche was now resorting to lies.

"He was attacked in Capitol Park, I might add."

She tried not to show her surprise.

The muscles in his face relaxed as he straightened. "I'm sure he carried a gun to scare off an attacker if he ever needed to, but he would never have carried a loaded gun because he would never want to harm anyone."

Not only was Roche full of himself; he seemed intent on trying to intimidate her while also making Parker Koontz into some pillar of perfection, which was one more reason why he'd probably agreed to speak to her. He wanted to take her down a notch.

"I am curious," he said. "Why exactly did you come to see me?"

"I'm an investigator. I talk to people and ask them questions. It's what I do. If I have to go against Nicholas Levine in court, I need to be prepared, which means I need to find out more about Parker Koontz. And who better to talk to than his good friend and business partner?"

"Well, I'm afraid I won't be any help to you, Ms. Cole. If anything, I'll probably do you more harm than good since I will be making sure the judge is aware of your reputation for being trigger-happy. In my opinion, you're a danger to society." He stood, letting her know their talk was over.

THIRTEEN

The house he'd been watching for more than a year now belonged to Mike and Natalie Bailey. From his perch in the highest branches of an oak tree, he had a perfect view of the kitchen window. He saw Mike Bailey step up behind his wife, kiss her cheek, and then wrap his arms around her waist while she rinsed the dishes. Under the soft glow of the kitchen light, he could make out the slight curve of her lips when she smiled.

He shifted his weight from his right hip to his left. He hadn't planned on sitting in the tree for so long. Usually that wouldn't be a problem since he'd been climbing trees for as long as he could remember. After mastering the art of climbing gangly-limbed oaks, he'd moved on to pines and redwoods. From there he'd conquered fences and walls. His ability to climb trees had often saved him from his father's tortuous whims.

Mike walked away, leaving Natalie alone.

His chest tightened. Tonight was the night.

He'd learned a lot about the couple just from picking through their garbage. Discovering where they hid the key to their house, though, had been a game changer.

He'd read every love letter he'd found hidden away in their closet. They'd met when Mike was a senior and Natalie was a sophomore in high school. Two days after Natalie graduated, they were married at a local courthouse. Hardworking people, they had toiled at odd jobs during the day and attended higher-education courses at night. Mike became a lawyer, and Natalie worked as a psychotherapist, which was surprising considering all her talk in her journal about wanting to be a social worker like her mother, Sue Sterling.

Which brought him to the reason he was here.

Sue Sterling was the social worker sent to his house when he was a child. By the time she came for a visit, there had to have been enough complaints and concerns about abuse and child neglect to fill a binder. He couldn't count the number of times teachers, neighbors, and doctors had commented on the cigarette burns and bite marks they'd seen on his bony arms and legs.

Why else would she have been sent to his house?

What nobody had witnessed were all the other unimaginable things he was forced to do on the farm. If he didn't submit to his father's demands, he was locked in the box for days.

He didn't question why his mother never left his father. The one time she'd tried, his father found her and dragged her home, shackled her wrists and ankles to the barn wall with metal cuffs, and made him, her only son, practice playing darts.

He was twelve by the time Natalie Bailey's mom arrived. Somehow his father had been warned that someone from Child Services would be paying them a visit, so he made him and his mother scrub floors, wash clothes, and makes themselves presentable.

Sue Sterling seemed impressed. Not only by his father's good looks but also by the cleanliness of their house. The second his father walked into the other room to stir the pot of stew on the stove, he'd lifted his shirt high enough so that Sue Sterling could see his chest was covered with infected crisscrosses made with a pair of rusty scissors.

Her breathing had hitched before she'd quickly looked away.

Ultimately he figured she must not have cared because she talked to his father one more time, shook his hand, and then left the premises, never to be heard from again.

He'd never forgotten her face or her name.

Many times after that day, he'd thought about running away, but he couldn't bring himself to leave Mom. But she was determined that he save himself. She knew he was smart. Dad had pulled him out of school after the Sue Sterling visit, so Mom tutored him every day. When he was old enough, she'd helped him apply to colleges. He'd gotten a full scholarship to UCI, and since he was growing big enough to fight back, Dad let him go. He majored in psychology and social work. And when he wasn't studying, he fought the demons within and did everything he could to keep the voices at bay. Two weeks before graduation, after discovering his mother had passed on, something had snapped.

He'd killed a cow and a dog, hoping the act of killing a living creature would help him release his never-ending frustration and hatred for life and people. Unfortunately the urge to harm others only grew from there, especially when he'd realized a lot of his hostility stemmed from Sue Sterling's visit.

It hadn't been too late. She could have saved him.

She'd seen.

She'd known.

And yet she'd done nothing.

The first human he'd killed was a homeless man. It had all happened in a blur. He'd snuck up behind the old man, leaned over his shoulder, and stabbed him in the chest. It was over in the blink of an eye. So he'd ripped out his heart in hopes that he would feel something more.

But it wasn't enough. He couldn't stop, didn't want to stop.

His next victim had been a hooker. She'd told him to call her Sugar. And that was what he'd done.

Without any prompting, she'd stripped off her clothes. She couldn't understand why he didn't jump her bones—then she'd seen the knife in his hand. That was when she'd panicked. Sugar had started talking real fast, every word tumbling over the next. Her eyes had become overly bright, and she began to shake, even peed right where she stood. Peed like a horse. He should know, since he'd grown up on a farm.

Sugar didn't run. Instead she froze in terror.

And he was fascinated.

For the first time in his life, he understood what fear did to people, and what his father must have felt every time he tortured him or his mother. Being in control of another human being gave him a high he'd never experienced before.

He was the Wizard of Oz, a force to be reckoned with.

He was all-powerful.

He had told her not to worry, calling her Sugar as he tied her to a tree. And he'd listened to her ramble on about all the reasons he should let her go as he used his knife to sharpen a couple of sticks that would be used to poke and prod.

Every time he'd given her hope by telling her he'd let her go when he was finished with her, she would relax. He'd told her to do all sorts of things, like dance and sing, and poke herself in the eye. She had done anything and everything he asked her to do, and his pulse quickened every time she obeyed.

But not in a sexual way. He didn't feel those kinds of things. Never had. He had no desire to touch a woman, let alone another human being. What he'd always wanted was to feel something other than anger. And for the first time in his life, he did.

Sugar had grown tired of his games, so he'd untied her. He knew she'd run, but he'd never expected her to be so fast after everything she'd been through. It hadn't been easy catching up to her. When he'd had her on the ground again, she'd kicked and clawed, bit down hard on his wrist. He still had the scar. She was a fighter, but she was no match for him. He'd easily taken control again, tied her to the tree, and began to remove her heart, slowly and methodically, while she screamed and spit fire. That time he'd been able to watch the pulsing, pounding organ as he felt his own heart beat within. It was magical.

Sugar was special. The one who made him recognize that control was power, and power was everything.

He'd found his passion.

So he'd moved back home and showed his father who was boss. Then he'd forced him to sell most of the farmland so that they would own the house, the barn, and ten acres of land, free and clear, allowing him to work from home and do what he loved best.

Natalie reached up and removed two cups and saucers from the cupboard, pulling him out of his reverie. A few minutes later, the lights went out, and he could no longer see Natalie through the kitchen window.

They would drink their tea while they read in bed.

He'd hidden in their house before. Spent more than one night huddled inside the attic, listening to them through the vents. He'd been watching Mike and Natalie for so long, he felt as if he knew them.

He shimmied down the trunk and jumped to the ground, then stood still, overcome with excitement. In a few hours, it would be time to introduce himself to Natalie Bailey.

FOURTEEN

Jessie awoke to the sound of a barking dog.

Even then it took her a moment to remember Higgins.

When she opened her eyes, she saw Olivia's cat, Cecil, sitting on the dresser straight ahead, staring at her with his one gold-speckled eye. "How did you get in here?"

Cecil meowed.

She threw off the covers, climbed out of bed, and walked into the main room, where she could see Olivia in the kitchen making a bag lunch for school.

"Good morning," she said to Olivia as she watched the dog use his three good legs to scoot across the wood floor. Cecil had followed her from the bedroom. His long tail brushed across her calf before he jumped on top of the couch and stared the dog down. Higgins was too focused on Olivia to notice.

"Morning," Olivia said. "I didn't think you were ever going to wake up."

"You should have woke me."

"Bella is picking me up. And I knew you needed sleep after spending the night in jail."

"Thanks," Jessie said with a roll of her eyes, knowing she would never live it down.

Olivia scrunched up her nose. "I never asked you about being in jail. Was it horrible?"

"It smelled like body odor and bleach. I'll leave it at that." Jessie scratched her head as she focused her attention on the dog. "Is Higgins hungry?"

"No. I fed him and then took him outside to do his thing."

"Can he walk?"

Olivia nodded. "I carried him down the stairs, but when I set him down on the patch of grass, he did pretty good keeping most of his weight on his three good legs. Will you be able to check on him during the day?"

Jessie stared at the dog. "Sure." She glanced at the clock. "What can I do to help you get ready?"

"Can you give Higgins his pills?" Olivia asked before she disappeared inside her bedroom, where Jessie could hear the hamster wheel going round and round.

Jessie went to the kitchen and read the labels on the pills, then grabbed a piece of cheese from the refrigerator and walked back to the dog.

Higgins growled.

"Stop it, or I'll change your name to Cujo."

Another low rumble came from the dog's throat.

"Do you want your pills or not?"

His ears perked up.

"That's what I thought." She wrapped the cheese around the biggest pill first, bent down on one knee, and held it toward the dog's nose. He sniffed before drawing back his lip.

Jessie straightened. "Listen, Higgins. You're in pain. I can see it in your eyes. You need to take these pills if you want to get better."

The dog whimpered as he tried to get up on all fours.

Enough was enough. She knelt down and forced the cheese into his mouth.

It worked. He ate it.

"Good dog," she said, surprised.

She repeated the process, stroking his back when he was done, ignoring his persistent growling. "You're all bark and no bite."

He whimpered.

"I know. I know." Jessie sat on the floor next to him and continued to brush her fingers through his wiry, patchy fur. "We both had a rough day yesterday, didn't we? The good news is you'll feel better in thirty minutes when the medication sets in."

Olivia came out of her room with her backpack, ready to go. Her face brightened when she saw Jessie petting Higgins. "He's warming up to you."

The dog growled.

"Oh, never mind."

Jessie's eyes narrowed. "Are you wearing makeup?"

"No."

"We have a pact, remember? We always tell each other the truth."

"It's just a little mascara. What's the big deal?"

A car honked.

"I've gotta go."

Jessie frowned. Although she wasn't Olivia's mother, she thought of herself as one. Lunches and carpools, homework and discipline, tended to do that to a person. But lecturing Olivia about makeup . . . when had she become one of those mothers? Everyone wore makeup in high school. What harm could it do?

She thought of her sister then, and that was when it dawned on her. Olivia had helped fill the void in her heart after Sophie disappeared, and now she was scared to death—panicked, even—by the idea of Olivia growing up too fast. She wasn't ready to let her go. And the worst part was, she might never be ready.

Colin had been at the lab talking to the people in forensics who had processed Erin Hayes's abandoned car when he got the call about Natalie Bailey's abduction.

As he walked up the path leading to the Bailey house, a two-story Victorian in Midtown, an officer lifted the yellow crime tape to make access easy for him.

The sun hit his back as he continued on to the wide-open front door. Inside, the house was crowded with technicians, who were busy collecting evidence and taking prints from doors and windows.

Gordon Douglas called his name from the living room.

He and Gordon had worked together for a number of years now. Gordon had given up his career as an urban sociologist after losing his brother to a habitual criminal. A good man, he had twelve years of field experience and multiple areas of expertise. His degree in sociology gave him a better understanding of criminal behavior and social influences on crime, making him a valuable asset.

Gordon met him halfway across the living room and then walked him back to where Mike Bailey, Natalie's husband, sat.

Colin had talked to Gordon on the phone on the way over. He knew Gordon had completed the initial walk-through to see whether or not anything had been moved or disturbed. A video had been taken along with photographs. They would go over all that later.

The living room appeared neat and orderly, like a picture in a magazine. Beige walls, polished tables, no knickknacks. Clean and simple. Colin took a seat on the leather ottoman so he could talk to Bailey face-to-face. The man was clearly distraught. His eyes were bloodshot, his short brown hair disheveled. "Mind if I ask you a few questions?"

Bailey shook his head.

"What time did you go to bed last night?"

"Around nine thirty, but Natalie was still reading a book on her Kindle when I fell asleep thirty minutes later."

"Did you ever wake up during the night?"

"Yes. I woke up a little before one in the morning to go to the bathroom. She was in the bed next to me."

"Are you sure?"

He blushed. "I'm positive. She snores. Her snoring was what woke me up."

"And when did you finally notice she was missing?" Colin asked.

"I had a nightmare where I was being attacked by a pack of wolves and I was bit in the arm. Semiawake, I jerked my arm away and fell back to sleep. I didn't wake up fully until six." He lifted his shirtsleeve. "After I started looking around for Natalie, I began to feel woozy. My arm was sore, and I noticed a drop of dried blood right there." He pointed to what could be a needle mark.

"We took a blood sample," Gordon said.

Colin nodded, made a note. "And your wife was gone?"

"Yes, but that didn't set off any alarms for me. She's an early riser. I got out of bed, went to the bathroom, and then headed downstairs. Nothing looked out of the ordinary, but Natalie was nowhere to be found. When I saw her car in the garage, I panicked and rushed back upstairs. Everything was there—purse, car keys, wallet, and cell phone. I called her dad, who lives nearby. He hadn't seen or talked to her in the past two days."

"Had she made any calls during the night?"

"No. I checked her phone. No incoming calls, either."

"She works?"

He nodded.

"What does she do?"

"She's a psychotherapist. She does inpatient work at a local hospital."

Colin made a note. "Has your wife had any trouble with anyone she's been helping?"

"Not that I know of."

"Would she tell you if there was a problem?"

"Absolutely," he blurted as if the question offended him. "We share everything. I would know if she was upset or having problems at work."

"Do you keep an extra key anywhere inside or outside of the house?"

"Yes. When we first moved in, Natalie put a key under the gnome in the planter box."

Colin made notes. Getting in and out of the house without being noticed or leaving any trace evidence had similarities to the Heartless Killer's MO. And yet it was way too early to make assumptions. One of the reasons the Heartless Killer had not been caught was that absolutely no one was safe. There was no connection to race, gender, or age that would indicate any one particular target. He'd taken people from their homes, bicyclists from the street, and kids from bus stops.

Colin looked up from his notepad and asked, "Is the planter box at the front of the house or the back?"

"Right outside the front door. I'll show you."

They followed him outside. The planter was filled with flowers.

Bailey picked up the gnome.

There was nothing there.

"It's gone," he said.

Fifteen

Jessie had been at the office for a while when she looked at the time and saw that it was already ten thirty. Looked like Ben Morrison was a no-show. She would give him until noon before she went to check on Higgins.

Her phone rang. It was Adelind Rain. "Sorry I had to run off yesterday," she said without prelude.

"No problem."

"I'm calling to let you know I quit my job. My parents are worried, and so am I. I'm moving back to Seattle."

"Did something happen since I saw you?"

Adelind hesitated before saying, "I got a call in the middle of the night. Heavy breathing. Are you sure Parker Koontz is still in the hospital?"

"I was told he's in a coma, but I'll call the hospital to see if there has been any change."

"If it's not him, who would be calling me? It makes no sense, and yet it can't be a coincidence."

Jessie didn't have an answer for her.

There was a long pause before Adelind said, "If you could let me know what I owe you, I can get that taken care of before I leave."

Jessie tapped her pencil against her desk. "You might be subpoenaed when I'm brought to court."

"I understand." Adelind proceeded to give Jessie her parents' address and phone number.

"Is there anything else I should know?" Jessie asked.

"Just be careful."

The call was disconnected.

As Jessie stared absently ahead, thinking about the Koontz problem, a short and extremely pale man entered her office. He marched right in and took a seat in the chair in front of her desk. His gray hair was messy, his jaw unshaven. The dark shadows under his eyes made him look as if he might be sick.

Without bothering to introduce himself, he reached for a tissue and used it to wipe the sweat from his forehead. The only person she'd been expecting was Ben Morrison, the crime reporter. And this man was definitely not him.

But something was seriously wrong. Jessie stood. "Do you need help?"

"Are you Jessie Cole, the private investigator?"

"I am."

"Then yes. I need help."

"Are you all right?" she asked.

"No," he answered sharply, his shoulders tense. "My daughter disappeared five days ago, and the police won't do anything about it. I am *not* all right."

Jessie kept a close eye on him as she slowly sank back down into her chair. He looked a bit unhinged, making her wonder if he was on drugs. She knew the best thing she could do was remain calm. "Did you fill out a missing person's report?"

"Of course I did."

"What makes you think the police aren't doing anything?"

"Because they said as much," he said, his shoulders relaxing some. "Zee has disappeared before. Many times, in fact. She has problems.

Don't we all? But she's a good person—kind and compassionate. The sort of person who would never harm a flea."

In a matter of seconds, his anger had changed to hopelessness. A part of her wanted to reach across her desk, place her hands on his, and tell him to take a breath. The other part wondered if the pepper spray was still in the drawer in front of her. "Exactly what sort of problems does your daughter have?"

"She's been diagnosed as a paranoid schizophrenic. She suffers from depression, hallucinations, and delirium, which sometimes happens when she overmedicates by mistake."

"How old is she?"

"Twenty-eight."

"You said she's disappeared before. Where does she usually go?"

His shoulders fell. "I have no idea. I work for a software company, and there were a couple of times I came home and she wasn't there. But she's also left the house in the middle of the night when I'm sleeping, so I've never had the chance to follow her. She's usually home within twenty-four hours." He looked down at his lap. "Until now."

"Was she left alone during the day?"

"The last caregiver quit within hours and didn't bother telling me until I called her looking for Zee."

"Is Zee her nickname?"

"It's short for Zinnia. Her mother named her after the flower. Is that important?"

"No," she said. "It's not. Has Zee ever told you anything about where she goes when she runs off?"

He shook his head. "She's usually disoriented and confused when she returns. That's what happens when she doesn't take her pills."

"I see."

"Do you really?" he asked, his face pinched. "Or are you saying that because you think I'm crazy?"

"Why would I think you were crazy?"

"Because of the way I look. I hear what people say behind my back. I'm not deaf." He huffed. "I'm as pale as a ghost. My head is way too big for my body. And throughout grade school my nickname was Dumbo, thanks to my enormous ears." His tone sharpened. "I've heard whispers about Zee running off because I'm so hideously ugly."

People's cruelty had no bounds. "You're not ugly."

"So why did you practically jump out of your skin when I took a seat?"

"Because you *are* unusually pale, just as you said. And between the dark circles and sheen of sweat on your brow, I thought you might be having a heart attack."

He seemed to ponder that before he said, "Fair enough."

"What's your name?" she asked, hoping to change the subject.

"Arlo Gatley."

She opened the top drawer, ignored the pepper spray rolling around, and grabbed a pricing sheet instead. She slid the paper across the desk in front of him. "As you can see, it can get costly for you to hire me to search for Zee, which is why you might want to reconsider letting the police handle this."

He closed his eyes—sort of a long, exasperated blink. "Money isn't a problem."

"I charge by the hour, and I would need a retainer," she said. "I'm going to assume you've already looked for your daughter in all of her favorite spots. I'll need you to fill out some paperwork if you're interested in moving forward."

She pulled out another small packet with a list of basic questions: name, address, telephone number, hobbies, favorite restaurants, friends and family, and so on. She was having a hard time building up enthusiasm for the job, mostly because she had a lot on her plate. But he looked into her eyes just then, and for the first time since Arlo entered her office, she saw through his frustration. His Adam's apple bobbed as he swallowed. His eyes welled with tears as he said, "I'll be forever in your debt. Thank you."

"You're welcome," she said with a smile.

"If I fill out these papers right now and write you a check, when would you be able to begin your search?"

"Today," she said. "Fill out those papers, and I'll get started."

He released a sob, and it took everything not to cry along with him. Seeing him so distraught reminded her of how she'd felt when Sophie had disappeared. She didn't wish that kind of pain on anyone.

He grabbed another tissue and wiped his nose. "There is one more thing you should know about Zee before you agree."

"What is it?"

"When you find her," he said as if that was a given, "you'll need to be careful."

Jessie lifted a questioning eyebrow.

"She's been known to be violent at times."

"How so?"

"She'll kick and bite if someone tries to restrain her. She's strong, too. She broke my finger once. She didn't mean to, of course; it was an accident."

"I'm sure I'll be fine, but I am curious about something."

He nodded, waited.

"How did you hear about me?"

"I saw you on the news recently, but that wasn't the reason I came to you. It was three or four years ago when you found that fifteen-year-old girl—"

He paused, trying to remember, so Jessie said, "Tonya Grimm?"

"Yes, that's the one. Everyone else had given up on finding her, thought she was a runaway. Some people even accused the parents of having something to do with her disappearance. But not you. You didn't give up. And you found her."

Sixteen

Arlo Gatley remained in Jessie's office for another hour and a half, filling out paperwork and talking about Zee. Apparently his daughter heard voices. Zee talked to herself, even got into arguments with her reflection in the mirror. She'd once hidden inside a mail truck, and twice she'd made herself at home at the neighbor's house. The first time she was making a sandwich, and the second time she was asleep in the master bedroom. Two years ago she was fired from her job at a large retailer after she slapped a customer across the face for being rude. All the stories combined made Jessie realize that this girl could be absolutely anywhere.

It was two o'clock by the time Jessie stepped outside and walked down the block toward home to check on Higgins. A few minutes later, she slipped the key into the lock on her front door when she heard someone call her name from across the street. Glancing over her shoulder, she noticed a tall, broad-shouldered man heading her way. She recognized him immediately.

Ben Morrison in the flesh. He appeared taller than the six foot three specified during her Internet search yesterday. His hair was longer, too, pulled back with a rubber band at his nape. She could see the scarring from third-degree burns on the left side of his face and neck. Part of his left ear was missing. The skin was pulled so tight she could see the formation of muscle and bone beneath.

"You must be Ben Morrison," she said, offering her hand as he approached.

His fingers were as big as sausages, his handshake firm. She could feel the hard texture of his skin on the palm of his hand where he'd been burned.

"Sorry I'm late," he told her. "I just pulled up when I saw you crossing the street. Is this where you live?"

Although she wasn't the trusting sort and didn't usually invite strangers into her home, she was worried about Higgins. She was also interested to know what Ben Morrison had to say about Sophie. Besides, she thought fleetingly, he was a well-known crime reporter in the area, and a family man. She opened the door wider. "I need to check on the dog. You're welcome to come in."

He nodded and followed her inside. As they walked up the stairs, she told him about Higgins and the hit-and-run.

When they reached the top of the stairs, they both stopped and stared. The place looked as if it had been ransacked. The synthetic stuffing had been removed from the couch and was littered about the floor, making it look as if it had snowed inside her house. An empty cereal box and assorted garbage made a trail from the kitchen.

Cecil was napping on the windowsill.

Higgins was nowhere to be seen, but Jessie followed the path of chewed-on shoes and debris through the hallway and into her bedroom. "Higgins," she said. He was lying in a corner of her closet. He gave her a guilty look. Although there was a small fenced-in area in the backyard, it had been too hot to leave the dog outside. Instead she'd set up a place in the kitchen, complete with newspapers, blanket, water, and food. She'd used furniture to block his exit.

Jessie looked at Ben Morrison and raised both arms. "You said you wanted to do a story about me and my family. Well, this is my life in a nutshell. Chaos. Come on," Jessie said to the dog. "Let's take you outside."

Higgins growled as she leaned over to pick him up.

"Here," Ben said. "Let me take him outside for you."

She backed away. "Be my guest. I'll grab his leash and a plastic bag."

Twenty minutes later, Jessie had picked up most of the garbage scattered about and was shoving the last of the stuffing back into the couch when Ben returned with Higgins. She used duct tape to cover the torn fabric, then held up the tape and said, "My go-to repair tool."

He smiled. "I can see that. I took Higgins around the neighborhood," he told her. "He's basically walking on three legs, but overall I think he'll make a quick recovery."

"Thank you for doing that."

"I'm sure you've already figured out that this dog has been abused. He's fearful and untrusting, and I think I know why he seems to have a problem trusting you specifically."

His statement took her by surprise. She straightened and plunked her hands on her hips. "Why is that?"

"There's a lot of foot traffic out there, but the only person he showed aggression toward was a brown-haired woman who was about your size. He had no problem with men, children, or other dogs. My guess is he associates his abuse with petite, dark-haired women."

"Interesting."

"My wife and I adopted an abused Labrador when we were first married. He was afraid of small children. We did some investigating and found out he'd been raised with children who kicked him and threw rocks at him. Higgins," he said, petting the dog, "got it much worse than that. He still has the scars to prove it."

"I thought those patchy spots were from malnutrition," she said.

"Some of them are, but if you look closely at his backside, you can see he's been whipped. Probably with a belt. He also has scars that appear to be burn marks, most likely from cigarettes."

She dropped her arms to her sides. "That's horrible." She wanted to go to Higgins, but it was easy to see that he was truly fearful of her. "How did you help your dog recover?"

"Patience, time, and lots of love." He removed the leash. "Where should I put this?"

She took it from him and put it aside. She then led Higgins into the kitchen to give him his pills and some food and water. He ate half the food and then plopped down on the blanket, exhausted.

"Go ahead and have a seat," Jessie told Ben.

She brought him a glass of cold water and then took a seat across from him. "I need to be straight with you. I've thought about what you said about wanting to do a story on my family, and I'm not sure it would be a good idea."

Before he could respond, she added, "My niece, Olivia, recently started high school, and I'm not sure how I feel about her mother's life being put out there again for public consumption."

"I understand what you're saying, but—"

"The truth is, I'm not sure how you could help. I've been to every place Sophie ever set foot in multiple times. I've talked to teachers, friends, the postman, and acquaintances—anyone who ever said two words to her. And yet I'm no closer today to finding out what happened to her than I was ten years ago. It's as if she vanished into thin air." Jessie leaned forward and tapped a finger on the coffee table. "Sophie was twenty when she disappeared. She hardly had any friends. I don't even know who the father of her child is."

As soon as the words were out, she berated herself for saying too much. She didn't know this man.

"In your line of work, I'm sure you've handled a few cold cases over the years," he said.

"Yes, I have," she said, wondering what he was getting at.

"Then you know there's nothing better than having a fresh pair of eyes to look things over. My helping would have nothing to do with critiquing an old investigation or making anyone who worked on the case look bad."

She crossed her arms over her chest. "I get that."

"The thing is," he went on, "most people investigators talk to are more likely to open up about an old case rather than a new one. Witnesses and friends tend not to be so secretive about something that happened a decade ago. Many people don't like to cooperate with authorities because of fear or disdain. But after the years pass by, things change. People grow up. Sometimes they grow a conscience. Minds muddled by drugs grow clearer."

Jessie met his gaze and wondered if she could trust him. Everything he said made sense. She found herself warming up to him and changed her mind. Besides, she really could use some help. She thought about Parker Koontz and Arlo Gatley and the stacks of files on her desk at the office. She needed him a lot more than he needed her.

"This isn't about dragging your family's name through the mud," he said. "I'm not interested in casting dark shadows of any kind on your family. My plan would be to start by retracing every detail of the last day your sister was seen."

"You said on the phone that you might have known Sophie. Is that true?"

"I have amnesia—"

"Yes. I did a search on the Internet. Retrograde amnesia. You were in a car accident."

He nodded. "The doctors had hoped I would regain memories by now, but that hasn't happened. Not until I saw your sister on television. It felt as if a switch had been flipped inside my head. I know I've met her," he continued, "but I have no idea when or where."

"Maybe your sudden interest in Sophie has more to do about discovering your past than mine."

He seemed to ponder that. "Perhaps."

"If this is about finding Sophie, then why bother doing a story about my family?"

"I needed to sell the idea to my boss so I could continue to collect a paycheck, and your story makes good copy."

She raised a questioning eyebrow.

"You and your sister were born and raised right here in the neighborhood," he explained. "Your mother leaves. Your father starts drinking. One sister goes missing and the other never stops looking."

"I appreciate your brutal honesty, but I'll need to talk to Olivia about this before I make my final decision."

"Talk to Olivia about what?"

Jessie looked across the room and saw Olivia standing at the top of the stairs. Jessie sighed. "This is Ben Morrison with the *Sacramento Tribune*. He's interested in helping us find out what happened to Sophie."

Olivia looked from Ben to Jessie. "You said yes, right?"

"Don't you think that might be a problem at school?" Jessie asked her. "Your friends will be reading about Sophie's life, which means they'll be asking questions about you, too."

"I don't care about that," Olivia said with a shrug. "My closest friends know everything anyhow."

Ben pushed himself to his feet. "I should go and let the two of you talk in private."

Jessie stood, too.

Ben looked at Olivia. "It was nice meeting you, Olivia."

"You, too," she said.

Jessie walked him out and then joined Olivia in the kitchen, where she hovered over the dog.

"I don't know why you would even think about turning down his offer," Olivia said. "Don't you want to find out what happened to Sophie?"

Olivia had stopped referring to Sophie as her mom years ago, and Jessie had never pressed her about it. But there were times like now when she wondered what was going through that head of hers. "Of course I do," Jessie said. "But you're older now, and I worry about people talking, saying unkind things. How would that make you feel, hearing things that may or may not be true about someone you love?"

"I guess I wouldn't like it if people were talking crap about her, but I'm tough. I can handle it." Olivia pushed herself to her feet and looked Jessie in the eyes. "I want to know—no, I *need* to know why Sophie left and whether or not she's ever coming back."

SEVENTEEN

Erin could hardly move. Her breathing quickened.

Don't panic.

She was on her back, faceup, arms at her sides.

When she tried to lift her head, her forehead smacked against wood. Closing her eyes, she forced herself to take calming breaths. But it was no use. She wanted to scream for help.

But then what? Would that alert the freak?

No. No. No. Don't scream.

She bit down on her lip and counted to five. The sound of her heartbeat pounded inside her head.

How had she come to be there?

The freak had been angry with her. She remembered that much. He'd said something about a box. That was the last thing she'd heard him say before everything went black. Had he hit her over the head? Drugged her? She had no recollection whatsoever.

She used the tips of her bare toes to feel around and get an idea of the length of the box. If she pointed her toe, she touched wood. Damp wood. She could raise her knee only a few inches before making contact. The wood was soft. She jerked her knee upward, quick, to see if she could make a dent, but the wood wouldn't give. She cried out in pain. *Shut up. Shut up.*

She stopped to listen. Was he coming?

Suddenly she recalled waking up once before. She'd thought she was having a nightmare. Every time she fell back asleep, Grandma Rose would appear and remind her of her first track meet. "Go for it," Grandma had whispered in her ear. "Set goals or you'll have nothing to strive for. And don't forget to imagine it—see it in your mind—and it will happen."

Go for it, Erin thought. *Go for what?*

She looked left, then right. Tiny pinpricks of sunlight had found their way through crevices in the wood. Daytime. Was she inside or outside?

She sniffed the air, concentrating, trying to figure out the smells. Horse manure and straw.

Outside.

There were other smells she couldn't quite figure out. Every once in a while she'd hear grunting. *Pigs?*

Shit. Shit. Shit.

How had she let this happen? She was smarter than this. She'd thought she could outsmart him, but she'd failed. He'd known exactly what she was going to do, and he'd been prepared.

Think, Erin. Think.

Stay positive. Stay strong.

She could breathe. That was a good thing. If the wooden box had been constructed of brand-new wood instead of old, she probably wouldn't have had enough oxygen to stay alive for long. The light coming through was also reassuring since it meant she hadn't been buried alive.

She couldn't hear anyone moving around outside, so it wouldn't do her any good to scream out and risk drawing the freak's attention. Besides, she didn't want to waste her energy. She'd watched a show with her mom once about getting out of crazy situations, like if you were trapped in a car that was sinking in water or an attacker came at you in a parking lot. She would have kneed her abductor in the groin if she hadn't had the Taser. What a waste of effort that had been. In all situations, though, there was one common denominator: never panic. Not panicking wasn't as easy as it sounded. Neither was getting the image of Garrett's bloated face and bulging eyes out of her mind.

She worked on keeping her breathing even as she tried to think.

"Start out slow. Finish fast." Those had been the last words she'd heard Grandma Rose say before she woke up.

Start out slow. Finish fast.

The coins! As he'd dragged her from the cell, before she'd blacked out, she'd felt the coins beneath the straw. Knowing he would take them away if he saw them, she'd quickly shoved one coin in each ear.

Had he taken them from her?

There wasn't much room to maneuver in the box. It was a tight squeeze, but if she bent her elbow and slid her forearm slowly across her stomach, she could move her hand up toward her face. She put her left finger inside her right ear and squeezed her eyes shut when she realized there was nothing there.

It's okay. Try the other ear.

She took a calming breath, then moved her right arm in the same fashion, breathing a sigh of relief when the tip of her finger made contact with something hard. She pulled the coin from her ear, taking her time, careful not to drop it as she transferred it from her left hand to her right. It felt about the size of a nickel.

The wood was damp. Could she dig her way out of the box?

She used the coin to poke and dig at the wood near her right hip. After a few minutes, she felt a tiny divot. Making a hole could take days, she realized. How long could she survive inside this box?

As she scraped and dug, she thought about Mom and Dad and how they'd all been arguing about school right before she'd gotten in the car and taken off. She didn't want to go to college. At the very least, she wanted to take a year off. But they wouldn't budge. Why did she always have to be so stubborn? It felt as if she'd been fighting with her parents since the day she was born. She couldn't even remember what they fought about most of the time. If she could find a way out of this, if she could escape the madman, if she could get back to her parents and her siblings and their chaotic lives, she would never argue with them again.

See it. Imagine it. Make it happen.

In her mind's eye, she imagined making a hole big enough to dig her way out. She watched herself climb out of the box. The sun shone in her eyes and warmed her back. She imagined her legs moving and her arms pumping as she ran from this place.

She could do this.

Coin against wood.

Scraping, scraping, scraping.

Eighteen

In the morning Jessie called the hospital to check on Parker Koontz. According to a nurse on the fifth floor, his condition had not changed. Although she wouldn't elaborate further, she was adamant that his current condition would have prevented him from making a phone call.

Next on the list was a visit to the coffee shop on Sixteenth Street where Adelind Rain had said she'd met a barista by the name of Fiona Hampton. According to Adelind, Fiona had also been stalked by Parker Koontz.

Jessie hopped into the car and started the engine, hoping Fiona would be willing to talk to her. So far her research had proven everything David Roche had said about Parker Koontz was true. He was a well-respected, hardworking attorney who volunteered his free time to worthy causes.

So why the hell had the man shot blanks at her?

He had a clean record, and nothing she could find so far indicated he might be suicidal.

After finding a parking spot on the street, Jessie got out and walked a half block to the coffee shop, glad to see it wasn't too busy. She ordered a large coffee and grabbed a granola bar to go with it. As the man behind the counter poured her coffee, she asked him if Fiona Hampton worked there.

"Here she comes now." He gestured behind her.

Jessie looked over her shoulder. The woman coming through the door caught more than a few people's attention as she removed the scarf from her head, revealing a shock of white hair that matched her skin.

"Hey, Reid," Fiona said before connecting gazes with Jessie. "What? Haven't you ever met an albino before?"

"Chill," Reid said. "The lady was just asking about you."

"Oh." She looked Jessie over. "Sorry."

"Not a problem. I was hoping you would answer a few questions about a man named Parker Koontz," Jessie said as she dropped her change into the tip jar.

Fiona sighed. "Sure. I guess. I'm early," she said. "I can spare a few minutes."

Jessie slipped the granola bar into her purse and then grabbed her coffee from the counter.

After Fiona put her things in the back room, she led Jessie to a table. "So, what's going on? Did that creep go after you, too?"

"No. I'm here because Adelind Rain told me you were once stalked by Parker Koontz."

"Ah. I see. Is she okay?"

"She quit her job and moved away."

Fiona whistled through her teeth.

"So it's true that he stalked you?"

"Yep. That guy is one sick puppy." She pointed a finger at Jessie. "Hey, wait a minute. I thought I recognized you. Are you the one who shot him at the park?"

"Unfortunately, yes. What I need to know is whether or not you ever called the police during the time Koontz was disturbing you."

Fiona nodded. "Dozens of times, but he always disappeared before they could get to wherever I happened to be."

"Did you ever file a report?"

"No. I guess I should have. I would call the police, they would come, the creep would disappear, and life would go on until the next time I saw him."

"It must have been frustrating."

"You have no idea. Longest two weeks of my life."

"Bottom line," Jessie said, "is that criminal charges have been filed against me. If I have to go to court, which is likely, any chance you would be willing to tell a judge what you just told me?"

"I'd be happy to help in any way I can. But you should know that whoever is going after you in court could try to use my albinism against me."

"How so?"

"A lot of people with albinism are considered legally blind. Vision problems resulting from abnormal development of the retina."

"But what about you? Can you see?"

Fiona's smile was infectious. "Like an eagle."

After they exchanged contact information, Fiona stood and said, "I better get to work. It's getting busy."

Jessie came to her feet. They shook hands. "I can't thank you enough."

"I'm the one who should be thanking you. Having a creep like Parker Koontz follow me around day and night and not being able to do a damn thing about it was a nightmare. I'll do whatever I can to help."

After leaving the coffee shop, Jessie headed straight for Arlo Gatley's house in Woodland. Feeling hopeful about her talk with Fiona, she prayed Fiona's and Adelind's testimony would be enough.

Twenty-five minutes later she pulled up to the curb outside Arlo Gatley's house on the outskirts of Woodland, about twenty miles north-west of Sacramento.

Arlo greeted her at the door and invited her inside. The dark circles around his eyes had faded a bit. His hair was combed back with gel, and he looked better than he had twenty-four hours ago. Except for the drop of blood on his thumb on his right hand. She felt queasy. He saw her looking and shoved his hand into his pocket.

The house was one story, the inside painted a muted green with white crown molding, hardwood floors, and lots of built-in shelving filled with assorted knickknacks.

"Would you like to see Zee's room?" he asked. She knew he had an important job to do at the tech company he worked for because he'd told her as much. When she'd called last night to let him know she wanted to come by and take a look around, he'd told her she'd have to come early.

"Your daughter's room would be a good place to start," Jessie said. She followed him down a narrow hallway. Walls on both sides were covered with an eclectic group of pictures. The frames were made of wood, shells, paper—all different sizes—and most of them were tilted at odd angles. Mostly school pictures, and a few of Arlo and his daughter when she was younger.

Jessie stopped to take a better look at his daughter. In almost every photo, Zee had a strange look on her face. Lost? Worried? It was hard to tell.

Arlo stood at the door at the end of the hallway, his arms crossed. Gone was the desperate and accommodating man of yesterday. Today Arlo appeared impatient and agitated.

Jessie peered into the laundry room as she passed by. Everything in the home appeared neat, nothing out of the ordinary. That was, until she walked into Zee's room.

The walls were covered with macabre pictures of skeletons with bloodshot eyeballs hanging by a thread from their sockets. Above the headboard was a poster of a cemetery, bloodied body parts scattered about like debris after a night of strong winds.

She looked to her feet, where a trail of ants had been hand-painted across the entirety of the wood floor, continuing up one side of the wall and across a stark white windowsill. The ants looked so real, she knelt down to brush her fingers over the smooth wood. On a low table beneath a curtained window were jars filled with incense and herbs. She straightened and walked that way. Bottles of potions labeled "Eye of Doe" and "Dragon Fire" sat in front of a stack of tarot cards. All of it contrasted with the stuffed teddy bear and the pink comforter spread neatly across the bed.

"It can be a little overwhelming," Arlo said.

That was putting it mildly, Jessie thought.

"She's fond of her tarot cards, and when she's not making potions, she likes to do readings and spells."

"Did she draw these pictures?" Jessie asked.

"Yes. She's quite talented. She enjoys drawing and painting images that shock people."

"I can see that. Where's her mother?"

"She died of cancer when Zee was six months old."

"I'm sorry."

Arlo said nothing.

Jessie couldn't stop thinking about the blood she'd seen on Arlo's thumb. She went to the notebook sitting on the bedside table and held it up. "Do you mind?"

"Go ahead. She's been writing in journals for as long as I can remember. Most are filled with recipes for potions or spells."

Jessie turned the pages, noticed that the dates coincided with the time right before Zee went missing. "Mind if I take this with me?"

"As long as I get it back when you're done."

"No problem," Jessie said. "I also need a recent picture of Zee. Do you have one?"

He nodded before disappearing for no more than thirty seconds, then returned with a photo of Zee. Jessie noticed that Zee wasn't smiling.

"She wasn't happy with me that day," Arlo offered, reading her mind. "But it's a good likeness of her."

Jessie slipped the photo into the journal, then walked to the closet and slid the mirrored door to the left. Dozens of black T-shirts were lined up on hangers along with black pants, black skirts, and a black leather jacket. Shoes and boots were lined up in neat rows on the floor. All black.

With Arlo's permission, she searched through dresser drawers and a vintage chest. Under the bed she found a shoe box. She placed it on the top of the bed and pulled off the lid. It was filled with Polaroid pictures and dried flower petals.

Arlo came closer and reached for a picture that showed Zee sitting in the middle of a field of cut grass. The smile on his daughter's face said it all. She was happy.

Jessie sifted through pictures of Zee on a swing at a park, on a retaining wall looking down into the camera lens, and sitting cross-legged while taking a whiff of a single rose.

Arlo gestured at one of the pictures and said, "That looks like it was taken at Rainbow Park, a few blocks from here." He frowned. "I wonder who took the picture."

Jessie handed Arlo a close-up of his daughter. "When would you guess this might have been taken?"

He used his right hand to hold the picture. It was definitely blood on his thumb. She looked away.

"Two weeks ago," Arlo said. "Zee cut her bangs, straight across, close to her hairline, as you can see in the pictures. My guess is that these were taken within days of her haircut, or maybe even the same day." He put the picture back in the box.

"You told me she didn't have any friends and that she was a loner."

Arlo looked through the contents of the box, a deep frown contorting his features. "Zee and I have always been close." He rubbed his temple. "Or at least I thought we were. Obviously I haven't been paying close enough attention to what she's been doing. I'm at a loss here."

"I'd like to take these things with me, too, if you don't mind?"

He nodded. "As long as you take good care of everything. Like the journal, I'd like it all back, you know, after you find her."

"Of course," Jessie told him. "What happened to your hand?" she asked, unable to let it go. "It looks like you're bleeding."

"It's nothing," he said, avoiding eye contact. "I was cutting some fruit before you came. I must have nicked myself."

"Would you mind if I have a quick look around the rest of the house? It will only take a minute."

His face flushed. He glanced at his watch and shook his head. "Maybe another time. I've got to get going. I—I'm late as it is."

Flummoxed, she said, "Okay. Another time, then." She looked around. "I don't see a computer. Did she use one?"

He rubbed the back of his neck and gave her a subtle nod. "She used mine. I can't part with that. Sorry." His eye twitched, and she wondered if that was a nervous habit of his. She couldn't remember his eye twitching when they'd first met. Arlo was acting so strange, she didn't know what to think.

"I have enough to work with here," she finally said as she piled the journal on top of the shoe box. "You might see me down the street on your way out. I want to knock on a few doors and talk to some of your neighbors, see if anyone spotted Zee coming or going."

"Good luck with that."

His statement baffled her. "What do you mean?"

"The neighbors and I have never seen eye to eye."

The man had a way of saying everything and nothing at the same time. "Why is that?"

"You know how neighbors can be . . . loud music, tall fences, barking dogs. The list is long." His eye twitched again. "Mrs. Dixon next door. Her husband died years ago. She's lonely and has nothing better to do than watch my every move. I'm sure you'll get an earful—that's all I'm saying."

"Is that the same neighbor whose house Zee broke into before?"

"Well, yes, but still, I see no reason for Mrs. Dixon to hold any grudges over such a silly thing."

Jessie nodded, but she couldn't help but think there was something extremely off about Arlo Gatley.

Why did he seem so nervous?

Had he lied to her about the blood on his hand?

Although she questioned what she might have gotten herself into, she was more determined than ever to find Zee. The girl was mentally unstable, lost, and scared.

Jessie needed to find her.

———

"Those two are strange," Mrs. Dixon, the widow and neighbor to the left of Arlo Gatley, said. "If you've met Arlo, which it sounds as if you have, you've probably already figured out that the apple doesn't fall far from the tree. I mean, who names their daughter Zebra?"

"She was named Zinnia, after the flower," Jessie explained. "Arlo calls her Zee."

The woman rolled her eyes.

"When you say the apple doesn't fall far from the tree, what do you mean?" Jessie asked. "Could you elaborate?"

"You've met him, talked to him. He's odd, plain and simple." She sighed and made a face as if she thought Jessie was a dimwit. "For instance, when Arlo pulls up into his driveway after work, I see him sitting in the car, sometimes for an hour. He's not texting or talking on the phone, just staring out the window with a blank look."

Jessie nodded, waited. Arlo might have been right about Mrs. Dixon being lonely.

"Elijah and Lettie Foxletter," Mrs. Dixon said next, pointing to a two-story colonial house not too far down the block, "are in charge of the neighborhood-watch group. You might want to talk to them."

"Before I go," Jessie said, "I was told that Arlo's daughter broke into your home more than once. Did you and Zee ever have a conversation?"

"No. Once she saw me, she just left the house without an explanation or apology. She's a strange one."

"What makes you say that?"

"Well, she did break into my house. That's strange enough, but it's more than that. She mutters to herself, and she's always wearing black." Mrs. Dixon sighed. "When the girl was younger, I use to wake up to her screaming for help in the middle of the night. It was a frightful time— let me tell you. I called the police every time it happened. And every time the police told me she had some sort of mental disorder and that her father was doing everything he could to keep her outbursts under control." She shrugged. "Her screams haven't woken me in years, but that bloodcurdling cry is still stuck in my mind. I've considered moving away. Many of us in the neighborhood have."

"Because you think Zee could be a danger to you?"

"Not the girl—her father," she said. "He's strange, yes. And if you ask me, there's also something disturbing about Arlo Gatley." Mrs. Dixon smoothed the front of her crisp, clean blouse and then peeked over Jessie's shoulder as if she was afraid someone might be listening in. "I'm going to have to say goodbye. Talk to the others. Maybe they can help."

"I will. Thanks for your time."

Before Jessie had a chance to turn away, the door clicked shut in her face.

As she walked on the sidewalk toward the house Mrs. Dixon had pointed out, she saw before her a quaint picture of a tree-lined street with white picket fences bordering newly mowed lawns. The click of her shoes was the only sound as she moved down the street. A hint of jasmine filled the air. If not for the disturbing images on Zee's wall and the thought of that same young woman screaming out for help in the dark of night, Jessie might have found a peaceful sort of solace on her short walk to the Foxletters' house.

Instead she felt chilled to the bone.

NINETEEN

Erin's eyes snapped open at the sound of heavy footsteps against the ground. Her space inside the box was so cramped she could hardly move.

Her claustrophobia was real, making her heart race. *Breathe. Calm down.*

Pressing her lips together, she forced herself to remain quiet. If the footsteps continued on, she would scream. Because that could mean there were other people, hired help who came by to feed the animals. Even now she could hear pigs grunting and ducks quacking. The rooster would crow at sunrise.

But if the footsteps stopped, that would mean it could be *him.* In that case, she would stay quiet. If he opened the lid, she could use the splinters of wood she'd collected to gouge his eyes out.

Being confined did strange things to her mind. She had no idea how long she'd been in the box. She'd been drifting in and out of sleep, hot during the day and cold at night.

Two nights or three?

If she thought about it for too long, she could convince herself she'd been trapped in the cramped space for a lifetime.

Dry mouth and stomach cramps made her crave water and food. She'd eaten a couple of bugs that had dared to creep inside her space. Or had she imagined eating the bugs?

Waiting, trying not to make a sound, she lifted her arms a few inches. *Up and down, up and down. Keep the muscles working.* Inwardly, she recited Lincoln's Gettysburg Address to keep her mind occupied on anything other than the footsteps. *Stay strong. Be ready.*

The footsteps stopped, seemingly right outside the box.

She froze. It was him.

Holding tight to the pieces of jagged wood, her fingers clenched tightly around her makeshift weapons.

"Good morning, Erin. Are you still in there?" he asked.

The sound of his voice gave her goose bumps. She closed her eyes, swallowed her fear.

"If you want any chance of getting out of there alive, you need to follow orders, my darling Erin. Do you hear me?"

The clinking of metal sounded. *A lock?*

Sunlight poured in. Blinding her.

And then she felt a single drop of water hit her forehead.

Squinting one eye, she saw that he hadn't opened the lid, but only a tiny door above her face. How had she missed that?

It was small. The size of a single pack of cigarettes. There was no way she could move her arms, let alone take a swing at him.

"You must be thirsty," he said. "Open your mouth."

She did as he said, her mouth parched.

A handful of dirt hit her face. She spit and coughed. Dirt got in her eye. Tears dribbled down both sides of her face. He was taunting her and enjoying it.

"Good girl," he said. "Just having a little fun. Come on. Open up. This time I'll give you some water. I promise."

She kept her mouth shut. Said nothing. If she opened her mouth, he might shove something worse than dirt inside.

He knelt down close enough that she could see his face clearly through a squinted eye. "You've spent two nights in the box without food or water. I know you're thirsty. So open up or I'll have to force the issue."

He knelt down and pinched her nose closed. When she opened her mouth to take a breath, he shoved an upside-down open water bottle into her mouth. She swallowed once before she felt as if she were drowning. She couldn't breathe. She yanked her head to one side, forcing him to let go of her nose and drop the water bottle.

She sucked in air through her nostrils, then coughed and wheezed.

"If you had followed orders," he told her, "you were going to get to feast on fresh vegetables and fine cheese." He laughed. She knew it was a lie. This was all part of his psychological torture.

"But now," he went on, his tone filled with false sorrow, "I can see that you're not ready to cooperate with me, which means you'll have to share your tiny space with my friend S-S-S-Stan. I found him in the garden. He looks pretty harmless—for a snake, that is."

She screamed as the heaviness of the snake's body slid across her face and neck. And then again when the tiny door above clicked shut.

He stood there for a moment, hands on hips, listening to her muffled screams and looking out at the pasture, where he could see the gray mare. The box used to be in the barn, but a few years ago he'd decided it was time to burn it and get rid of it once and for all. He'd dragged it down the dirt path toward the house, but it was heavy, and he'd gotten only halfway before changing his mind. Now the box sat in a grassy spot at the side of the pathway leading from the house to the barn.

After Erin stopped screaming, he walked away, surprised to realize how much he missed Garrett. Garrett had been the only one of his sheep who had done everything he asked and more. He'd never complained, never cried or whined. And now he was dead, thanks to the bitch in the box.

The box was not a fun place to be, and it might teach Erin Hayes a lesson, just as it had taught him once. His father used to put him in the box a few times a year. The first time he'd thought he would die and nobody would ever find him.

When he'd turned twelve, not long after Sue Sterling had paid them a visit, things had changed.

For the worse.

His father had become creative with his methods of torture. Instead of putting his only son's splayed hands on a red-hot burner, beating him with a belt, or throwing him in the box, he'd found ways to exploit his fears and phobias. His dad had begun to threaten to cut off his feet or his ears or peel off his fingernails. Psychological torture at its best. Designed to mess with his mind and cause stress. He'd lost sleep thinking about what his father might do. Never mind what he'd already done.

He'd once found a book his father had been reading about torture from medieval times to modern day. After Sue Sterling's visit, his father had learned to torture in ways that didn't leave marks. He used a cane to whip the soles of his feet. The worst pain was when his father had extracted a sore tooth because Mom was not allowed to take him to the dentist. After his dad had attempted to pull the molar, part of the bone that had supported the tooth had shifted and poked through his gum. It took about a year for the exposed bone to erode and for the pain to subside.

After feeding the chickens and collecting eggs from the coop, he gathered a tin can of oats, a brush, and a shovel before making his way to the pasture, where he clicked his tongue and waited for Misty, an old swayback mare, to see him and come his way. Misty was his best friend. The only living creature in the world he cared about.

As soon as Misty spotted him, she trotted his way. As she ate the oats he'd brought her, he pulled the brush from his back pocket and used the soft bristles to rub the horse's neck. "How are you doing, girl? You look good."

Misty lifted her head and looked toward the barn, ears perked.

"It's okay, girl. He's not going to hurt you. Never again. Dog is locked up in the basement, remember? He's living in the cell he built with his own two hands."

Misty went back to eating.

"I know. I should have killed him already, but that would have been much too easy—for him, not me. The man caused Mom and me and you nothing but grief. Not a day went by that he didn't call me weak and stupid. He needs more time to think about the things he did wrong. He deserves to be punished, maybe for eternity."

Even as he spoke the words out loud, he knew they weren't true. He wasn't weak and stupid. He was strong. He was a survivor. He didn't want to hurt people, but he felt as if he had no choice. Sue Sterling could have stopped his father, but she'd chosen to ignore what she'd seen with her own eyes.

And what about all those other people who'd seen the cigarette burns on his hand and the infected bite marks all over his body? In the end, nobody cared. He wasn't heartless. They were.

After Misty finished the oats, he surprised her with a carrot. Then he patted her on the rump, grabbed the shovel, and made his way to the big oak tree in the middle of the pasture.

As he'd been doing for as long as he could remember, he put his ear against the trunk and listened to the vibration as the tree hummed with life. Seconds passed before he gazed out at the tall grass and weeds, then turned so that he faced west. He then counted his steps until he found a plot of ground that had not been disturbed and began to dig.

He would need two holes. Or maybe just one this time. He had an idea. It had been a while since he'd purposely staged a corpse for the authorities to find. If his calculations were correct, there were six bodies buried in the pasture. Every once in a while he liked to change things up, though, and leave a corpse or two somewhere shocking, somewhere small kids and their uptight parents would run into the dead body, a sight that would be forever ingrained in their brains.

It was always risky, but also exciting, making what he did for a living so much more fun.

At that very moment, he remembered the girls stored away in the extra refrigerator in the garage. He'd been so busy he'd forgotten all about them. How long had they been in there, he wondered. *A year? Maybe two?*

One thing for sure, he needed to get Garrett out of the house. The stench of his decaying body had already filled the basement and the room above.

His mind was made up.

One hole was all he needed.

He had no idea how long Erin Hayes would last in the box, especially since he planned to torture her with hope, his favorite kind of torture. He would give her enough water and food to keep her hanging on by a thread. And he would feed her words of encouragement. Tell her everyone was looking for her and that he was even thinking about letting her go.

All lies.

"What are you doing?"

His head snapped up at the sound of a female voice. She stood there, watching him work. He dropped his shovel. How had he not seen her standing there before? "Zee? What are you doing here?"

"I spent all day in the park waiting for you to come. When you didn't show up, I decided it was time to go in search of you."

Her straight black hair was a tangled mess, and her long dark jacket that flared at the knees was torn and dirty. Her face was smudged with dirt and blood. He leaned closer. *Yep.* She'd definitely suffered a bloody nose.

There were many miles between Rainbow Park and his small farm. How could she have possibly found him? It defied reason. He'd known within minutes of their first meeting that she was highly irrational. She had multiple brain disorders, including schizophrenia. He'd studied mental disorders in college. He knew all about her illness, which was why she'd fascinated him the moment he met her. Without medication and therapy, she had to be a walking time bomb. "Have you been taking your medication?"

"What are you digging a hole for?" she asked, ignoring his question. She looked around, then marched through high grass and stopped at a rectangular-shaped patch of ground that had been disturbed.

Garrett's wife was buried there. Grass and weeds had sprouted, but it would take a while before Mother Nature did its thing and the grass grew tall enough to hide the spot from curious eyes.

"That was my last compost area," he said happily. "It was time to make a new one. Once I dig the hole, I'll add newspaper clippings, wood chips, and dry leaves to get it started. After that I can put kitchen waste, food scraps, et cetera, into the pile, and it'll all make for a wonderful fertilizer for my garden." He pointed to his right, where even from here he could see juicy red tomatoes growing from a vine. He'd always prized himself on his green thumb.

She looked semi-impressed. But then, in the blink of an eye, she pointed to the house. "Is that where you live?"

He raked his dirty fingers through his hair. "Why are you here, Zee?"

"Why didn't you come to see me?" she shot back, angry.

He wasn't ready to tell her the truth, that he'd come upon a young woman stranded on the side of the road and couldn't pass up such a golden opportunity. So he asked, "Can I be honest with you?"

"You know you can."

"I was afraid that if I kept coming around, you would grow tired of me," he lied. "I couldn't let that happen." He did his best to appear forlorn, as if he gave one shit about her.

She wasn't the touchy-feely sort. He knew that because his hand had accidentally brushed against hers once in the park, and she'd had a conniption. But still, he thought she'd at least try to comfort him with kind words. Instead she started walking across the pasture, following the path toward the house.

Damn it! He grabbed the shovel and started after her.

Zee was only a few feet from the box when Erin decided to yell for help. Zee ran that way, stopping right outside the box. "Is someone in there?"

"Help! Get me out of here!"

Zee looked over her shoulder at him, her eyes wide and questioning.

He hated to hurt her, but she'd left him with no other choice. "This is your fault," he told Zee as he raised the shovel and swung hard.

Bam. Zee fell to the ground.

"What's going on?" Erin cried. "Who's out there?"

"You should have kept your mouth shut," he told the stupid girl in the box as he knelt down close to Zee's crumpled body and watched the thin line of blood trickle down from the top of her head and across her nose. "Look what the bitch made me do."

He dropped the shovel, grabbed two fistfuls of Zee's hair, and dragged her toward the house.

TWENTY

After spending the afternoon going door-to-door talking to Arlo's neighbors, Jessie wasn't any closer to finding his daughter. Arlo had been right. His neighbors didn't like him. More than a few of his neighbors had talked about the Gatleys as if they were a disgrace to humanity and deserved to be carted off and locked behind bars. Their reasoning had boiled down to the simple fact that Arlo and Zee looked and acted different than most "normal" people did. Zee wore dark lipstick, dark nail polish, and apparently a long dark coat that one of the neighbors described as "Goth," and the other called "witchy." Others had refused to answer the door at all, peeking through their curtains or telling her through the door to go away.

Back at the office, Jessie sat at her desk, staring at a long list of things to get done. There were subpoenas to serve and a deadbeat dad who needed to be hunted down. It had taken her years to acquire the skills needed to find her niche in the investigative business. She preferred to focus on looking for people, which included missing person cases, skip traces (people who owed a debt), or finding the birth parents of adopted children. Finding a birth parent could be rewarding but also emotionally draining. Sometimes parents were found who didn't want anything to do with the people looking for them.

Her business had been growing at a nice rate, but the Parker Koontz incident had thrown her off her game. For the first time since starting her investigative business, she realized she needed help. If she had time to train someone, she might consider hiring an assistant. Although staying out of jail was her number one priority, she still needed to pay the rent and keep food on the table. As she picked up a subpoena and looked at the address, her cell phone buzzed. Distracted, she hit the "Talk" button and said hello.

"Hello. It's Ben Morrison. I was wondering if you could head over with me to the Wild West in Auburn later this afternoon?"

The Wild West was the last place Sophie had been seen. Jessie had been there many times. "I'm neck-deep in work right now. A young woman is missing, and her father is frantic. I—"

"This could be an important lead. I think you'll want to be there when I talk to one of the employees. She remembers seeing your sister there that night."

"What's her name?"

"Leanne."

Leanne Baxter. Jessie remembered her well. "You're wasting your time. I've talked to her multiple times over the years. She told me she left early the night Sophie was there. I showed her Sophie's picture, and she was adamant about never having seen her before."

"How long ago was that?"

"At least three years ago."

"You need to come," he said. "Leanne told me she's been haunted by your sister's story for years and wants to come clean."

Jessie thought about Olivia and what her niece had said about *needing* to know what happened to her mom. Her chest tightened. "Why would Leanne decide to talk now?"

"Because I offered her a bribe. After talking to her landlord, I discovered he was ready to kick her to the street. I told her I would pay for her next two months of rent."

"Jesus," Jessie said. "So this is how you get people to talk."

"Not always," he said, sounding unrepentant. "But when I'm desperate? Sure."

"If you already met with her, why didn't she tell you what she knew?"

"We haven't met face-to-face, and she didn't want to tell me anything over the phone."

She sighed as she looked at the stack of unopened mail. "Okay. I'll be there."

"I'll pick you up at three forty-five."

"No need. I can drive myself."

"If we're going to work together to find your sister, I think it's best if we get to know each other. And it makes sense, especially with your busy schedule, that we use the driving time to do that."

"You want to pick my brain—is that what you're saying?"

"Yes. One more thing," he said before she could hang up.

"What is it?"

"Do you have any of Sophie's old high school yearbooks lying around?"

"I think so. Why?"

"I'd like to take a look at the people she went to school with. That sort of thing."

"No problem. Anything else?"

"That's it for now. See you soon."

———

Jessie was in the kitchen when Olivia returned from taking Higgins for a walk. She was sweaty and red in the face. "Looks like Higgins gave you a workout," Jessie said.

"Yeah. He's getting faster." Olivia hung the leash on the wall hook. "It's hard to believe he has a broken leg."

Higgins's cast clicked against the wood floor as he made his way to his water bowl. The dog was starting to feel comfortable in his new home. Even Cecil was getting used to him.

"Oh," Olivia said, gesturing toward the stairs, "that crime reporter guy is outside. He said he was early and didn't mind waiting." Olivia looked at Jessie with curious eyes. "Where are you guys going? Did he discover something new about Sophie?"

"I'm not sure yet." Jessie went to the window overlooking the street, where she could see Ben Morrison leaning against the hood of a black Toyota Highlander, both hands stuffed in his pants pockets as he gazed straight ahead.

As she watched him, she tried to put herself in his shoes and imagine having no memories whatsoever of her childhood. Despite her dysfunctional upbringing, she would never want to part with all the good memories she still held so dear to her heart.

There was something mysterious about Ben Morrison. It was in his eyes, she decided. The first time they'd met, she'd felt as if he could see right through her. And although she tried to give him the benefit of the doubt, she found herself wondering if his amnesia was merely an excuse, and that maybe he knew more about what happened to Sophie than he was letting on.

"Are you okay?"

Olivia's voice pulled Jessie from her thoughts. She looked at her niece, feeling a little guilty about being less than enthusiastic about looking for Sophie. Ten years had passed since her sister's disappearance, the event that had shaped her and Olivia's lives. Not a day went by that Jessie didn't think about her sister and wonder where she was. And yet once Ben had called her, she'd realized somewhere along the way she'd begun to move on with her life.

"What's wrong?" Olivia asked again.

"Nothing. I'm fine."

"So where are you going?"

"To the Wild West in Auburn."

"Isn't that where Sophie was seen last?"

"It is. Basically we're starting over."

"Can I go with you?"

"No. I need you to watch Higgins. You wanted a dog, and now you have one. I'll help out while you're in school, but he's your responsibility. I expect you to do your homework, too. No television until it's done."

"Fine. I have a paper to write anyhow. I had to pick a fictional character to write about, so I picked Sherlock Holmes."

Jessie grabbed the backpack she used for a purse and slid the straps over her shoulders. "Interesting choice. What made you pick Sherlock?"

"I thought it would be a good place to start since I've decided after I graduate I want to be a private eye like you."

"No, you don't."

"What do you mean?"

Jessie raised her arms. "Look around you. You want to live my glamorous life?"

"I thought you were happy."

"I can barely pay the bills, let alone buy dog food for Higgins. You can be anything you desire. You have the freedom to choose any occupation at all."

"Are you telling me that you didn't have a choice?"

Jessie's arms fell to her sides. "Never mind. This is way too soon to be talking about this. First you need to go to college."

Olivia crossed her arms. "I'm planning on it. I've already decided that I want to get a degree in criminal justice."

Jessie groaned. "I've got to go. We'll talk about this later."

"Nice ride," Jessie said when Ben Morrison opened the door for her, and she slid into the passenger seat.

"It's the wife's car. Mine isn't so nice. No air-conditioning and an engine that hisses at stoplights."

"Sounds a lot like my car," Jessie said with a laugh.

He merged into traffic.

She unzipped her backpack, pulled out the yearbook, and placed it on the back seat.

"Thanks."

"You're welcome."

She looked at his profile. "What's really going on here?" she asked.

"I'm not sure what you mean."

She exhaled. "Never mind. I've got a lot on my mind. Forget I said anything."

"You still have doubts about me—don't you?"

"I guess I do."

"You sound upset."

"You're right. I'm sorry. I'm just feeling a little overwhelmed right now. I could end up in jail for shooting a man in self-defense. I need to find a missing girl with schizophrenia. I have an injured dog at home that hates me and a niece who just told me she wants to be a private eye when she grows up."

"There's more, isn't there? Come on," he said. "Go ahead and get it all out."

"Are you sure about that?"

"Absolutely. The whole point of driving together was to get to know each other."

"Okay, fine. I'm just not sure I have time for this. I've spent the last ten years going over and over Sophie's last day. I was there when they were doing ground searches in a vast field not too far from here, uniformed officers and volunteers poking long sticks into rock and terrain. I was more afraid of finding her dead than not finding her at all."

Thinking about her sister always brought her back to that empty spot inside of her—a lonely, dark cave filled with sorrow.

"And later?" Ben asked.

"When the searches stopped and the cameras disappeared," she continued, "I felt differently. Sophie, it seemed, had vanished into thin air. I was heartbroken and numb, but also more determined than ever to find her. I became obsessed to the point that it was all I ever thought about. Year after year I continued the search. Eventually the trauma and stress from getting nowhere began to take their toll. And only recently did I realize my obsession was also affecting Olivia." She took a breath. "Every day I was inadvertently reminding my niece that she'd been abandoned. Not only by her mother but by me. I think that's why she no longer refers to Sophie as her mother." As she stared out the window, she added, "I finally decided to start focusing on Olivia and her needs. I began to believe that maybe Olivia and I could find a way to move forward together. And then you popped into our lives, and here we go again, taking another ride on an endless train to nowhere."

He said nothing.

"And it doesn't help," she said, now that she'd opened the floodgates, "that I have no idea who you are or what your true agenda is. In fact, I can't help but wonder if your amnesia is something you hide behind. A convenient wall you can use to conceal your ugliest secrets or any part of yourself you might be uncomfortable with."

"What are you basing this on?"

"Everybody and their cousin is hiding something," she blurted, unable to rein in her frustration. "Parker Koontz, a seemingly outstanding citizen, shoots blanks at me. Why? Leanne Baxter might have been withholding information for ten years. Why? Then you come along, a crime reporter with amnesia, convince her to talk, and the timing just seems a little too convenient." She studied his profile while he drove. "I can't help but wonder if you're hiding something, too."

After a long bout of silence, he said, "You're the first person who's ever accused me of being a fraud. My amnesia is real. I have no memories of my parents, who passed away when I was a teen. My older sister, the person one would think might have known me best, won't have anything to do with me. She told me we were never close, and it was better for her if she kept her distance. I would do anything to have a wall where I could simply reach over and pluck the memories back at random."

"I'm sorry," Jessie said, sensing genuine sincerity. "That wasn't fair of me to accuse you of deceit."

His shoulders relaxed. "You're not a trusting person. I could see that during our first meeting. And yet you came with me anyway."

He was right. He'd called, and she'd jumped. Maybe that was how it would always be. Sophie first. Everything else second.

"You're right about one thing," he said after a while. "This is about me. Seeing your sister's image on television and feeling . . . knowing we had met before did something to me. It made me realize that there was hope and that maybe my memories would begin to return after all these years." He released a long breath. "But this is about you, too. When I watched that show, I heard the desperation in your voice when you talked about what it was like to have a family member disappear—the not knowing, always wondering. Imagining the worst does something to a person. And in that moment I hoped maybe we could help each other."

TWENTY-ONE

Jessie and Ben exited the car and then walked side by side toward the entrance of the Wild West. The place was well hidden, not far from trails for hiking and horseback riding amid foothills and waterfalls. The building looked like an old Western saloon with a wide boardwalk that flanked the dusty, unpaved parking area. A couple of hitching posts completed the look.

The Wild West was known for its whiskey and loud music. The regulars wore cowboy boots and wide-brim hats. It was past four when they pushed through the swing doors and walked inside. The wood floors creaked under their feet. Chairs were made from wine barrels, and the tables were mostly warped and scarred.

There were a few customers scattered about, since they served hot soup and sandwiches during the day.

Ben introduced himself to the bartender and asked if Leanne Baxter was around. The bartender disappeared inside the back room, and a minute later Leanne appeared. Leanne looked the same—round face, sky-blue eyes, and curly blonde hair that stopped at her shoulders. She wore a plaid shirt, jeans, and a pair of distressed leather boots with a Western stitch. Her cheeks reddened when she spotted Jessie. Then her gaze settled on Ben, and she stopped in her tracks, looking momentarily taken aback.

"What is it?" Ben asked.

Her blonde curls bobbed when she shook her head. "Have we met before?"

Ben shook his head. "We talked on the phone earlier about Sophie Cole." He gestured toward Jessie. "I believe you've met Jessie Cole. I figured you wouldn't mind if she came along to hear what you had to say."

"Sure," she muttered without bothering to look Jessie's way. "Did you take care of the rent?"

"I did."

Leanne gestured toward the back of the room. "Why don't we sit over there?"

They followed her across the room to the booth with cracked leather seats. Jessie slid in first. Ben took a seat next to her, leaving Leanne to sit across from them.

The bartender brought them a round of waters, then disappeared.

Ben pulled out a pad of paper and a pen, then complimented Leanne on her bolo tie, which made her face brighten. And then he got right to it. "If you don't mind, I'd appreciate it if you told us everything you remember about the same night ten years ago."

"I don't remember much," she said before clearing her throat. "If you've ever been here in the evening, you would know the lights are kept dim, which makes it hard to see clearly."

It didn't take much to make Jessie's ire grow. Leanne was being vague and seemed to be throwing out a few disclaimers for good measure. The woman hadn't changed one bit.

Ben must have sensed Jessie's frustrations because he leaned forward. "Don't worry about getting everything right," he told Leanne. "We're not here to judge you, and everything you say is off the record."

Leanne visibly relaxed. "The night in question wasn't the first night I'd seen her here."

Jessie clenched her teeth and remained silent.

"Sophie was beautiful," Leanne continued. "Men adored her, and women wanted to be her. Heads turned when she walked through a door. But all the adoration stopped the minute she opened her mouth."

"Why is that?" Ben asked.

"She was mean, bordering on cruel. The words that came out of her mouth were usually spiteful or condescending."

Jessie stiffened. "My sister was one of the most compassionate, caring people I've ever known."

Leanne lifted a shoulder in a shrug. "I'm just telling you what I saw. Should I go on or not?"

Ben looked at Jessie. "Do you want to take a look around while I finish this?"

He wanted to get rid of her. *Too bad.* She was staying. "No. I'd like to hear what she has to say."

"All right then," he said, turning back to face Leanne. He propped his elbows on the table in front of him, fingers entwined. "So what was Sophie doing on the night you saw her last?"

"She was dancing with Frank."

"Frank?" he asked.

The name meant nothing to Jessie.

Leanne nodded. "Frank was my fiancé at that time."

"I take it you didn't appreciate another woman dancing with your fiancé."

"That's right," she said. "I weaved my way through the crowded dance floor, pried her hands off Frank, and told her to back the fuck off."

Ben kept his gaze on Leanne. "And what happened after that?"

Leanne shrugged. "She found someone else to dance with."

"Who?"

"A scraggly-looking guy with bad teeth and wearing gaudy jewelry."

Ben scribbled on his notepad. "A gold chain?"

"No," Leanne said. "Rings. One on each of his middle fingers. One of them reminded me of the ring Johnny Depp wore when he played the pirate."

"Jack Sparrow in the *Pirates of the Caribbean*?" Ben asked.

"Yeah, that's the one." She drank some water. "When we get busy around here, I usually end up helping the bartender. The guy was sitting at the bar that night, twirling his rings. The skull ring on one hand and a gold band with a purple stone on the other."

Jessie felt Ben stiffen next to her.

Eyes squeezed shut, he pressed his fingers to his temples.

"What's wrong with him?" Leanne asked.

"I don't know." Jessie touched his shoulder. "Ben. Are you all right?"

He nodded. "Migraine." He slid out of the booth. "I'll be right back."

They watched him go.

"He's a big man—isn't he?" Leanne asked. "What's with the limp and all the scars?"

Jessie hadn't noticed a limp, but Leanne was right. He definitely had an uneven gait. "He was in a car accident."

Leanne nodded as she glanced at her phone. "I'm on duty in ten minutes."

Jessie needed to keep her talking. If Leanne was telling the truth, then this could be her best chance of finally getting information about Sophie's last day. "How long would you guess Sophie danced with the man wearing the skull ring?"

"Not long. If you ask me, he wasn't her type. It took her less than a minute to find someone better-looking—a tall, decent-looking guy with broad shoulders. About the same height as your partner, Ben."

Jessie didn't bother correcting her. "And then what? Did they dance?"

"This is where things get a little hazy," Leanne explained. "I don't think he was interested in dancing. Instead they sat at the bar talking. I remember thinking she looked frustrated with him. It must have been an hour later when I saw Sophie leave. I know this because I wanted to make sure Frank didn't follow her. He didn't, but the guy wearing the skull ring did."

"He followed Sophie out the front door?"

Leanne nodded. "Next thing you know, I see the tall man leave, too. That's when I figured there was going to be trouble."

"Why?"

"Two men who've been drinking whiskey and a pretty lady equals trouble. Anyway, I ran to the kitchen"—she pointed that way—"slipped out the back door, and crept around the side of the building so I could see what was going on."

Leanne had Jessie's full attention. Her stomach tightened. "And what did you see?"

Ben returned before Leanne could answer.

After Jessie filled him in, telling him everything Leanne had told her, Leanne stood, and they followed her through the kitchen and out the back door. Everything looked the same as the last time Jessie had visited—an unpaved area with a dumpster and stacks of boxes and crates.

Gravel crunched beneath their feet as they walked to the side of the building. Leanne stopped and then pointed toward the parking lot. "See the truck over there? The charcoal truck next to the blue Honda? That's about how far away Sophie and the two men were by the time I got out here. It looked to me as if the guy wearing the rings was making a move on Sophie."

Jessie frowned. "Did he touch her?"

"He grabbed her from behind, his arms circling her waist." Leanne made the motions, her arms wrapping around air. "That's when the tall guy pulled him off her and punched him in the face. Skull Ring Man fell to the ground, and I hoped that would be the end of it. But it wasn't."

Jessie and Ben didn't say a word. They just listened.

"Sophie smashed the bottle of beer she'd been holding against one of those concrete parking blocks over there. The music was loud that night, but not loud enough to cover the sound of shattering glass. Next thing I knew, she was on top of Skull Ring Man."

Leanne's voice hitched, and she was trembling, which made it difficult not to believe her.

Ben rested a hand on Leanne's shoulder and told her it was okay.

"I'm sorry," Leanne said, "but the sound he made when she jammed that broken bottle into his chest, or maybe his neck—I'm not sure—was a sound I will never forget for as long as I live."

Jessie thought she might be sick. "Are you suggesting that Sophie might have seriously hurt the guy?"

Ben lifted a hand to stop Jessie from saying anything else. "So what did you do next?" he asked Leanne.

"I ran back through the kitchen to get help, but the cook had cut off half his finger." She shook her head. "I'm not shitting you. There was nothing but chaos that night. But I had to do something, so I ran around the place like a fucking idiot until I found Frank." She anchored her hair behind her ears. "Guess where I found him?"

Ben shifted his weight from one foot to the other. "Where?"

"In the boss's office, happy as a clam, getting blown by the new girl."

Jessie felt heat rise through her body. Every time she'd talked to the woman in the past, Leanne had either said she'd never seen Sophie in her life, she didn't remember the night in question, or she'd left early. Now suddenly she could clearly recount everything that happened in detail.

Jessie knew Sophie had been a partier and a bit of a wild thing, but she couldn't imagine her sister ever hurting anyone. That was what she'd been telling people all her life. But if Sophie had been threatened in some way, then of course she would defend herself. Besides, why would Leanne lie, especially after all this time?

"Everything went to shit after that," Leanne said, her gaze on Ben. "By the time I got my wits back and remembered why I'd been searching for Frank in the first place, I grabbed a flashlight and headed back outside. And guess what?"

"What did you see?" Ben asked.

Leanne shook her head in wonder. "There was nothing there. I didn't sleep well that night. The next day, even though I was off work, I stopped by to take a look at the place where I'd seen it all go down. I found a few pieces of broken glass, but it could have been from another time—who knows?"

"No blood?" Ben asked.

Leanne shook her head. "Nothing."

"And you never thought to call the police?" Jessie asked.

"Why would I? There was nothing there. No proof at all of what I'd seen."

"At the very least," Jessie said, "you could have told *me* what you saw. I talked to you three times."

"Frank didn't want me to say anything to anyone," she shot back. "He'd been in and out of jail and didn't want the cops, let alone the FBI, hanging around asking questions."

Jessie rubbed her forehead. "The last time we spoke, you told me you left early that night. Why should we believe you now?"

Leanne looked at Ben. "You promised nobody would judge me or point fingers." She looked around. "I need to get to work. I think we're done here."

"You've been a big help," Ben assured her, "but I have one more question before we go."

"What is it?"

"Did you happen to see what kind of car Sophie or either of the men were driving that night? Color, model, anything at all?"

Leanne shook her head.

"And you never heard either of the men's names?"

"Nope. That's all I got."

After watching Leanne walk off, Jessie turned around and headed for Ben's car. She felt sick to her stomach, and she wanted to get away from this place.

Awkward silence filled the car as they drove home. Ten minutes passed before Ben broke it. "Why don't you say what's on your mind?"

"I don't know if it's a good idea."

"Why not?"

"Because I'm pissed. I asked Leanne Baxter the same damn questions more than once, and I got nothing. And now suddenly she not only remembers Sophie but also the men she danced with. Her story is a little over the top—don't you think?"

"People change. You heard her. She was scared. And Frank told her not to talk."

"I wasn't a cop," Jessie said.

"To Leanne you were worse than a cop. You were her sister. I'm not saying she was right to keep quiet, but she'd obviously been holding on to some guilt for not telling someone sooner. Maybe she was still with Frank the last time you talked to her."

Jessie's arms were tightly drawn over her chest. She tried to relax, but she couldn't get the image of Sophie stabbing a man with a broken bottle out of her head.

"Might I suggest," Ben said, keeping his eyes on the road, "that next time you interview someone, you attempt to warm them up first. Compliment them, ask questions about their life, questions that have nothing to do with the case you're working on. It's easier to get people to open up if you gain their trust first."

"You're right. I'm a fucking amateur." *God.* Not only was she pissed; she was feeling sorry for herself. *Damn.*

"I've researched a few of your cases," Ben said. "You're no amateur."

"Colin, a close friend of mine, has always told me that I'm too close to the case. Maybe he's right. Maybe it's better if I take a step back and stay out of your way. That was a shit show back there. I'm too close, too involved, and for the first time since Sophie disappeared, I'm beginning to wonder if I can look at things objectively."

"That's exactly why I need you," Ben said. "You know details about this case and about your sister that I need, data that would take me months to gather. You might not like her, but Leanne is all we've got at this point. She says there were two men with Sophie when she left the Wild West. Skull Ring Man and another guy."

It wasn't easy trying to think logically at a moment when her world felt as if it were spinning off its axis, but he was right.

"I'm going to find a forensic artist," Ben told her. "If Leanne agrees, we could have composite drawings of two men, both possible suspects, by the end of the week."

A sense of calm swept over Jessie. What if they could locate even one of the men Leanne had seen that night? If so, he might be able to shed some light on what happened. For the first time in forever, she felt hopeful.

TWENTY-TWO

I'm going to kill him.

You're not going to kill him because when I'm done with him, he's going to be blood and guts, splattered to bits like a bug on a windshield.

"Shut up," Zee told the voices in her head as she looked around. She was inside an ugly, straw-covered, stench-filled cell, and through a shared wall of metal bars, she saw a naked woman curled into a ball, lying on the ground in the cell next to her.

"Hey, you!" Zee shouted.

No response.

"Are you dead?"

Who cares? You're going to be dead if you don't find a way out of here!

I told you not to try to find that weirdo, but you wouldn't listen. You never listen.

Zee rubbed the knot on the back of her head. It hurt like hell.

The voices weren't the only ones who wanted blood.

A minute later she heard footsteps coming down the narrow wooden stairs at the far end of what looked to her like a shitty basement.

When she'd first met the socially awkward man at Rainbow Park six months ago, he'd told her his name was Scar, which she'd figured he'd picked up from the movie *The Lion King*. At the time she'd thought it was cool, but not any longer.

Dealing with schizophrenia wasn't easy. She had good days and bad days. More often than not, she heard voices. Sometimes Francis, a deep, gravelly, and convincing voice inside her head, would remind her how well she was doing and suggest she stop taking her medication. When that happened, she often wandered from the house.

This last time she'd wandered too far.

Her dad was probably worried. The thought of him worrying made her feel sick to her stomach. She and Dad had their differences, but he loved her for who she was, and she was lucky to have him in her life.

"You never should have followed me here," Scar said in a cheerful voice as if nothing had changed between them.

"No shit, Sherlock," Zee spat back. "My head still hurts."

"Are you hungry?" he asked, seemingly determined to get on her good side.

"Fuck you."

He made a sad face. "I've never heard you curse before. It's unbecoming."

She shot to her feet, wrapped her fingers around the metal bars between her and him, and rattled the cage. "I no longer care what you think. I want out!"

"You should have minded your own business," he told her.

"You've never met any of my friends," she said. "But you're going to be meeting a lot of new people if you don't let me out right this minute."

He answered with a creepy smile.

"He's not going to let either of us go," the woman in the cell next to her said.

The woman had lifted her head. Her eyes were wide-open.

"Who is that?" Zee asked Scar.

"Natalie Bailey," he said.

"Why is she naked?"

"Because he wants to humiliate me," Natalie answered.

"Is that true?"

His answer was half shrug, half nod, which Zee took as a yes. Zee narrowed her eyes at him. "What is this all about? Why are we here?"

"*You're* here because you're one messed-up crazy chick," Scar said. "And she's here because of her mother."

Natalie Bailey sat up, her spine stiff, straw sticking out of her hair, making her look a bit deranged. Zee blinked a couple of times to make sure the woman wasn't a figment of her imagination.

"He's a liar," Natalie said. "He never met my mother."

"Sue Sterling," Scar stated, his tone clipped. "A social worker born September 16, 1953, to Myriam and Rafael Potts. I met her for the first and last time on Friday, May 14, 1999."

Natalie's lips flattened. If looks could kill, Zee was pretty sure Scar would be dead.

"Her job on that particular day," he said through gritted teeth, "was to investigate a report of child abuse. It was Sue Sterling's responsibility to examine the home, *this* home, and talk to neighbors, teachers, friends—anyone who might have come into contact with said child."

Zee knew he was different, quirky, and quick to anger, but she'd never seen him quite like this. At the moment his face was red and blotchy, his body shook, and spittle flew from his mouth as he spoke. His narrow chest still rose and fell from all that emotion.

"Did she follow you here, too?" Zee asked him.

"No," he said. "Not exactly."

"No. Not exactly," Zee mimicked, irritated by his nonanswer.

"You know I don't like that."

"You know I don't like that," Zee repeated, imitating him, mocking him.

"If you do it again," he said, pointing a finger at her, "you're going to be punished."

"If you do it again," she said, "you're going to be punished."

He snarled.

Zee held tight to the bars, leaned close, and spit at him, missing his boots by a few inches. He wasn't the only one who was angry. She was livid, and he had no idea whom he was dealing with.

"You're going to regret that."

"My dad is looking for me. He's rich, and he's smart, too, and I know he'll find me soon!"

He turned, marched across the room, and disappeared up the stairs.

"They're watching you!" she shouted after him. "They're coming!"

When he got to the top of the stairs, he slammed the wooden hatch shut, then made his way to the living room and turned on the TV, switching from one news channel to another, his heart racing the entire time.

If Zee Gatley had somehow managed to mess things up for him, he would hang her by her toes and gouge her eyes out.

But there was nothing being reported on the news about a missing girl.

Calmer now, he went to his bedroom and crossed the room to where his desk sat in the corner, and turned on the computer. As he waited for it to boot up, he spotted the picture of him and his mom that was tacked to the wall. It was the only picture he had of the two of them. He'd been a baby at the time, and she was looking down at him with so much love.

He closed his eyes, imagining the feel of her arms wrapped around him, holding him so close he could hear the rhythmic beat of her heart.

If only she were here with him now.

A beep sounded, and it took him a few seconds to return to reality.

He typed "Missing girl in Yolo County" into the search bar. Dozens of headers with links popped up:

Missing Woman Chained, Battered When Found

FBI Offers Reward for Missing Girl
Missing Northern California Woman Found
The Heartless Killer Strikes Again? Erin Hayes Missing

He clicked on the link having to do with the Heartless Killer, which took him to online news reported by the *Sacramento Tribune*. On the right-hand side was a list of recent news stories. The name Arlo Gatley caught his eye. He clicked on that particular link and then felt a tingling in his limbs as he read every word.

Zee was right. Her father had hired a private investigator in Sacramento named Jessie Cole.

His stomach churned as he did a little research on the private investigator. Apparently she had a decent track record when it came to locating people.

He found a bunch of images of Jessie Cole, including one from the time she'd appeared on *Cold Case TV*. Leaning back in his chair, he wrung his hands together as he thought about what he should do with her.

Doing nothing was out of the question. It took him less than a minute to make up his mind. Swallowing hard, he stared into her eyes.

Jessie Cole was as good as dead.

———

"Hey there," Ben said when he walked into his house and found Melony sitting on the bottom step waiting for him. Her blonde hair was pinned at the top of her head, accentuating her long, pale neck. The top buttons of her silk blouse revealed enough cleavage to catch his attention. When he shut the door and stepped closer, he got a whiff of perfume. He realized then that the house was abnormally quiet.

Ben looked around. "Where are the kids?"

"Across the street. They were invited for a sleepover." She stood, brushed her fingers across his neck and then slowly downward over his collarbone, where she began unbuttoning the top buttons of his shirt.

It wasn't often they were able to get time alone, just the two of them.

He brushed his lips across hers.

That was all it took.

They were all fumbling hands after that, leaving a trail of clothes from the front entry to their bed upstairs. Melony covered his chest with feathered kisses, giving as much attention to his left side as his right, making sure he never felt insecure about his disfigurement. For their entire married life, she'd worried as much about his emotional scars as his physical ones. It didn't matter how many times he told her he was fine with the way he looked, wasn't bothered by people who ogled; she couldn't stop herself. It was who she was. And who could fault the one they loved for caring too much?

He grew hard beneath her caresses, flipped her over so the length of her was beneath him, her leg moving between his, brushing against him, driving him crazy. His breathing grew ragged; his eyes closed as he nibbled on her ear, every part of her ready and wanting as they lost themselves in the moment.

A whimper, as if from a distant dream, brought him back to the moment. He opened his eyes, confused by what he was seeing. Golden-brown hair framed a creamy oval face and exotic brown eyes. She pulled him closer.

He didn't understand. Who was she?

He wanted to stop, but he couldn't bring himself to do so. Instead he drove deeper into her. The more she squirmed beneath him, the faster his pulse raced. Her hips grinded against him, her tongue hot inside his mouth.

"You're hurting me," she said.

She tasted like a sweet honeycomb. Her hair was smooth and silky within his grasp, his movements bordering on frantic. He was on the edge of release when she screamed out for him to stop, her fingernails digging into his shoulders.

He opened his eyes and saw Melony, her blonde hair clutched tightly within his grasp, her eyes fearful and wet with tears.

"I'm sorry." He released his hold on her hair and backed off, unsure of what had just happened. It was as if someone else had taken over his body and soul. Confused, he wanted to give her an explanation, but he had none. He'd completely lost control and didn't know why or how that could have happened.

Sobbing, she slid off the bed and ran to the bathroom. The door clicked shut behind her.

He climbed off the bed and looked around, everything hazy, especially his thoughts. He'd hurt his wife, the woman he loved more than anything. Disgusted with himself, he paced the room. Was he losing his mind?

"I'm so sorry," he said again through the door when she still hadn't exited moments later.

The door came open. Melony tightened the sash around her robe as she headed past him, taking a seat on the edge of the bed. Her eyes met his. "I don't know what's going on with you, Ben, but you need to get help."

He shoved his fingers through his hair. She was right. The gruesome bloody images he'd been seeing, and now this. It wasn't normal. He needed to do something right away. He went to her and kneeled on the floor in front of her, his eyes watering. "I will. I promise."

TWENTY-THREE

It was late that same night when Jessie heard a knock at the door. She crept down the stairs and peeked through the peephole. It was Colin. She opened the door. He looked like hell. "What's going on?"

"Did I wake you?"

"No." She'd been reading through old files on her sister's case. "Come inside." She led the way up the stairs and then followed him around the house as he checked the locks on windows and doors. "What are you doing? What's going on?"

"It's happening again," he said. "The Heartless Killer has struck again."

"Are you sure?"

He turned to face her. Dark shadows appeared as half-moons beneath his eyes. "The mayor isn't convinced. He doesn't want to panic the public, but we're seeing the same pattern as last time. A group of people goes missing, and dead bodies from his last hunt begin to emerge. Last year it was a married couple, Garrett and Robin Ramsey, taken while picnicking in a wooded area. Two days later, a teenage boy disappeared after leaving a party—"

"And then the twin girls abducted on their way to the bus stop," Jessie finished. "So what happened?"

"An abandoned car with a flat tire was found on a road just off Highway 99. No sign of the driver, Erin Hayes, eighteen. This followed by Natalie Bailey, a psychotherapist taken from her bed while her husband lay sleeping. Test results haven't come back yet, but we believe he was drugged."

"That's horrible."

"Yeah, and a few hours ago, Garrett Ramsey's elderly father found his dead son sitting in the back seat of a vintage car propped on blocks in the side yard. The missing twin girls were also inside the car. Their decomposing bodies had been set up, one on each side of Garrett."

Jessie had no words.

He looked around. "I needed to know you were safe. Where's Higgins?"

"He's been sleeping with Olivia."

"I'm sending someone over tomorrow to put a dead bolt on both doors."

Before she could answer, he said, "Natalie Bailey lives a block away. Humor me."

"Okay," she said.

He kissed her forehead. "Thanks."

She frowned when he turned and headed for the stairs. Ever since he'd come back into her life she'd been holding back, afraid to get too close too fast. Not having him around for the past six weeks, though, had made her realize that not only did she need him; she wanted him to be a part of her life. "Leaving already?"

"My night is only just beginning. Talk to Olivia in the morning—will you?"

"I will."

"Lock up behind me."

She followed him down the stairs. "Stay safe," she told him before shutting and locking the door.

———

Erin woke up shivering again. It was dark. She could hear the sprinklers and droplets of water hitting the outside of the box.

Hot during the day. Cold at night. She wasn't sure which was worse.

She was always thirsty. She couldn't remember if she'd gone twenty-four hours without water or forty-eight. Her mouth felt like sandpaper. She'd read somewhere that a person could live three days without water.

The smell inside her confined space was becoming unbearable. But that was the least of her worries. She dragged the coin against the decaying wood, back and forth, back and forth.

Scraping, scraping, scraping.

Crack.

Had that really happened?

Did the wood just crack?

It did. It did. It did. Be careful. Do not drop the coin.

Despite losing a few pounds since being thrown in the box, moving her arm from her side to the top of her stomach was still a tight squeeze. But she did it. Very carefully she placed the coin snugly atop her belly button, then moved her arm back to her side and used the tips of her fingers to push against the wood where she'd been working. One of her fingers poked through decayed wood.

She stifled a giggle.

Stop it.

She couldn't allow herself to get overly excited. Not yet. Too early.

She pulled and dug at the wood until two of her fingers slid through the hole. The tips of dewy grass brushed against her fingertips as a lone tear slid down her cheek.

———

Early the next morning, Jessie sat at the kitchen table across from Olivia and looked through Zee's Polaroid pictures, examining each one closely while Olivia read Zee's journal.

"It's says here," Olivia said, "that Zee hears voices in her head. The voices even have names. Lucy is the most outspoken and is easily angered. Marion is the clever one, the one who knows how to make potions and put spells on people. And Francis is the troublemaker."

"She has schizophrenia," Jessie said without looking up. "You should be working on your report."

"I am. This is research. If I can help you solve the case, then I'll be able to relate with Sherlock Holmes, which will make it so much easier to write my paper. And since I'll be helping you for the next few days, you can think of me as a consulting detective."

Jessie rolled her eyes.

"Sherlock was known for his keen observation," Olivia said. "We have to be sure to look at every detail. We must look at every word she wrote and every item in that box as a clue."

Jessie ignored her as she examined the picture in her hand closely and then set it aside after failing to see anything unusual. She was careful with the dried flower petals as she sifted through the box. She put all the photos with scribbled, hard-to-decipher words in the margins to the side. At the bottom of the box were two pictures that were stuck together, image to image. Zee must have piled them together before giving the ink a chance to dry. She peeled them slowly apart, careful not to ruin the photos.

Olivia left the table to grab a snack and a glass of milk. When she returned she stood looking over Jessie's shoulder and pointed at one of the pictures Jessie had put to the side. "Those are supercool sunglasses she's wearing in the photo."

Jessie looked closer. The cat-eye sunglasses were lined with tortoise shell. Zee definitely appeared to have a unique fashion style.

Olivia picked up the picture. "Look at that! You can see a reflection of a guy in her sunglasses. Do you think that's Zee's boyfriend?"

Jessie frowned. She hadn't seen anyone but Zee in the pictures. "What guy?"

"The guy taking the picture. Here. Look."

Jessie examined the photo. The man's reflection was hard to see at first glance, but it was there. Her heart thumped inside her chest. Olivia was right. It looked like a young man holding the camera. "With the sun shining on him," Jessie commented, "his reflection is sort of distorted, and his face looks kind of blurry."

"Yeah, you're right."

"What is he wearing?"

"Looks like a pair of jeans," Olivia said. "And a short-sleeved blue-collared shirt."

"No, not a short-sleeved shirt, but long sleeves rolled up to his elbows," Jessie amended, her face pressed close to Olivia's as they both stared at the picture. "I'd say his hair is light brown and short."

Olivia agreed. "He could be anybody," she said. "I mean, there's nothing about him that stands out. We can't see his eyes or his nose. It's almost impossible to tell how tall he is. Talk about looking for a needle in a haystack."

"It's a place to start."

"What do you do now?"

"I'm going to have this image blown up, and then I'm going to show it to people living in the Gatleys' neighborhood and see if anyone recognizes him. But first I need to show it to Zee's father."

"Cool. Why don't you make two copies? That way we can show twice as many people in the same amount of time."

"We?"

"I want to go with you. I'll have plenty of time later to work on my report. Please?"

Jessie thought about leaving Olivia at home, but then she was reminded of the look on Colin's face the last time she'd seen him. Only a few blocks away, a woman had been taken from her home. Olivia was coming with her.

"Fine," Jessie said. "I'm going to get ready. Then we'll take Higgins for a walk around the block before we go."

"I can take him."

"No. I want to go with you. We'll go together."

TWENTY-FOUR

When Colin walked into the crime lab, Evelyn Klein, longtime friend and forensic pathologist, was waiting for him. They both wore blue, ankle-length, long-sleeve surgical gowns, shoe covers, and latex gloves.

On the steel table in front of Evelyn was Garrett Ramsey, his pale, ashy flesh stretched tautly over bone. His feet were swollen, blackening; his eyes were bulging, marked by severe trauma; and his throat stretched and circled with a reddish-purple welt.

"His expression says it all," Evelyn said.

Colin nodded as he continued his own examination. The burn marks on Garrett Ramsey's legs were easy to identify, same with the markings made from a whip or belt across his abdomen. He pointed to the bloody holes in the man's hands. "Any idea what caused those?"

"Looks like nails." She picked up a hand to show him that the hole went clear through. "This man was tortured in every way imaginable. These stab wounds," she said, her gloved finger following the path along the length of his arm, "were made postmortem." She sighed. "This is what I do every day. I thought I'd seen it all. But this nonsensical mutilation after a body has already begun to decompose is beyond comprehension. Plainly put," she went on, "we've got one sick fuck out there roaming the streets, and I'll be sleeping with one eye open."

"What about the twins?"

"One of them was hung by the feet. That would have been a slow, painful death. The other girl looks a lot like this man. Poked and prodded, burned and mutilated with multiple objects. We'll know more later, but it's my opinion the twins have been dead over a month. Some of the injuries had time to heal; others were newer, which tells me, based on the dates they were reported missing, they were tortured continuously during their captivity. Once they passed, their bodies were preserved in cold storage before the final staging."

"How could you tell?"

"The photographs taken at the site of disposal show surface ice crystals and condensation on the skin. By the time the bodies got to me, the bodies had thawed, but some of the organs were still hard. The freezing didn't hide the mutilation or torture, but it does make it more difficult to calculate time of death." She gestured toward pictures clipped to a corkboard. "I was using pictures to see if I could make comparisons between the twins and Garrett Ramsey. You can see that the girls' skin, after thawing, is red, fading to a leathery brown instead of yellow. Nose, ears, and tips of fingers on both girls are blackened."

He walked that way to examine the pictures. Sure enough, the areas mentioned looked like freezer burn. Feeling nauseated, he went back to his place on the other side of the dead man and decided not to absorb the information until later. To think about what those girls had been put through would not help him move forward. "What about sexual abuse?"

She shook her head. "Hymens are intact—both girls. No signs of sexual abuse on any of the three victims."

That information was consistent with the Heartless Killer's MO. He wasn't a sexual predator. This was about control. He tortured and killed because it made him feel powerful. Some might argue he was simply a psycho who gained pleasure from the acts he committed.

"After CT scans were completed and blood was drawn," Evelyn said, "my preliminary examination revealed something I knew you would want to see."

He followed her to the counter that ran along the back wall by the sink. She removed a green surgical towel from atop a metal tray. Underneath was what looked like a small, bloodied organ about the size of his thumb. "What is it?"

"The heart of a chicken," Evelyn said. "It was found lodged in Garrett Ramsey's throat."

Before he could ask, she added, "Same with the girls." Evelyn then reached for a lone glass slide, the kind you would put under a microscope, and held it up for him to see.

"It looks like a hair."

She nodded. "Identical hairs were found on both girls."

"Human or animal?"

"The lab is still processing, but I think you should know I grew up on a horse farm. The hairs found are coarse and have a mosaic pattern, which are consistent with horsehairs. I should note, however, that animal hairs, as a rule, do not possess enough individual microscopic characteristics to be associated with a particular animal to the exclusion of other similar animals."

He felt lightness in his chest. "So, there's a good chance the killer could be living on a farm?"

She shrugged. "Could be a ranch, a farm, someone who owns or works with horses. But you didn't hear that from me," she said. "It would be wrong of me to suggest one thing or another before the final analysis and diagnosis has been reached."

"Got it." Although it was too early to jump to any conclusion—especially one that could easily lead him and his team down the wrong path—he was hopeful. If the final analysis proved that the hairs could be identified as horsehair, it was more than they had at the moment. And it was the first time a hair from a victim of the Heartless Killer had been identified as not belonging to the victim. There were few, if any, cases he could think of where the case was solved as a result of animal-hair findings. But this was different from finding a cat or dog hair. "Anything else I should know?" he asked Evelyn.

"No. I'll call you if anything else comes up."

"Thanks." Colin peeled off his gloves and tossed them in the garbage.

When he got to the door, she said, "Catch that guy, would you? I need to get some sleep."

TWENTY-FIVE

Jessie parked in front of Arlo's house, but before she or Olivia could climb out of the car, she saw the front door open.

"Stay here," she told Olivia as she reached for the picture, "while I talk to Zee's dad."

Arlo stepped out of the house and shut the door behind him. "What are you doing here?" he asked, seemingly put out by her visit.

Ignoring his bluster, she handed him the eight-by-ten photo she'd had blown up and pointed at the man in the reflection of Zee's sunglasses. "Look at that man," she said. "He's holding a Polaroid camera and taking Zee's picture. Have you ever seen him before?"

He looked at it for a long while, his trembling hands causing the photo to shake. A light sheen of sweat covered his forehead, and for the life of her, she had no idea what was going through his mind. Afraid to ask him if he was okay, since that hadn't gone well the first time she'd met him, she simply waited for him to talk.

A solid two minutes passed before he looked back at Jessie. His eyes appeared glossy. Was he going to cry? "What is it?" she asked.

He handed her the picture, pushing it into her hands as if he wanted nothing more to do with it. "I've never seen him before."

The shocker was when he turned away and headed back for the front door.

"Arlo," she said, stopping him in his tracks, "this is our best clue so far. If you want me to find Zee, then you're going to need to help me."

He turned to her and said, "What do you want me to do? I'm paying you to do your job, so do it."

She held her ground. "There has to be someone who might be able to tell me who this man is. You and Zee must have friends or family or someone—anyone at all—who might know who this man is."

"I filled out your paperwork."

"And I read every word," she said.

"Then you know there's nobody for you to talk to."

"You don't have a brother, sister, or parents?"

"I have a brother in Minnesota who I haven't seen or talked to in twenty years. That's it."

"Can you tell me his name?"

He sighed. "Zee has never met him, and I've never spoken to her of my brother, but his name is Waylon. There. I hope that helps. I've got to go."

With that said, Arlo walked back into his house and shut the door behind him, leaving Jessie to wonder if all his neighbors were right about the man. And then she thought of Zee and headed back to the car. "Come on," she said to Olivia when she climbed out. "We'll leave the car parked here while we go door-to-door."

"He looked angry. Was he mad at you?"

Jessie lifted her arms in frustration. "I have no idea. But I've made the decision not to give up on Zee."

"Yeah," Olivia said. "I agree. I just hope she's okay."

"Me, too."

Jessie was worn-out by the time she knocked on the front door of a one-story yellow house with a green roof and white shutters. Directly across the street, she saw Olivia talking to a woman with small kids clinging to her legs. They had been at it for two hours, showing the blown-up blurry image of a man's reflection to anyone who would take a look. No luck so far, which was understandable, considering the picture they had to work with.

Like the last time she'd been in the neighborhood, many of Arlo's neighbors were reluctant to talk, especially after they realized she was working for Arlo Gatley. His neighbors were wary of him. Arlo was odd, they would say. He drove too fast. He never waved hello as they drove by, and he was quick to call city officials to complain if they didn't cut their lawns, and so on, and so on.

Most of the people she'd talked to so far knew Arlo and his daughter. They also knew Zee was missing but were convinced she'd simply run away. Although a few of the neighbors had made a halfhearted attempt to assure Jessie she would show up sooner rather than later, it was obvious by their tone of voice and mannerisms that they didn't care one way or another.

When no one answered the door, Jessie turned to leave. Before she took more than two steps, she heard a quiet voice. It took her a second to realize someone was talking to her through a partially opened window.

"Are you Jessie Cole, the investigator everyone says is making the rounds?"

Jessie squinted her eyes but still couldn't make out a shape. The voice definitely sounded female. "That's me," Jessie said. "I was hoping you could tell me if you recognize the man in this picture." She held up the photo.

"Meet me at the gate to the side yard. I'll be right there."

Jessie took the long way around so she wouldn't step on the grass. The gate creaked open, and she joined the woman on the other side. The woman looked to be in her late forties, with auburn hair and a friendly face.

"I'm Gina. Let's see what you have there."

Jessie handed her the photo and pointed out the person in the reflection of Zee's sunglasses.

"My husband and I try to stay out of all the drama that goes on around here," she said as she examined the photo.

Jessie said nothing.

Gina straightened and handed the picture back. "I don't recognize him. I'm sorry."

"What about Zee Gatley?" Jessie asked. "Before she went missing, did you ever see her pass by?"

"I work from home, so, yes, I see her walk by fairly often. I'd be surprised if there was even one person in the neighborhood who hadn't seen Zee walking along the street at some point or another."

"Have you ever seen her with anyone?"

Gina considered that for a moment. "No. My windows are usually open, and I do hear her talking to herself on occasion." She frowned. "What's wrong with her—do you know?"

"She has schizophrenia, which has caused her to suffer from a faulty perception of reality."

"How sad. I've never talked to her, but I should have at least tried." She shifted her weight from one side to the other. "I'm sure you've heard that Zee isn't the first young woman to disappear from this area."

"Nobody has mentioned anything," Jessie said.

"Four years ago Beth Cordell, a sixteen-year-old girl who lived two doors down, went to get the mail and was never seen again. It was all over the news. There were search parties, all the usual events that happen when a child goes missing, but she was never found, and her parents have since moved away."

Jessie wondered why Arlo hadn't mentioned Beth Cordell's name. "Is there anything else you think might be helpful for me to know?"

"Afraid that's all I've got. I should go now, but I do hope you find her."

Jessie thanked her before heading out through the gate. She jogged across the street. Olivia was no longer talking to the woman with the young kids, so she continued on down the road.

The names Zee Gatley and Beth Cordell swirled about in her mind as she picked up her pace, keeping an eye out for Olivia as she went along.

Two girls on the same block had gone missing.

Shivers raced up her spine.

A car drove slowly by. An old man in the back seat stared at her. His lips were moving. He was telling the driver to stop and let him out. The car made a left at the corner and disappeared.

She felt as if she were in *The Twilight Zone.*

A dog barked in the distance. Where was Olivia?

She spotted an open garage. There was a man fiddling around inside. "Excuse me," Jessie called to him. "Did you happen to see anyone walk by here in the last five to ten minutes?"

"No. Sorry."

"Are you sure?" Jessie asked, trying not to panic. "She's fourteen, and she has brown hair." Jessie touched her own hair. "Darker than mine."

"I'm sure I didn't see anyone," he said with a tinge of annoyance. "But I did go inside for some water, and she could have snuck by without my noticing."

She thanked him as she walked off, looking both ways, seeing nothing. "Olivia!" she called out as she pulled out her cell phone and dialed her number. Her call went directly to voice mail. "Olivia, where are you? Call me right back."

Maybe Olivia had headed back for the car, Jessie thought as she turned around, calling her name as she went. All the emotions from the days after Sophie went missing came rushing back.

"Olivia!" she called out once again, louder this time. Before she reached the car, she spotted Olivia up ahead, exiting the same house where Jessie had seen her last.

Olivia looked her way and waved, oblivious to the turmoil Jessie was experiencing.

"Don't ever do that again," Jessie said when she approached, trying hard to catch her breath, angry and relieved at the same time.

"Do what?"

"I had no idea where you went."

"I saw you slip through the side gate across the street," Olivia said, "so when Mrs. Goodman invited me inside, I figured it would be fine."

Jessie started walking toward her car parked at the curb. She could hear Olivia's footsteps directly behind her on the sidewalk.

"Are you mad at me?"

Jessie stopped and turned around. "No." She took a breath. "I was scared. It turns out that Zee might not be the only young woman who disappeared from this area." She paused, thought about what she was feeling. "When I couldn't find you, I panicked. It was my fault. I never should have let you out of my sight."

"I was right by the front door the entire time. I'm not a little kid."

"You're right. I have a lot going on right now. Colin stopped by last night to let me know the Heartless Killer is on the prowl again. My every nerve is shot."

Jessie opened the car door and climbed in behind the wheel.

Olivia opened the passenger door and said, "Can I drive?"

"No."

"I'll be fifteen soon. I need to learn to drive sooner or later."

"No. Get in."

Olivia shut the door and buckled her seat belt.

Neither of them said a word for the rest of the drive. Jessie's adrenaline was still working overtime when they reached Sacramento. For a moment in time, she'd thought she might have lost Olivia. It was something she never wanted to experience again.

TWENTY-SIX

The most important part of Ben's job as a crime reporter was spending time on the crime beat. He hung around police stations, firehouses, and medical technicians. He'd gone on countless ride-alongs and had been walked through unsolved cases with a number of homicide detectives. He knew the judicial process because of long hours spent in the courthouse. He knew what police officers and detectives dealt with on a daily basis.

Too often reporters merely wrote accounts of a crime as it occurred, using little background or depth. A good reporter needed to do his homework, which is why Ben had spent enough time with these guys to earn their respect. They knew he cared about trends and the impact crimes had on a community. And for that reason, he was granted access to things many reporters were not.

Today Ben was at the Auburn Police Department, waiting to talk to Police Lieutenant Anne Garcia. He liked Anne. She was professional and seemed to see things many people didn't. She'd always been a good listener with a keen eye to conscious and unconscious gestures and body movements.

Lieutenant Garcia had been the first officer to arrive at the scene of Ben's car accident ten years ago. The vehicle, a stolen 1974 Ford Pinto, had crashed head-on into a tree and exploded after veering off Highway 49 onto a secluded side road and into an area known for hiking and rock climbing. The crash occurred at one in the morning on August 18, 2007. The driver, identified as Vernon Doherty, a young man he had never heard of, was found dead at the scene, 90 percent of his body burned to a crisp.

Ben was led to a conference room, where Lieutenant Garcia was waiting for him. They shook hands, and the door was closed behind him as they sat across from each other.

"How are you doing, Ben? Busy working the Heartless Killer case?"

"Gavin is covering the case for the *Tribune*, but he keeps me in the loop. I heard about Natalie Bailey being taken from her bed while her husband slept. Any evidence her abduction is connected?"

Anne shook her head. "It's too early to tell."

At forty-five, Anne was five years older than he was, but she took good care of herself and looked years younger. She also had a practiced charm about her and a wide smile that drew people in.

Despite the oddity surrounding the crash—stolen car, drug-and-alcohol level of the driver, and Ben's amnesia diagnosis—it was determined that Ben must have been working on a lead and was a victim of circumstance. Why else would he be in a stolen car with Doherty? Nobody, including Ben himself, had ever questioned his innocence.

The reason Ben had come today was because Leanne Baxter had mentioned seeing Sophie Cole with two men that night. One of them had been wearing a skull ring. The moment Leanne had mentioned the ring, Ben had seen an image in his mind. A hand falling through a wall of fire before landing on the console next to him. Fingers limp, skin melting from bone, and a skull ring on the middle finger. Like other images he'd seen lately, this one had been vividly clear, nothing like a hazy dream after a long night of tossing and turning.

If the man driving the stolen Ford Pinto was the same man Leanne Baxter had seen with Sophie Cole, did that mean Ben had also been at the Wild West that night? Was that why he'd seen Sophie Cole's image on TV and felt as if they'd met? For the past ten years he'd wondered how in the world he'd ended up in a stolen car with Vernon Doherty. Sophie Cole might be part of the puzzle. It was time to take a fresh look at his accident.

"So," Lieutenant Garcia said, "what can I do for you?"

"I've been thinking about the crash lately," he said, not ready to give her too many details, "and I wanted to shoot a few things past you."

"Go ahead."

"As you know, I've read the reports so many times I've got most of the details memorized verbatim. But a few things have been bothering me. If Vernon Doherty was driving the car that night, why didn't the autopsy report show any signs of smoke inhalation as cause of death?"

Lieutenant Garcia thought about it for a moment. "If I remember correctly, Doherty's alcohol level was double the limit, and he had drugs in his system, which made for an open-and-shut case."

Ben raised a brow. "Meaning?"

"Meaning that the reason for the crash was obvious. The man was intoxicated, swerved off the road, and hit a tree. You had been in the passenger seat. You had diagonal cuts from the seat belt to prove it. Two men. One dead. One with amnesia. No witnesses."

He nodded, waited for her to continue.

"Although he was badly burned, I believe severe head trauma was cited as the cause of his death."

"Correct."

"If smoke inhalation isn't listed on the autopsy report," Lieutenant Garcia went on, "I would assume Doherty died on impact, before he was consumed by the fire, and therefore there was no reason for the coroner to list any other causes."

Ben wasn't satisfied, and yet he couldn't rationalize his wayward thinking. "I'd like to talk to the coroner," he told her. "But since you were lead investigator on the case, I thought I'd check with you and make sure that wouldn't be a problem."

She frowned. "Is there anything you want to talk about? Are you regaining some of your memory?"

"No," Ben said. "At least I don't think so. I've had what I would call visions, but I'm not sure if any of the things I'm seeing have any relevance to my accident or to cases I reported on in the past."

"Must be frustrating for you."

"You have no idea," Ben said. "I also wanted to talk to you about the items found at the scene."

She looked through the file. "Jewelry, a key, pocketknife, and some coins."

"That's right. How long do you keep those items?"

"In other words, if we still have them, you'd like to take another look?"

"I would appreciate it."

"Hoping something will jog your memory?" she asked.

"Yes."

Anne nodded and then made a quick call. "Barbara is bringing the box of items from the evidence room. She also has the name of the coroner. If you do talk to him, tell him I sent you. If he has any problem talking to you about the case, have him call me."

"I know you're busy. Thank you for your help. I appreciate it."

"Not a problem. We all want answers. If you don't have any further questions, I'm going to get back to my office. Barbara will be here soon."

They both stood and shook hands before she left the room.

Ben rubbed his left leg below the knee, where it often ached. He sat down again, looked around the room, and suddenly wondered why he was there. What was he trying to prove? For the first time in more than a decade, he wondered if maybe his past was best left in the past. The flashbacks and the extra time spent on Sophie Cole's case were wearing him down, causing him to do crazy things. Melony had forgiven him after he'd left a message with his therapist asking her to call him, telling her it was an emergency. What had happened between him and Melony last night disturbed him beyond words. He loved his wife more than anything in the world. He would never do anything to harm her or the kids. But it was as if he'd been in a trance. The woman he'd seen in his mind's eye was a stranger without a name, a woman he'd never seen before. And the worst part was that he'd meant to inflict harm. He pulled out his phone. No missed call from his therapist.

Before he could call again, Barbara entered the room and left him with a small dusty box no bigger than a loaf of bread.

The door clicked shut again, and he was alone.

He stared at the box for a long moment. The seal had been broken many times. Ben had looked through the items before. He knew what he'd see: a key, two rings, a pocketknife, and some coins.

The first time he'd been shown the items, he'd felt nothing. He'd touched and held everything, hoping to summon a memory, anything.

The second time he'd looked inside the box, he'd felt confident that he'd never seen the objects before. The third time he'd been desperate for answers, and he'd held the key between his fingers and then tried on the rings. But again he'd left disappointed.

The bloody images, the headaches, the screams for help, crackling fire, and a skull ring worn by a man he couldn't remember.

Were his memories finally coming back?

If so, he had a feeling he needed to brace himself.

He slipped the lid off. Everything looked the same. He picked up the silver skull ring and slid it onto his finger. It was handcrafted and highly detailed.

He stared at the ring for a moment longer, waiting for images or flashbacks to come forward.

When nothing happened, he stood, looked around, and then slipped the ring into his coat pocket and left the room.

TWENTY-SEVEN

Natalie Bailey couldn't stop thinking about Mike. Was her husband okay? She prayed he was okay. And if he was okay, that would mean he'd be frantic. And yet there was nothing she could do to help either one of them.

She was trapped. Locked in an ancient-looking handcrafted cell that had been welded together with rebar that was bent and rusting in places. She had no idea how she'd ended up in this place with its cracked, uneven cement walls and moldy smell. Beneath the fresh straw, she could smell a hint of bleach.

How many people had been locked up before her?

And who was in the enclosed cell nearby? Every once in a while she'd hear a long, mournful cry. At first she'd thought it was a wolf. Now she wasn't so sure.

The last thing she remembered before waking up in her own personal hell was being home in her warm bed. Sometime well after midnight, she'd felt the weight of a hand clamped tightly over her mouth. Her eyes had shot open, and she'd seen a shadowy figure hovering over her. Her muffled screams had gone unnoticed, which made her think her abductor had already done something with Mike. At one point she'd managed to kick her abductor in the groin, and he'd grunted in pain. But then she'd felt a pinch in her side right before everything went black.

She looked at Zee, who was preoccupied at the moment, talking to herself. Natalie had been awake the other day when the poor girl was dragged down the stairs, her head thumping against each step.

Their abductor, a skinny man with a pale face and big blue eyes, stood at about five foot ten. His wheat-colored hair was straight, cut short and at odd angles. He'd struggled with Zee's deadweight, huffing and puffing until he'd finally left the girl in a heap in the middle of the cell next door before locking her in.

When he'd returned the second time, Natalie had been shocked to discover that he blamed her mother for what he'd become. He'd said he'd met her mother, Sue Sterling, on May 14, 1999. He was gone now, but Natalie knew he'd come back sooner or later.

She still couldn't stop thinking about what he'd said about her mother. Natalie would have been seventeen at the time. Mom and Dad had divorced two years before that. Her mother used to come home exhausted, overwhelmed by the sheer number of children who were being abused and needed help.

But that Friday, May 14, 1999, was especially memorable to Natalie for another reason. That was the same day her mother had been diagnosed with breast cancer.

And that was when it came to her. Her heart raced as she realized she knew who he was. Mom had talked about him often, more worried about the abused boy than her cancer diagnosis. She'd made multiple phone calls until a caseworker had assured her that she would follow up.

His name wasn't Scar, as Zee referred to him. His name was Forrest Bloom.

With renewed determination to get out of there alive, Natalie got to her feet and walked around the cell, examining every nook and cranny. She pushed the straw away from the walls, making a pile in the center of the room. Then she examined the cracks in the floor, looking for anything that might help them escape.

She ran her hands over the rough metal, looking for flaws. In the cell next to her, Zee still stood by the door, her fingers curled tightly around the bars as she rocked back and forth. She hadn't moved since the last time the madman had marched from the room.

"He never should have done that," Zee said when she saw Natalie walking around. "He's a very bad man and will be punished."

Natalie glanced at Zee. "What did you say?"

"Shut up, Lucy," Zee said. "You don't know what you're talking about."

"Who are you talking to?" Natalie asked.

"Nobody," Zee said as she continued to sway back and forth, causing the metal bars to squeak in protest.

Natalie looked up. There it was, about a foot above Zee's right hand. A fragile link in the rebar. How much effort, she wondered, would it take to break one of the bars? Would Zee be able to shimmy her way up the rebar and squeeze through the space?

"Zee," she said, "look up. Every time you shake that bar, it squeaks. There's a weak point above your right hand. If you can break it loose, you might be able to get out of here and save us both."

"I could be a hero," Zee said.

"That's true," Natalie agreed.

Zee's eyes narrowed. "I really thought he liked me."

Natalie didn't say a word. Zee was obviously at war with the demons inside, muttering to herself, her body tense.

Zee's face turned red, and she began to shake the bars again, harder this time, the noise deafening.

Suddenly she stopped and looked up at the spot Natalie had pointed to. She stared, her eyes narrowing, and then shook the bars again. She did the same thing again and again, stopping, looking, shaking.

The bar was loosening.

Zee looked over at Natalie and smiled.

Twenty-Eight

After driving to the Wild West in Auburn and being told that Leanne Baxter had the day off, Ben drove to the apartment building where he knew she lived, since he'd talked to her landlord a few days ago. Calling it a shithole was being kind. Trash, piles of it, littered the parking lot and the edges of the property. Windows were covered with sheets, and more than one rat scurried past him before he made it to the stairs. A shouting match between a man and a woman was taking place inside one of the apartments.

He stopped in front of 5B and knocked.

The curtain moved. A few seconds later the door opened, but only an inch. He recognized Leanne as the one peeking through the crack. A TV blared in the background.

"What are you doing here?" she asked. "How did you get my home address? That bitch at the bar, the one who—"

"I found you on my own," Ben said, cutting her off. "I talked to your landlord, remember?"

"Oh."

"I want to show you something, and then I'll leave. I promise."

Reluctantly she opened the door wider and gestured for him to come in.

He stepped inside, but when he turned to shut the door behind him, she stopped him. "Leave it open."

She obviously didn't trust him. He pulled the skull ring from his pocket and held it out for her to see. "Is this the ring you saw that night?"

Her arms were crossed over her chest. Her jaw dropped, and her eyes widened. "That's it! How did you get that?"

Ignoring her question, he said, "I was hoping you wouldn't mind working with a forensic artist to identify the two men who left with Sophie Cole the night in question."

"No need to hire a forensic artist," she told him.

"Why is that?"

"When I saw you yesterday, there was something about you that looked familiar, so I looked you up on the Internet. I read all about the accident you were in the very same night Sophie Cole disappeared. You have amnesia, and you don't remember anything. But I do."

Ben knew Sophie had gone missing around the same time of his accident, but until now there had been no reason whatsoever to connect her disappearance to what had happened to him. Sophie Cole had gone missing on a Friday. His accident had happened early Saturday morning.

"The man driving the car," Leanne said, "the one who died that night, was Vernon Doherty. I saw more than one image, and I can guarantee you that it was him. He was the one wearing the skull ring, the man Sophie attacked with the broken bottle. And *you*," she said with an accusing finger, "were the other man in the parking lot that night."

Ben looked her square in the eyes. His heart skipped a beat. "You're sure it was me?"

"Positive—tall, broad-shouldered, square jaw. The accident obviously did some damage, but you haven't changed all that much."

She took a tentative backward step. Was she afraid of him?

"Did I dance with Sophie that night?"

"I told you yesterday. Oh, that's right—something was wrong with you, and you ran off. You and Sophie never danced. She approached you at the bar, and the two of you talked for a long while."

"And you're certain she left the bar first?"

"Definitely. She whispered in your ear, but you didn't respond to whatever it was she told you, and that's when she left. She looked annoyed. I figured you turned her down."

"Turned her down?"

"Oh, come on. You know, turned down her offer for a quick lay. She was one of those girls. Like I said before, that wasn't her first time coming to the Wild West. She came alone, but she always left with someone."

He said nothing.

"You really don't remember—do you?"

He shook his head. "Not a thing." But then he saw Sophie's face in his mind's eye, and he knew that wasn't completely true.

TWENTY-NINE

"I'm going to take Higgins for a walk," Jessie told Olivia. She needed to get out, get some air. She didn't want Olivia to know she was still wound up after thinking she'd lost her.

Olivia waved a hand above her head to let Jessie know she'd heard. She was watching TV and eating a grilled cheese sandwich.

"Maybe you should work on your report."

Another wave of the hand.

Jessie sighed, grabbed the leash, and called Higgins's name.

The dog lifted his head and scurried around, his cast slipping on the floor before he finally got to his feet. Less than a week, and the dog already responded to his new name. He didn't seem to know he had a broken leg, either.

"You're starting to like me—aren't you, Higgins?"

Higgins ignored her. He was halfway down the stairs, eager to get to the dog park. Overall, he was a good dog. He never made trouble with other dogs, and as long as she and Olivia kept things put away in the house, he mostly chewed on his rubber toys and bones she'd bought him. As Ben had pointed out, Higgins seemed to have a problem only with dark-haired females. The thought of someone purposely hurting the poor animal broke her heart.

The second her feet hit the pavement, Higgins pulled her along at a good pace. She wondered about Parker Koontz and whether or not he was still in a coma. David Roche had told her he was going to do everything possible to see her in jail. He'd made it clear that she'd messed with the smooth running of his firm. He obviously believed she'd been stalking his partner, too.

Although thankful that Fiona Hampton was willing to talk on her behalf in court, Jessie knew she needed more. Someone had to know about Parker Koontz and his stealthy pursuit of young women. But who?

She pulled out her phone and called Andriana, hoping she had an idea about whom she might talk to about Koontz, but there was no answer. It was the weekend, which meant she was probably puttering around in her garden. Her thoughts quickly turned to Zee Gatley. Everything about the case was odd, starting with Arlo and how he'd rushed her out of the house and acted so strange whenever she saw him. What was he hiding?

She thought of his neighbors. Many of them came across as judgmental and secretive. And what about the other girl who went missing on the same block? Was there any correlation to Zee Gatley's disappearance? Many of the neighbors had refused to talk, unwilling to help a father in his search for his mentally ill daughter. Why wouldn't they all want to work together to help find Zee? It defied reason.

And then there was Mrs. Dixon, who'd said she'd heard screaming and loud noises coming from the Gatley house. Zee was a schizophrenic. Jessie had been reading about the mental illness. Many people with the disorder failed to understand what was real and what wasn't. Common symptoms included confusion, hearing voices that no one else heard, false beliefs, and abnormal social behavior. Maybe things had been worse at home than Arlo let on. He'd seemed nervous. And yet he was the one who'd sought her help, which made Jessie consider the possibility that he was simply a socially awkward man, and his nervous mannerisms had nothing to do with Zee and everything to do with who he was as a person.

A low growl brought her back to earth. Hackles rose from the top of Higgins's neck, down his backbone, and to the base of his tail.

"Come on," she said, trying to pull him along.

He wouldn't budge. She'd never seen Higgins like this before. Jessie bent down, hoping to see what might be bothering him. There were houses on both sides of the street. No cars coming or going. Not one pedestrian in sight.

Higgins set off again at a fast walk, his ears straight, his body stiff. She stood and let him pull her across the street and into the alleyway. There was a dumpster to her left overflowing with trash.

Higgins's pace slowed, his limp more noticeable, the cast on his foot making an uneven clip-clop across the pavement. But there was another noise, too. The sound of paper crunching beneath a shoe.

Higgins growled again, his ears set, body tense.

The hairs at the back of her neck stood on end. Using her free hand, she reached into her back pants pocket for her pepper spray at the same moment a man wearing a baseball cap jumped out from behind the dumpster.

He lunged for her, taking her to the ground, the weight of his body pinning her against asphalt. Pain shot through her head and her elbow.

Higgins barked.

The pepper spray rolled across the pavement, out of reach.

Her attacker was Caucasian, midthirties, blue eyes. His right ear had a missing chunk of flesh, as if someone had taken a bite out of it.

"You should have minded your own business," he told her.

Having no idea what he was talking about, she grunted, still struggling to get out from under him. She saw the blade of a knife coming at her.

She tried to pull away, but he held tight and struck fast, slicing the side of her face. It all happened in a flash. There was no pain, only shock and blood, lots of blood dripping down her neck and shoulder as Higgins continued to bark.

She had an aversion to blood.

Don't look at the blood.

She gritted her teeth as she tried again to free her arm. His knees were crushing her chest, making it hard to breathe. He raised his weapon again. He was going to kill her. She could see it in his eyes. It was over. She screamed.

And Higgins lunged, sunk sharp teeth into the man's arm. Spittle flew from her attacker's mouth as he cursed the dog, his movements giving Jessie enough wriggle room to pull her arm free and use his own weight to knock him off her. She punched him in the groin, then rolled across the pavement and grabbed the pepper spray. With the flick of her thumb, she released the tab, jumped to her feet, and sprayed him in the face as he battled with Higgins.

His elbow made contact with Higgins's side. The dog yelped and released his hold. But Higgins continued to bark and nip at the man as he got to his feet and made a blind zigzag path out of the alleyway.

Jessie held a hand to the side of her neck and headed back the way she'd come. By the time she crossed the street, Higgins was at her side, the leash dragging behind him. She felt dizzy and had to work to keep her focus. Just another block to go.

A woman across the street stopped to look at her.

Jessie didn't pause.

Higgins whimpered at her side, and she wondered if he'd been hurt. And then she saw Colin up ahead, climbing out of his car parked at the curb. He glanced her way and did a double take before running toward her. "Jessie! What happened?"

"I was attacked."

"By who?"

"I don't know. A man with a knife. Higgins might be hurt."

Her legs wobbled right before Colin scooped her into his arms and rushed toward her house. As he rang the doorbell, he called out Olivia's name.

The door came open, and Olivia saw Jessie in his arms. "Oh my God," she cried. "What happened?"

"She's going to be fine," he told her. "Take the dog, and then lock the door, and don't open it again until I return. I'm taking her to the hospital."

Olivia grabbed the leash and shut the door just before Jessie felt her body go limp, and everything went black.

THIRTY

Zee stood motionless at the door of her cell. She had given up trying to break the weakened rebar for now. Her arms still hurt from the effort. The voices in her head had finally calmed, but the howling in the enclosed cell next to her had started up again. She looked at Natalie. She was sitting on the ground, her back and shoulders leaning against the wall, her head tilted forward so that her chin rested on her chest.

Zee wasn't sure if the woman was awake, but she talked loud enough to be heard over the din. "Do you think that's man or beast making all that noise?"

"Man," Natalie said without looking up.

"Yeah, that's what I thought." After a short pause, Zee said, "We need to find a way out of here."

The woman lifted her head. "Agreed."

"Sorry if I went a little crazy earlier. Without my medication, it's not easy being me."

"Do you have an illness?"

"I have schizophrenia," Zee said. "A disease of the brain. The doctor told me there are abnormalities in my brain's structure and function."

"Then it seems we're both in a bit of a pickle."

"You have schizophrenia?"

"Type 1 diabetes. I wear a device that pumps insulin into my body, but he must have taken it."

"You don't look too good. You're not going to die and leave me here alone—are you?" For the most part, Zee didn't like being around people, especially strangers. But the woman was sick. She looked deathly pale. And nothing bonded two people faster than having a creepy man lock you up in his basement.

She's probably a spy. You better be careful.

"I'm not going to leave you," Natalie said. "I promise."

Zee wasn't sure how Natalie could make such a promise under the circumstances, but she let it go. What would be the point of arguing with her? Since the woman was naked, Zee thought about taking off her coat and handing it to her through the bars, but the voices in her head stopped her.

What if you need it later? It might get cold, and you hate being cold.

Zee had to stifle a giggle by slapping a hand over her mouth. Not because there was anything particularly funny going on, but because she just couldn't help it. If she started laughing, though, she wouldn't be able to stop herself.

The howling stopped. Abruptly. Like a faucet being shut off.

Thank you, Jesus!

"I wasn't laughing at you," Zee found herself saying. "Sometimes I just laugh at inappropriate times."

"I understand."

Zee narrowed her eyes. "You do?"

Natalie nodded. "Stress will make people do things they wouldn't normally do."

"What are you, some sort of therapist?"

"A psychotherapist."

"No shit?"

Natalie smiled.

"Maybe you can help me while we're stuck in here?"

"Maybe."

"Do you think he's going to come back?"

"I do."

"He seemed like a nice guy when I met him at the park. Sure, I thought he was a bit off and sort of quirky, but aren't we all?"

"You know him?"

Zee nodded. "I met him six months ago. I'm not a big fan of people in general, but we hit it off, talked about everything. He used my Polaroid camera to take pictures of me but wouldn't let me take a picture of him. Now I know why."

"Why?"

"Because of all this," Zee said, opening her arms wide. "It makes sense that a crazy man wouldn't want any record at all that he even existed." She paused before adding, "He was supposed to meet me at Rainbow Park, but when he didn't show up, I decided to go looking for him."

"So you know where he lives?"

Zee grunted. "On a small farm in Woodland, at least ten miles from Rainbow Park. That's all I know." She scratched her leg. "I should have been paying better attention, but I wasn't. After he didn't show up at the park, I headed toward the wooded area. I've never wandered that far before. It's not like there were road signs and streets," she said defensively. "There was nothing but trees forever and ever, it seemed. Once the trees disappeared, I crossed over a lot of farmland and tall grass."

Zee liked the way Natalie looked at her when she talked—as if she really was interested in what she had to say. One thing she'd noticed in her lifetime was that nobody listened. "It got dark," Zee went on, "and cold real quick. That's when I started seeing strange things."

"What sort of things?"

"Mostly circus people. But also an elephant and a tiger, and all the usual stuff you would expect to see at a traveling show. It was the clowns, though, who kept pointing and telling me I was almost there, so I kept going. I walked for days."

"You spent the night in the woods?"

Duh. She's not a good listener, after all. Hasn't she heard a word you've said? How do you walk for days without spending the night in the woods?

"Four nights," Zee said, ignoring the voice in her head. "Scar had said something about owning a horse, an old gray mare with a sway-back, so when I—"

"What city do you live in?"

"Woodland," Zee told her, trying not to get overly annoyed by the interruption. "Anyway, I passed a few horses on the way, but when I saw the gray horse with the swayback, I was pretty sure it had to be his horse and that I was on the right track. Sure enough, there he was in the middle of a field, digging a hole in the ground."

Zee frowned. "He was digging a hole when I found him. Do you think he's going to kill us and bury us in that hole?" She shivered. She didn't like being confined, trapped in small places. The cell was bad enough, but being put in a hole didn't sit well with her. *And what about the person in the box?* she wondered. For the first time since being thrown down here, she remembered the box. "When I was outside walking toward the house," Zee told Natalie, "there was a box, the same size as a small coffin. I think someone was inside, pounding their fists against the wood." Zee grabbed both sides of her head and squeezed. She could feel her heart thumping against her ribs. "That's when he hit me over the head with his shovel."

"I think we should concentrate on getting out of here," Natalie told her.

Zee looked up at the rebar.

You're weak and dumb. You'll never get out of here.

"I'm pretty strong," Zee said, "but I don't know if I can break through these bars."

Natalie pushed herself to her feet. "That's okay. We'll just have to think of something else."

"I know!" Zee rushed over to their shared wall of rebar. "If he enters your cage, try to get him to stand over here so I can grab him." She reached both arms through the space between the bars to demonstrate. "I'll lock my elbow around his neck so you can get the keys out of his pocket, or wherever he keeps them, and get us out of here."

"I think that's a great plan."

For the first time in a long while, Zee felt proud of herself. She opened her mouth to say thanks when the door above the stairs creaked open. She couldn't see the door from her cell, but she could hear someone rustling about at the top of the landing. She hoped he was bringing food and water. Her mouth was dry, and she couldn't remember the last time she'd been so thirsty.

Natalie hurried back to the far corner of her cell while Zee returned to her door and wrapped her fingers around the bars.

He's coming. He's going to kill you. I told you months ago that he was bad news. You should have listened to me.

"It stinks in here," the asshole said as his feet hit the cement.

He set his canvas bag on the floor and lit one of the kerosene lamps. Then he fished around in his bag and pulled out a dead chicken, feathers and all, opened the mail-slot-like door in the cell where the howling came from, and shoved the dead bird inside. She heard a thump when it hit the ground on the other side.

"Hey, Dog," he called through the opening. "I brought you some food." He tossed a couple of water bottles inside, too, then let the metal door fall back in place with a loud clang.

Zee heard chains clinking as someone moved about inside. Why would his prisoner be chained? It wasn't good enough that he was locked inside an enclosed cell? She looked over at Natalie, who was sitting with her knees up close to her chest and her head down.

"Who do you have locked up in that cell?" Zee asked him.

"None of your business."

"Why are your eyes so red?" She crinkled her nose. "And your neck is bleeding. Did you get into a fight?"

"Why did you have to show up here and ruin everything?" he asked, still angry. "I thought we were friends."

Zee stiffened. "You said you would meet me at the park."

"I got sidetracked."

"With what?"

"A stranded girl on the side of the road," he stated proudly, all anger gone.

Who's the schizo now? she wondered.

"Her car had a flat tire," Scar said. "She needed help."

"Where is she now?"

"In a box."

So she *had* heard someone in the box. She knew it!

Natalie stirred, rustling the straw.

The young man Zee no longer recognized as the guy she once thought was sort of cool walked over to Natalie's cell and pressed his face up against the bars. "Are you awake?"

Nothing.

He chuckled. "I know you are."

"She's sick," Zee told him. "She's a diabetic and needs her medicine."

"What about you?" he asked, turning to face Zee. "Don't you need your medicine?"

"I can take it or leave it," she lied. Even when she took her pills, she still heard voices, but her medication eliminated other problems, like hallucinations. She wanted out of there. "Let me go."

"It's too late for that."

"Why are you doing this?"

"I already told you," he said, his attention back on Natalie. "Natalie's mother could have saved me, but she did nothing. She simply looked the other way. Someone had to pay. Since I couldn't locate Sue Sterling,

I figured her daughter should be punished in her place." He sighed. "Look at me, Natalie."

When she failed to move a muscle, he walked back to the stairs and disappeared within the dark space behind the steps. When he returned, he was pulling what looked like a fire hose along with him. "Nobody cared about me growing up," he said as he approached. "I was tortured all my life, and yet nobody cared. How does it feel, Natalie, to be trapped and suffering and to have no one help you?"

Natalie lifted her head; the anger scrawled across her face matched his. "On May 14, 1999," she said through gritted teeth, "the same day my mother visited you, she was diagnosed with breast cancer. My mother was more concerned about *you* than her diagnosis. She spent days making phone calls, pleading your case to get you the help you needed, but—"

The lines in his forehead deepened. He turned the nozzle, spraying Natalie in the face with a gushing stream of water, pushing her back against the cement and forcing her to turn her head to one side and gulp for breath.

"Stop it!" Zee cried.

A few more seconds passed before he finally shut off the water.

"My mom wanted to help you," Natalie cried, water dripping from her face.

"Bullshit! She shook my father's hand, the same hand that had been torturing me and my mother since the day I was born, and left without another glance my way."

"She didn't want your father to know that she was on to him. She knew you were suffering, and she wanted to help, but she was dead within weeks of visiting your home."

Chills swept up Zee's spine as she watched Scar's expression change. *He's gone from slightly deranged to full-blown cray-cray.* His face was red, eyes bulging, the muscles in his neck thick like corded rope.

"You're a liar!" he shouted.

"It's true," Natalie said. "She was worried about you. Your name is Forrest Bloom. I only know that because you're all she talked about. Years later, I looked you up and saw that you were enrolled in college and doing well."

"After your mother left," he said, his voice an octave higher than before, "Dad made my mother homeschool me so I would no longer have contact with the outside world." His hands trembled. "Do you have any idea what my life was like after your mother left me to rot in hell?"

Nobody said a word.

"Dad liked to pull my teeth out with pliers just for fun, just because he could. If I wet my bed, he put me in a box outside, kept me there for days. He enjoyed throwing darts at my mom and me. He made me do unspeakable things. My own grandmother purposely starved herself so she wouldn't have to watch us all suffer. I would have done the same if I could have found the courage to leave my mom alone with the bastard. He did all of these things to me because he enjoyed it. So, no," he said, calmly now, "I was never doing well. I was never fine. My mom filled out applications and begged me to go to college after I was accepted." His jaw hardened. "When I found out my mother passed away, I left school early so I could return home and take care of some unfinished business."

Natalie lifted her chin a notch. "So now you spend your days hurting others just as your father hurt you?"

He smiled, a wicked smile that silenced all the voices inside Zee's head.

"By George, I think you've got it!" he said, startling Zee. He turned the nozzle and sprayed Natalie again, forcing her to turn away. When he shut the hose off, Zee watched the excess water circle the drain in Natalie's cell and disappear. A tiny stream of water trickled into her cell. She dropped to the ground and began to lap it up with her tongue.

"Is that tasty, Zee?"

She ignored him.

"I have something for you, too," he said, which made Zee look over at him. He was holding a small box. Her stomach growled. She was starving.

He stood next to her door, close enough for her to reach out and touch him.

"Come and get it," he said.

He likes you. It's food! Reach through the bars and get it! Hurry before he feeds it to the bitch in the other cell!

She was confused, wasn't sure what to do. She stood, then looked over at Natalie, who very subtly shook her head. *She's a smart lady,* another voice warned. *Don't go over there.*

You're an idiot! She wants the food for herself. Go get it before that lady eats it all!

Zee walked over to him, her body pressed against metal as she reached through the bars and wiggled her fingers. "Give it to me," she said. "I'm hungry."

"Are you sure?"

"Yes. Don't be an ass."

He pulled off the lid, raised the box high in the air, and then slammed the open end of the box against the metal bars above her head so that the contents spilled out over her. Tiny little legs skittered through her hair, down her face and neck. They were everywhere.

Terror froze her in place.

Spiders.

He knew she hated spiders. He knew her worst fear, and he was using it against her. There was one crawling inside her ear. The tiny creepy crawlers tickled her flesh as they worked their way into her shirt.

Move, you idiot! Walk. Dance. Hop. Jump up and down! Do something!

Her feet wouldn't budge. She couldn't move a muscle. She didn't make a sound, either, not even when a spider darted into her mouth.

The monster laughed, guffawed as if he'd never seen anything so hilarious. His face changed again right before her eyes. He was suddenly one of the circus clowns she'd passed on her way there. Tufts of red, wiry hair above his ears vibrated with laughter. His mouth was wide-open, his brown-stained teeth pointy and revolting. Like most clowns, he had a red ball for a nose. It cracked and fell off. Blood oozed from both nostrils, but he didn't seem to notice or care. He wouldn't stop laughing.

The howling wolf man began shrieking and beating his fists against the wall closest to her. She wondered if he was laughing at her, too, or if he just wanted out.

Before today Zee had thought she knew crazy better than most. But this guy, Forrest Bloom, or whoever he was, gave *crazy* a whole new meaning.

THIRTY-ONE

Jessie had returned from the hospital fifteen minutes ago. After being interrogated by Olivia about what had happened during the attack, Jessie had escaped to the bathroom.

As she washed her hands, she looked at her reflection in the mirror. Her right eye was puffy and shaded with a half-moon of grayish black. She'd needed nine stitches under the left side of her chin. Gauze and tape covered her wound. The doctor had told her she'd been lucky. If the cut had been any deeper, she could have suffered nerve damage, or worse.

Before she'd run into Colin, she'd been in shock. Seeing all that blood had made her dizzy, barely able to walk. If she closed her eyes, she could see her attacker. Average height and build. No identifying tattoos or marks. He had expressive eyes. Angry eyes.

When she walked out of the bathroom, Colin was exiting the kitchen carrying a bowl of soup that he'd warmed up in the microwave. He set it next to the hot tea waiting for her on the table in front of the couch.

Olivia stood off to the side, a worried look on her face. Colin was watching her, too, but neither of them said a word.

"I'm okay," Jessie said. "You both know how I get when I see blood. That's the only reason I passed out. It got to me, but I'm fine now. You can both relax."

"I'm not worried about you passing out," Olivia said. "You were attacked a few blocks from here!"

Jessie's gaze fell on Higgins. He was lying beneath the window and hadn't stirred. "You can thank Higgins for saving my life," she said. "Higgins went right for the man's arm, the one holding the knife, and he wouldn't let go."

"He's a good dog," Olivia agreed. "I gave him extra treats. He's worn-out, but I think he's okay." Olivia crossed her arms. "Now stop trying to change the subject."

"Eat something," Colin cut in, nudging Jessie along until she took a seat and ate a spoonful of chicken soup.

Olivia couldn't let it go. She came around the other side of the couch, took a seat next to her, and read from her notebook. "You said your attacker was Caucasian, midthirties, intense blue eyes, and he had a bite out of his right ear."

Jessie swallowed another spoonful of soup. She was hungrier than she'd thought.

"Do you think the attack has anything to do with your missing person investigation?" Olivia asked next.

"I doubt it. Arlo and Zee live in Woodland, twenty minutes away," Jessie reminded her. She'd filled Colin in on the way home, told him all about the report Olivia was doing on Sherlock Holmes and how she suddenly had a newfound passion for investigative work. "Besides," Jessie went on, "Zee's case isn't high profile, and she's run away before."

"So?"

"So, it's highly unlikely anyone would know or care if I was helping Arlo Gatley search for his daughter. I think there's a good chance that without her medication, Zee got confused and is now lost or staying with a friend."

Olivia frowned. "If you really believe that, then why did we blow up that picture and take it door-to-door?"

"Because I was hoping someone would recognize the man in the picture. Maybe Zee is staying with him but doesn't want her father to know, for whatever reason."

"You two should talk about this later, after Jessie has eaten and gotten some rest," Colin said.

"You don't need to mother me," Jessie told him.

"Agree to disagree," he said.

When Jessie saw the scowl on Olivia's face, she set her spoon down and said, "Listen, you're right. It's perfectly reasonable for you to deduce that I was being followed by someone connected to a case I'm working on."

"Thank you," Olivia said, looking smug.

"But," Jessie continued, "if the attack was not connected to Zee, then maybe it had something to do with Parker Koontz." Jessie thought about what Adelind Rain had told her about the call she'd received in the middle of the night. The nurse at the hospital had assured Jessie that Koontz was in a coma. Following that path, if it was true that the attack was connected to Koontz, then that would mean someone else was making phone calls and possibly wanted her out of the picture completely.

But who?

David Roche's name popped into her head, but she knew that wasn't fair. She had no evidence whatsoever that he would want to do her physical harm. She didn't like him, but that didn't make him evil.

The ring of Colin's phone brought all thoughts and conversation to a halt. When Colin disconnected the call, Jessie could tell by the concerned expression that something was going on. "What happened?"

"Andriana," he said. "An armed man broke into her house, tied her up, and then ransacked her home."

"Is she okay?" Jessie asked, her mind swirling with speculation.

"She's shook up. She'll be fine. I'm going to head over there now."

Jessie started to stand up.

Colin pointed a finger at her and gave her one of his looks. "Don't even think about it."

———

Ben stood on the dirt road, looking down over the edge of the same steep slope where first responders had found him unconscious ten years ago. According to the police report, the weather had been extraordinarily warm then, as it was now. Ben had escaped the burning vehicle, but not before suffering third-degree burns over more than half his body. He'd also ended up with broken ribs, multiple fractures in his foot and legs, and a traumatic brain injury.

Beyond the hill was a steep embankment, a ravine full of trees with lots of dry, overgrown brush and weeds. A thick tangle of vigorously growing blackberry shrubs covered much of the land. They appeared so unruly, he wondered if he would have survived had he rolled past the tree and into the gorge.

He looked at the skull ring on his finger. He'd been wearing it since he'd met with Leanne Baxter. He closed his eyes and saw the same image as before—a hand, flesh melting off bone, splayed fingers, the ring. He waited for the sharp pain in his head that usually accompanied the images.

Nothing happened.

He opened his eyes. Still nothing. Ever since talking to Leanne, he'd been having a difficult time coming to terms with the truth. Vernon Doherty, the driver on the night of Ben's crash, was the same man who had followed Sophie as she exited the Wild West. And that meant Ben had to be "the other man" Leanne had seen that night.

The notion greatly disturbed him.

For ten years he'd tried to find a connection between himself, Vernon Doherty, and the stolen car, but he'd ended up with nothing.

Thanks to his wife and his therapist, he'd finally been able to let the matter go and move on with his life. But seeing Sophie Cole on TV had changed everything. And standing here now, he had new questions: What had really happened that night ten years ago? Why had he been at the Wild West, and what the hell had happened to Sophie Cole?

Ben stepped forward, heading farther down the hill, hoping to conjure images from that night. He slid most of the way down, kicking up dust and dirt, until he made it to the oak. From there he had a better view of the ravine and the brown hills and trees beyond.

He stood there for a good long while.

But nothing came to him.

Not until he started the trek back up and found himself on his knees when the slope became too steep. He grabbed on to a clump of weeds to help him gain traction, and that was when it hit him.

He squeezed his eyes shut, waited for the pain to subside, but that didn't happen. The pain grew in intensity, forcing him to roll onto his back, the palms of his hands clutching both sides of his head.

And there she was, plain as day.

Sophie Cole.

She was kneeling on the ground, hovering over someone. When she looked up at him, her beauty took him aback—flawless skin, piercing eyes, thick, shiny hair. She didn't appear to be worried about the person lying on the ground, just curiously surprised. Her head tilted slightly, and she said, "I think he's dead."

Five minutes after leaving Jessie, Colin was climbing out of his car in front of Andriana's house in East Sacramento. There were three cruisers at the scene. A uniformed police officer joined him and walked at his side. "It looks like the suspect came through the garage door at the side of the house. No fingerprints. We're in the process of canvasing the neighborhood for witnesses."

Colin nodded. "Where is she?"

"Inside. Ren is with her."

Colin found Andriana in the living room, sitting on a vintage purple-velvet love seat. Ren Howe, rookie investigator and pain-in-the-ass kid who wouldn't know tact if it bit him on the nose, saw him coming and met him halfway.

Ren's father worked for the FBI, which had allowed Ren to skip more than a few years of training, making him an easy target for officers who felt as if they were overlooked for the investigative position. It didn't help that Ren seemed to be oblivious to anyone who had a problem with his speedy climb to the top. "She didn't want to talk to anyone but you," Ren said with a long sigh.

"Do you have a problem with that?"

Ren gave a half shrug. "No, I guess not."

"Good." Colin had been to the house many times before. Andriana and Jessie had been friends for as long as he'd known Jessie. He looked around, wondering where her ten-year-old son was as he walked across the living room.

He leaned down and gave Andriana a quick hug. Her tangle of red hair was all over the place. A thin red line of dried blood made a path down one side of her face, ending just past her earlobe.

"Where's Dylan?"

"Thankfully," she said, "he spent the night at a friend's last night. He has no idea what happened, and I'd like to keep it that way."

Colin pulled out a notebook. "Why don't you start from the beginning, and tell me everything you remember."

She nodded, then relayed her story: It was Saturday. She slept in until seven, then spent the cooler part of the morning doing some gardening in her backyard. She came back inside about ten or ten thirty and made herself an egg on toast. An hour later, she heard a loud crash that sounded as if it had come from upstairs. Thinking a picture had fallen from a wall, she took a look around upstairs but found nothing out of the ordinary. When she returned to the main floor, a man dressed in black from head to toe stood at the bottom of the stairs. She pivoted, tried to run, but he struck her over the head, gagged her, and dragged her to the dining room, where he used duct tape to secure her to a heavy wooden chair.

For the next thirty minutes, she heard the masked man rummaging through drawers and closets. After spending some time upstairs, he finally left. It had taken her twenty minutes to get the gag from her mouth and another three hours to escape. Bruises marked her arms, neck, and wrists. Understandably she was still visibly shaken.

"Did he ever speak to you?"

"Not one word." She frowned. "I take that back. He cursed at me after I kicked him in the shin and struggled to get away."

"Is anything missing?"

"He didn't take any jewelry, which I found surprising since I have a few nice pieces. The contents of my purse were scattered across my bed, but nothing missing as far as I could tell, although I haven't been able to find Jessie's GoPro."

He raised a questioning brow.

"The GoPro," she repeated. "The one Jessie used to video Parker Koontz while she followed him."

He nodded his understanding. Jessie had made a point of wearing the GoPro ever since the shooting incident three years ago. Colin looked over his shoulder at Ren. "Call the hospital and find out what's going on with Parker Koontz?"

"I'm on it." Ren pulled out his phone and walked out of earshot.

"So, how are you holding up?" Colin asked Andriana. "Do you need to see a doctor?"

"No. I need to clean up and be here when Dylan is dropped off. I'll be fine."

He rubbed his chin. "You should know that Jessie was attacked."

"What happened? Is she okay?"

"She says it was a younger man. He pulled a knife on her, but she was lucky she had the dog with her."

"What dog?"

"Long story, but I'm sure she'll fill you in later. Nine stitches under her chin. She'll be okay."

"Thank goodness."

Ren was back at his side. "Nothing has changed," Ren said. "Koontz is in a coma, still critical. The doctors have given him a fifty-fifty chance of survival."

"So, we know it wasn't Koontz," Andriana said. "But possibly someone connected to him? Why else would this guy have taken the GoPro?"

Jessie was attacked around five. Had the man with the knife attacked her after he'd left Andriana's place? Seemed unlikely, since he would have been in a hurry to get away.

"What about hair color?"

"I saw black hair peeking out at the back of his neck."

"Eye color?"

"Also dark."

"About the video device," he said. "Are you absolutely certain the camera is missing?"

"Positive. It was next to my computer. I was going to upload the video and watch it over the weekend."

"The first time you noticed him was around eleven?"

"Somewhere between eleven and eleven thirty."

"You said he was wearing black from head to toe. A black baseball cap?"

"No. It was a ski mask, pulled down to his neck, but it didn't completely cover his hair."

"How tall would you guess?"

"Six feet, at the very least."

"If you don't mind, tell me again what happened from the start."

It was usually helpful in cases like this to have the victim repeat, blow-by-blow, what happened. Now that Andriana was calm, they might find that she'd inadvertently left something out.

As Andriana obliged, telling them everything from the beginning, Colin's instincts told him that this incident has nothing to do with the Heartless Killer. His next thought was that Andriana's attack was driven solely by someone's desire to get their hands on the video. Why would anyone go to that much trouble unless they were afraid of what might be on the video? And if that was true, then it was likely connected to the Parker Koontz incident. Since the two events appeared to involve two different men, based on physical attributes, Colin suspected Jessie's and Andriana's attacks were not connected. The man with the knife never went through Jessie's pockets, nor did he attempt to steal her bag. He wanted to harm her, maybe kill her. That thought not only left him fearful for her life but also pointed to something darker, something they had yet to uncover.

"I'll make sure everything is secure before I leave," Ren told him.

Andriana walked Colin to the door. "Call me if you think of anything else," he told her.

"I will."

THIRTY-TWO

Ben's first stop after watching his oldest kid play soccer was John Hardcastle's house off Gunn Road in Carmichael. John, a tech writer, had retired from the *Tribune* eleven months ago. It was his HTML skills, not stringing words together, that had landed him a job with his first tech publication back in the day. But along the way, John had fallen in love with journalism. Before he retired, he'd often entertained Ben with stories about how serious and socially inept Ben had been when he'd first come to work for the newspaper. Although Ben couldn't say whether the stories were true or not, the two men had become fast friends after Ben's accident. Although Ben tended to be an introvert, he honestly missed having John around.

Ben had to knock on the door quite a few times before he heard movement inside the house. The door came open. "Hey there, pal. Long time no see."

"Mind if I come in?"

John scratched the salt-and-pepper scruff covering his chin before gesturing inside. "Come on. Make yourself at home."

Ben followed him through the small living area, where piles of newspapers and tech publications were stacked high against one of the walls. On the TV screen was a grid-shaped maze, a giant game that had been paused. A remote rested on the recliner in front of the big-screen TV. When they reached the kitchen. John opened two cans of beer and handed him one. "So what brings you here on a Sunday, my day of rest?" he asked with a chuckle.

Ben took a swallow. It tasted better than he'd expected, soothing his parched throat. "I'm hoping you can help me with something."

"What sort of something?"

"I'm investigating the disappearance of a woman who went missing ten years ago. There's not a lot to go by, since she didn't seem to have many friends. But there's a yearbook that points to a woman named Juliette Farris. I was hoping you could unlock the universe to her social-media life."

John frowned. "I'm offended."

"Why?"

"That's for babies. But come on," he said with a wave of his hand toward the living room. "Let's see what we can do."

"Looks like you've been keeping busy," Ben said after John grabbed his laptop and took a seat in his recliner.

"Don't be a smart-ass. Most people want to travel when they retire, but not me. For thirty-five years I couldn't wait to sit in my favorite chair and play games. Not just any game, either. Right now I'm playing *The Witness*. Took six years to develop at a cost of more than five million dollars. If I wanted to waste my time, I would go on because it would blow your mind, but enough about me."

Ben smiled. "It's good to see you doing what you love. You've earned it."

"Damn straight."

It didn't take long for his computer to light up. He punched away at the keys and said, "Juliette Farris? Was that the name?"

"That's right."

"Thirty years of age? McClatchy High School?"

Ben set his beer down and came to his side to take a look. "That was quick, but that's definitely her. What I need to know is whether or not she hung out with Sophie Cole. Juliette wrote a note in Sophie's yearbook. It's not much, but it's all I've got. I have an appointment to talk to her later on today. I need to know if there's anything—"

"Jackpot!" John turned the laptop so Ben could have a look.

"What site is that?"

"You knew what it was before the accident messed up your brain," John said. "It's called Myspace, a social-networking website that was founded in 2003. In 2008 it was overtaken by Facebook in sheer number of unique visitors. Here, take a look. Read the profile, group photos, blogs, et cetera, and you'll see both girls' names mentioned in the captions. My guess is they were good friends, indeed."

Ben took the laptop to another chair and scrolled through the images. John wasn't kidding. He'd hit the jackpot. "You're a genius."

"Tell me something I don't know."

"I could kiss you right now."

John gave him a worried look.

"Kidding."

"Not funny."

"You wouldn't happen to have a printer, would you?"

"I hope that's another stupid joke."

"Yeah," Ben said. "Can I use it?"

"Help yourself. Down the hall. First room to the right."

Ben took the computer that way. Behind him he could hear John clacking away, playing his mind-blowing game.

An hour later, Ben was in Elk Grove, knocking on the front door of a one-story house that belonged to the parents of Juliette Farris.

Prior to his visit with John Hardcastle, he'd used his own sources to find out what he could about the woman. The yearbook pictures had shown her to be tall and vivacious. Yesterday he'd made dozens of phone calls until he finally reached Juliette. Although it took some prodding, she had agreed to meet with him at her parents' house. He didn't know whether she lived with her parents on a permanent basis, but at this point in his investigation, he didn't care one way or another. He wanted to have a chat with her.

When he saw Juliette in the flesh, he couldn't hide his surprise. She looked nothing like the pictures he'd seen in the yearbook. She wore a bright-red head covering. Her face was thin, and once-lively eyes were now buried in deep sockets. The dark lipstick accentuated the lines around her mouth, and she reeked of stale tobacco. Juliette was thirty, yet she looked twenty years older than that, battle worn and wary.

"I'm Juliette," she said as she gestured for him to come inside, and then promptly closed the door behind him. He followed her to the kitchen, where she motioned for him to take a seat on one of three stools lined up at the kitchen counter.

"My parents should be gone for another hour. I prefer not to talk about any of this in front of them, so let's get to it." She grabbed a glass from the cupboard, filled it with water from the tap, and slid it across the counter in front of him. Unidentified particles floated to the top.

Ignoring the glass of water and pretending not to notice the mouse that skittered across the kitchen floor and disappeared beneath the refrigerator, he pulled out his notebook and pen. "So, I've been told you were one of Sophie Cole's closest friends."

She nodded, lit a cigarette, then sucked in a lungful of nicotine.

"You're on record as saying you had no idea what men, if any, Sophie hung out with during high school, but it's become apparent that she made the rounds at any number of random bars from Placer to Sacramento County."

She gave a tiny shrug of one shoulder.

"Is that a yes?"

"That sounds about right," she said flippantly.

"You two were close," he said.

She nodded.

"Did you visit these bars with her?"

"Maybe. Sure. I don't really remember."

He sighed, opened the file he'd brought with him, and then showed her the pictures he'd had printed.

Her face paled. "Where did you get those?"

"Myspace."

"You've got to be kidding me. I deleted my account ages ago."

It was his turn to shrug. "I have a friend. You could say he's sort of a techno whiz at that kind of thing. Your account popped right up."

"When did you meet Sophie?"

"Oh, God, I don't know . . . middle school. I was probably twelve."

"So you hung out from the age of twelve until she disappeared."

"Yeah."

He laid the pictures across the counter. There were six total, blown up to eight-by-tens. Juliette and Sophie were in every one. The first four were group pictures, Sophie, Juliette, and unidentified men, everyone making silly faces. The last two were Juliette and Sophie alone in semi-intimate positions. He looked at Juliette and waited for her to meet his gaze. It didn't take long.

He raised an eyebrow. "Do I even need to ask?"

"No. We were more than just friends."

"So she was bisexual?"

"No," she said, sounding possessive.

"Why all the men in the bars?"

"We needed money, and Sophie was good at getting it."

"You two were a team," he said when he finally caught on to what she was saying. "She'd pick a guy up at a bar, bring them to a hotel, and you would rob them?"

"Something like that," Juliette said before taking another hit of her cigarette. "Let's put it this way—hotels were costly."

He understood. "So, she brought him to her car, and that's when the two of you would take his money."

"Close," she said. "Sophie would get him in the car, drive down the road, pump the brakes, pretend she had a flat tire, then pull over to the side of the road . . ."

"Where you would be waiting," he said when she failed to finish her thought.

"That sounds about right."

"And yet nobody ever turned either of you in?"

She shook her head. "Mostly I think they felt like idiots. And we rarely went to the same bar twice, so it would have been difficult to track us down."

"What about the Wild West in Auburn?"

"Doesn't ring a bell."

Ben let that go for now. "All anybody had to do back then was describe what Sophie looked like and then report the make and model of the car or license-plate number."

She laughed. "Neither of us owned a car."

"So whose car did you drive?"

"Take a guess," she said, still chuckling as if he was the biggest moron she'd ever met.

"You stole a car, drove to a bar, zeroed in on some fool, robbed him, and then left the car on the side of the road."

She stubbed her cigarette out on a dirty plate. "More often than not, we returned the car to its original owner."

"I'm sure they appreciated you returning their vehicle."

"I'm sure."

Judging by her mannerisms and the tone of her voice, it wasn't that Juliette didn't have a care in the world, Ben thought. She just plain didn't care. "You never thought to tell the police any of this?"

"Why? I couldn't tell you the name of even one man we robbed. It's not like we killed anybody."

"You never stopped to think that maybe one of these men might have wanted revenge?"

"Nope. That would take brains and balls." She laughed.

"You talked to Sophie's sister, Jessie, on more than one occasion after Sophie disappeared. Is that right?"

"Yes."

"But you didn't tell her much—why is that?"

"It was Sophie's sister, for God's sake. How do you tell someone that their sister lies, cheats, and steals on a daily basis?"

"You sound bitter."

"I was. Maybe I still am. I loved Sophie, but the truth is, she was bad news. She taught me how to disengage a car alarm and hot-wire an engine. Then she showed me how to make a living by robbing men who think with their dicks. My parents didn't like me hanging around her, but Sophie Cole was addicting. I couldn't let go."

"What about the pregnancy?" Ben cut in. "How close were you two by then?"

"Close enough. She was raped."

"Are you sure about that?" He pulled out one last photo from the manila folder and slapped it on the counter. This picture was of Sophie and a good-looking fellow with light hair and a friendly smile. A young Robert Redford look-alike. Sophie was sitting on his lap, her long arms hooked around his neck as she gave him one of her winning smiles and gazed longingly into his eyes.

"She looks pretty happy to me," Ben said.

Juliette's face twisted, her anger palpable, making him wonder for the first time whether or not she had something to do with Sophie's disappearance.

"Where did you find that?" she asked.

"Like I said, I have a buddy who—"

"It's time for you to go. I never should have agreed to talk to you in the first place."

"Why did you?"

"Because you aren't the only one who wants to know what happened to Sophie."

She didn't do it, Ben thought. She loved Sophie, and she wanted to know what happened to her. And there was more to it. His gaze roamed over bony shoulders and eyes shadowed with death. "How long do you have?"

"Doctors aren't sure. Could be three months, could be six."

"I'm sorry."

"We all gotta go sometime."

"If you tell me what you know about this guy, I can track him down, talk to him, see if he knows anything."

She lit another cigarette. "I know he was a loser," she said. "He didn't deserve her. Besides, she didn't love him. Not like she loved me."

"I need a name," he said. "It might take me a few hours, a day at most, but I'll figure it out with or without your help."

"Jimmy Rhodes," she said with a cough. "He meant nothing to Sophie."

"Are you sure about that?" Ben asked as he glanced at the picture of Sophie and Jimmy. "A picture is worth a thousand words."

"He dumped her," she said, her tone spiteful. "Started dating another girl. I remember hearing through the grapevine that he moved out of the country." Her hand trembled as she brought the cigarette to her mouth and took another drag. "It took Sophie a while to figure it out, but she finally realized it was for the best."

"What was for the best?"

"Jimmy finding someone else."

"Why was that for the best?"

"I already told you. She loved me."

THIRTY-THREE

With raw, bloodied fingers, Erin removed the last of the rotted wood from around the lock. Her shoulders relaxed, and she took a breath before she lifted the lid. It was dark, which meant it was time to make her escape.

Too weak from lack of food and water to push the lid all the way to the other side, she twisted her body in such a way that she could reach both arms out of the box, grab clumps of grass and weeds, and pull herself free. Wood scraped against her head and then her back as she pulled and pushed, grunted and groaned.

She ignored the sharp pain pressing against her skull as her fingers dug into hard clumps of dirt. All her energy was focused on holding tight to the prickly weeds and grass. Finally, she was able to use her legs to push herself from the box.

She lay there for a moment, her chest heaving. The night air was cold. Goose bumps covered her body.

Her gaze darted about, then followed a dirt path to a barn. Staying low, she crawled on her belly in the opposite direction of the barn, cringing at the sight of the box as she passed by. She hadn't gotten very far when the snap of a branch stopped her cold. Her heart raced. Was he close by? Was he watching her?

Hoping a squirrel or some other creature had caused the noise, minutes passed before she set off again. The moon was bright, forcing her to stay low as she crawled across clods of dirt and grass. Farther along she heard chickens clucking and then the chirping of crickets in the distance.

Adrenaline kept her moving.

She focused on living to see her parents and her siblings again. She wanted to spend an entire morning watching the sun rise, write Grandma a long letter, take piano lessons, and learn to paddleboard. More than anything, she never wanted to end up back in that box.

Up ahead was a fence. Three wooden slats that she could easily climb through. She slithered beneath the lowest board, continued on all fours across grass and thorns until her knees and hands were raw and she couldn't take it any longer. She pushed herself to her feet and tried to stand perfectly still. Her knees wobbled like a newborn colt's. In the moonlight straight ahead, she saw nothing but fields and trees. When she finally dared to glance over her shoulder, she saw a farmhouse. There was a light on inside, shedding a yellow glow into one of the rooms.

Panic clogged her throat, and she set off, running as fast as her legs would carry her. She tripped and fell more than once, but she scrambled upward each time and kept on running.

She could hear every breath thrashing inside her ears. She kept looking over her shoulder, making sure nobody had seen her and that she wasn't being followed. Nobody was there.

Run. Run. Run.

Her body trembled, but she couldn't slow down. A noise sounded, and when she looked to her left, she found herself falling into a hole. It was only four feet deep, but she fell hard and hit her chin against hard-packed soil. She tasted blood as she dragged herself out. It wasn't until she was back on her feet that she realized she'd hurt her ankle.

Gritting her teeth, she limped onward, determined to find help.

THIRTY-FOUR

Ten o'clock the next day, Jessie was getting ready to head to the office when a knock at the door prompted Higgins to jump to his feet. The dog was filling out, had some meat on his ribs, and his patchy fur was looking better.

"It's okay," Jessie told Higgins as she made her way to the window.

Ben Morrison stood at the front door. He looked up, saw her standing there, and waved.

"It's Ben," she told the dog. "You've met him before." But Higgins didn't care who it was. He stayed close to her heels, growling all the way down the stairs. Holding tight to his collar, she opened the door.

It took Ben only a moment to calm Higgins down. When he finally straightened, he looked at her and frowned. "What happened to you?"

"I was attacked yesterday. Nine stitches. I look worse than I feel." She gave the dog a pat on the head. "Thanks to Higgins, I was able to use my pepper spray and get away."

"Good dog." He stroked the animal's back. "Where did it happen?"

"A few blocks from here."

"I'm glad you're okay. I went to your office first, but I realize now I should have called."

"No worries. Come on in." She headed up the stairs, leaving him to shut the door.

"Random attacker or something else?" he asked when they reached the living room.

"Not sure, but there's a chance it could have something to do with Parker Koontz."

"Why do you say that?"

"My lawyer, who also happens to be a good friend, lives a few miles from here. She was also attacked yesterday. Tied up inside her home while the place was ransacked. The only thing they took was the device I had used to get a video of Parker Koontz as I followed him across town."

"Last I heard he was in critical condition."

She nodded. "Nothing has changed in that regard. But this whole Koontz thing has spiraled out of control. My friends and loved ones are at risk, and yet so far I have found nothing to point me in a particular direction."

It was quiet as he appeared to mull the news over.

"The police are looking into it." Gazing at Ben, she noticed the telltale signs of little sleep: frumpy hair, wrinkled shirt, and heavy eyelids. Her gaze fell to the leather case at his side. "I'm assuming you came to talk to me about Sophie?"

"Correct."

"Have a seat. Olivia is at a friend's house, so now is a good time to talk. Can I get you anything?"

"No, thanks." He took a seat and then picked up a book on the table in front of him: *The Sherlock Holmes Book, Big Ideas Simply Explained*. "You've been studying, I see."

Jessie smiled. "Olivia is doing a report on Sherlock Holmes."

"Following in her aunt's footsteps?"

"Seems so. She believes investigative work might be her calling."

"What do you think?"

"She's only fourteen. I'm sure she'll change her mind a dozen times before she graduates high school."

"What about you?" he asked.

She sat in the chair across from him. "What about me?"

"Is what you do your calling? Your passion?"

She didn't know what to think about the man. Even if he didn't have amnesia, she had a feeling he would be a mystery to her. Although she hadn't known him for long, he was easy to talk to. But something in those eyes of his told a different story, a dark story filled with twists and turns. Who was he, really? Even he didn't know.

"My wife tells me I have a tendency to get overly personal. I didn't mean to pry."

"I'm sure you didn't."

He chuckled.

"When I was Olivia's age, I wanted to be a doctor," she told him without further prompting. "But that plan was shot to hell when my friend rode her bike straight into a mailbox. Seeing all that blood did me in."

"Did you faint?"

"Nope. Just stood there like an idiot. My blood pressure dropped, and I couldn't function."

"And you didn't know about your aversion to blood before that?"

"No. Not until that day. And I knew it was worse than I thought when years later my sister was cutting a piece of fruit and sliced right through the tip of her finger. I froze. It was as if I was having an out-of-body experience. I could see her, the knife, the blood, the look of surprise on her face, but I was unable to do anything about it. Seeing her blood was too much. I've read that my reaction to blood is supposed to be unique to humans and primates, but possums and some breeds of goats also become unresponsive when they see blood. It supposedly triggers something inside that tells them they're in danger." She paused to take a breath. "After being cut open yesterday, I realized nothing had changed. I had hoped I would grow out of it, but I barely made it home after the attack."

"But at least you didn't freeze."

"True. I could feel the blood oozing down my neck, but I refused to look. But enough about that—you asked about my dreams and passion in life."

He said nothing.

"Two years after Mom left," she said, "I was putting myself through school at Sac State when I discovered Dad was falling apart and Sophie was pregnant." Jessie shrugged. "It didn't really matter what my dreams and life goals were after that. My sister needed help."

"So you quit school."

She nodded. "I'm four years older than Sophie. She was sixteen when she got pregnant. By the time Olivia was born, Dad's drinking had gotten out of hand, and I knew I needed to get a job and find somewhere else to live. I could make the most money as a cocktail waitress, so that's what I did. And then I lucked out when I met a guy who said he had a run-down house in Midtown. We made a deal. He'd keep the rent low if I agreed not to ask him to fix leaky faucets or creaky wooden steps." She sighed. "We've been here ever since."

"And Sophie and Olivia moved in with you right away?"

"Yes. Sophie needed to finish high school, so I took care of Olivia during the day, and Sophie took over at night. I was too busy and too tired to worry about life dreams."

"And then Sophie disappeared."

"In the blink of an eye, it seemed."

"And that brings me to the reason I came here today," he said.

She waited.

"I want to talk to you about Sophie's last day."

When Ben Morrison had first contacted her, Jessie had been worried about Olivia, but she'd also worried about whether she could handle starting over again. In the past, every time new evidence was brought to her attention, she would start from the beginning and find herself reliving the nightmare. But after hearing Olivia talk about needing to know what happened to Sophie, she'd had a change of heart and found herself thinking that maybe this time things would be different.

"Would you rather do this another time?"

"No," she said. "Let's do this now."

He pulled a manila file from his case. He then slipped a ring from his finger and set it on the table in front of her.

She picked it up. "What's this?"

"I believe it's the same ring the man who followed Sophie out of the Wild West was wearing the night she disappeared."

She dropped it as if it were on fire. It clinked and then rolled across the table. "How? Where did you find it?"

"I'll explain, but if you don't mind, I'd rather start from the beginning."

"Go ahead."

"As you know, I've been seeing images—flashbacks, if you will—which could be the return of some forgotten memories, which possibly include remnants of things I saw when I was reporting on one case or another before the accident."

"Okay," she said anxiously.

"When we were talking to Leanne Baxter at the Wild West the other day, she mentioned a skull ring. No sooner were the words out of her mouth than my head felt as if it were about to explode—"

"I remember. You excused yourself for a few minutes."

"That's right."

She did her best to sit quietly and listen.

"Months after my accident, after I was released from the hospital, the lead investigator called me into her office and showed me objects that were found at the scene of the crash. A pocketknife, two rings, some coins, and a key. She wanted to see if any of the items belonged to me, but she also hoped that one of the objects might help bring back memories of that night."

"But that didn't happen? The objects meant nothing to you?"

"No. Not until Leanne mentioned the skull ring."

It took a second for it all to sink in. Jessie straightened. "I don't understand—wait a minute. Are you telling me that whoever was in the car with you on the night of *your* accident"—she pointed at the skull ring on the table in front of her—"was wearing this ring?"

He nodded.

She felt the blood rush from her face. "But that would mean you were the other man Leanne saw walk out of the bar that night."

"I'm left to assume the same thing," he said.

Jessie jumped from her chair, grimacing from the pain that caused, since she was still bruised and sore from the attack. "This is crazy."

He said nothing.

She pointed an accusing finger at him. "You were there," she said, unable to fully comprehend what he'd just told her.

He nodded.

Unable to contain her anger and frustration, she felt her hands shaking. "So where the hell is she?"

"I don't know."

"Oh, come on." She pushed her hair out of her face. "How convenient. My sister walks out of a bar after midnight. Two men follow her. One of those men is now dead, and my sister is missing. The one man who survives, the one man who holds all the answers, happens to have amnesia."

"I'm as frustrated as you."

"No, I don't think you are," she told him. "I've been raising a young girl for the past ten years—a young girl who has no idea who her father is—or who her mother is, for that matter, or why she disappeared. Not a day goes by that I don't wonder what I could have done differently to stop Sophie from leaving the house that night. Have you ever felt so much guilt that it eats at you every single day until you feel less than whole? I don't think anyone truly knows what it's like to have someone you love go missing unless it happens to them."

"You're right. I'm sorry."

She drew in a breath, tried to calm herself by taking a seat again. "So you must know who this ring belongs to. What's his name?"

"Vernon Doherty."

"He was driving the night of your accident?"

"A stolen Ford Pinto," Ben said with a nod as he pulled out a copy of the accident report and handed it to her.

She read it over before she looked at him. "Why were you at the bar that night?"

He sighed. "I have no idea. Nobody knows. I must have been working a case. I've gone through the files at work a dozen times, hoping to find something to point me to a case I might have been working on at the time." He shook his head. "I've found nothing. I have no idea what might have led me to the Wild West."

"Fair enough," she said. "So what do you know about this Doherty guy?"

"I know he was bad news. Years ago I tracked down his parents in New Jersey. Vernon was the youngest of three boys. They said Vernon had been trouble since the day he was born. Judging from his rap sheet, they were being kind."

Her head pounded. She stood, went to the kitchen, and took some ibuprofen, figuring she'd save the pain pills the doctor had prescribed for tonight. "So," she said after she was sitting again, "you contacted me after you recognized Sophie's image on TV."

"That's right."

If he had anything to do with Sophie's disappearance, would he be here now? Maybe he would be. Most of his life was a blank slate. Even he didn't know how far his involvement in the case went.

He opened his mouth to say something, but she raised a hand to stop him. "For some reason," she went on, "I find myself liking you. You're good with animals. Olivia liked you right off. You talk well about your kids and your wife. Overall, you seem like a decent man, a family man. But beneath it all you're a complete mystery." She angled her head. "Or maybe a puzzle would better describe you. A puzzle with pieces missing."

He said nothing, which was good because she wasn't finished.

"For instance, I'm curious to know what else you haven't told me. Maybe you know more than you're letting on. How much did you remember about Sophie and that night at the Wild West before you called me about doing this story on my family?"

"Maybe this isn't going to work, after all," he said.

"Why?" she asked, surprised by his sudden change of heart. "Because I'm being honest with you?"

"No, because you don't trust me."

"I thought trust was something people earned."

"The thing is," he said, "I can't tell you things I don't know or simply don't remember. And if you believe I have motives or reasons to keep the facts from you, then I don't see how we can work as a team." He scratched his chin. "From the first moment we met, you were wary of me."

She started to protest, but he stopped her. "I could see it in your eyes and in your quickness in telling me that you had already done all you could to find your sister, and it was time to move on."

Guilt. It swept through her in waves, her conscience reminding her that he was right. After all these years, she'd been ready to tamp down everything that had happened, bury it like a dog buried a bone, because that sounded a hell of a lot easier than carrying the shame on her shoulders, day after day. "You're right on both accounts," she said. "I thought I could forget and move on. But then you came along, and I realized pretending it never happened wouldn't resolve anything. Eventually the sorrow and memories would leach through cracks and crevices and find a way to torment me. And I need to think of Olivia, too." Her gaze met his. "Despite my concern over your motives, we need your help."

THIRTY-FIVE

Nothing was working out as planned.

He'd enjoyed having someone to talk to, but Zee had ruined everything. The fact that she was certifiably crazy had made her interesting to be around. But he'd never once thought of bringing her here.

He'd had so many ideas about what to do with Natalie, but having Zee in the cell next to her made it difficult to concentrate. He thought about throwing Zee in the box for a few days, but she was a big girl, and the box would never fit her. He could kill her, but last night he'd had an epiphany. All he had to do was build the perfect place to keep Zee. If he could do that, he would always have someone to talk to. She wouldn't die without her meds, and although she might be angry with him now, she would come around eventually. Anyone with two eyes could see she was infatuated with him. The notion amused him. Only a schizo could fall in love with the man dubbed the Heartless Killer. They were meant to be.

The stacks of cement bags piled in the corner of the barn gave him an idea. He had plenty of wood planks. He could clean out the far corner of the barn and build a nifty room where he would keep Zee forever, or at least until she no longer entertained him, whichever came first.

What he needed were a couple of poles or stakes for support. He grabbed the wheelbarrow and headed for the old corral, figuring he could use the wood posts from there as the main beams to frame the structure.

As he pushed the wheelbarrow down the dirt path toward the corral, he realized he'd almost forgotten about Erin Hayes. He stopped next to the box, tapped his toe against the wood, and called out her name. He said her name twice more before he caught a glimpse of the broken hinges.

For a split second everything became hazy. He dropped to his knees, pulled the lid off, and saw that it was empty.

His heart drummed fast and hard against his chest. He looked around until his attention fell on handprints in the dirt path ahead. He followed the trail until he came to the fence, where the handprints disappeared. The grassy field had been flattened in certain areas, making it easy to follow her past the hole he'd dug and through the other side of the fence. The thick clods of hard dirt in his neighbor's field made it difficult to walk fast. His neighbors rarely visited these days. They had moved to Europe years ago, leaving acres of unused land.

Ten minutes later he looked around, wondering which way Erin had gone. Had she stopped at the neighbors' farmhouse or slept inside their barn? She would have wanted to find shelter and food, he thought. But more than that, she would have sought help.

He headed for the farmhouse. And as he marched angrily across the field, his thoughts returned to Zee. This was her fault. If she hadn't come, he would never have forgotten about the girl in the box. His fingers curled into fists at his sides. His body tensed. If he didn't find Erin, he would kill Natalie and Zee and bury their bodies together in the hole he'd already dug. He could move and start over or—

A sound in the distance caught his attention. The sun had yet to rise, but it wasn't so dark that he couldn't see. Behind him, to his left, he saw the barn door creaking open. He raced to the nearest tree and climbed until he knew there was no way anyone would see him.

Had the neighbors returned from Europe, after all?

No. They had not. It was Erin. She'd fashioned a gunnysack into clothes. And she had a noticeable limp. He watched her look around, the whites of her eyes visible as she headed cautiously toward the house. When she reached the door, she knocked, waited, then went to the hose and drank her fill of water. She then turned and looked his way.

He remained still. Hardly breathed. If he didn't know better, he would swear she had spotted him, but then why would she be headed in his direction if she knew he was there?

He nearly laughed out loud when he realized she'd climbed an apple tree. The poor girl was hungry. As he watched her approach, he admired her gumption. The will to live was strong in most humans. But there were some, like Garrett's wife, who caved quickly and would rather die than fight to survive. Those sorts of people were wearisome. The sort of people he would never understand. If he could live through it, so could they.

He watched Erin look up into the higher branches. His pulse quickened at the thought of her seeing him. But she merely reached up and grabbed an apple from a low branch. She pulled hard until the apple came free, and the branch snapped back into place.

She gathered more apples, scooping them into the hem of her gunnysack dress before walking off.

He waited a few minutes before dropping to the ground and gathering a few apples of his own. Standing in the direct line of his intended target, he wound his arm and let the first apple fly. The fruit smacked her in the back of the head and caused her to topple over. It was no use; he couldn't hold back the laughter another second.

She looked behind her.

The expression on her face when she saw him was priceless. Apples forgotten, she pushed herself to her feet and ran, dragging her bad leg along.

He continued toward her at a slow pace, throwing the fruit at her, laughing each time he hit his mark. The next time she fell, he thought she might be dead since he couldn't see any sign of movement. But on closer examination, he found her on her back, eyes wide-open, the gunnysack rising and falling with every breath.

"You never should have run."

Her eyes narrowed.

"Come on," he said, leaning forward. "Back to the box you go."

Before he could grab her by the hair, her arm slid out from behind her, and she swung hard, hitting him with such force and speed he never saw it coming.

Grimacing, he staggered backward and fell to the dirt. He'd been struck in the arm with a bale hook made of steel. For a second he simply sat there in disbelief. And then he rolled his neck back and forth, taking it all in, enjoying the fiery pain as his arm pulsed and throbbed. It had been so long since he'd been tortured, he'd forgotten what physical pain felt like. It was intense. Indescribable. Awesome.

As much as he was enjoying himself, he knew he couldn't sit there forever. Afraid he might bleed out if he removed the hook, he left it in his arm and pushed himself to his feet. Anger overrode all else. "Stupid, stupid, girl," he said as he followed her along, laughing every time she tripped and fell. It didn't take him long to catch up to her.

"You're a monster," she said, arms flailing as she tried to run faster.

"Sticks and stones," he said before he kicked her in the back of the knee, sending her flat to the ground. He bent over, used his good arm to grab a fistful of hair, and began to drag her toward home.

"Why are you doing this?" she cried.

"Because I can."

THIRTY-SIX

Jessie walked Ben Morrison outside to his car just as Colin was crossing the street. She made quick introductions. "Colin Grayson, homicide detective with the Sacramento Police Department, I'd like you to meet Ben Morrison, crime reporter with the *Sacramento Tribune*."

"I've heard of you," Colin said, "but I don't believe we've ever met in person."

Ben nodded as they shook hands.

"So, what's going on?" Colin asked, turning toward Jessie.

"Ben is doing his own investigation on Sophie's disappearance."

"I thought you had decided to move on?"

Her chin came up a notch. "I changed my mind."

"I should get going," Ben said. "Good to finally meet you."

"Yeah, you, too." Colin looked at Jessie. "You should be resting."

"I took some ibuprofen. I'll be fine." Jessie stepped around Colin so she could thank Ben for coming. After he drove off, she looked at Colin for a long moment.

"Are you okay?"

She hooked her thumbs in the front pockets of her jeans and smiled at him. "I am now that you're here."

He raised both hands in surrender. "Is this a trick?"

She laughed. "No. It's just that I haven't been honest with you."

He waited for her to go on.

"Those six weeks that I didn't see you were the longest weeks of my life."

He rubbed his chin. "Are you trying to tell me that you missed having me around?"

She nodded. "I never should have pushed you away."

"I should have called you after the divorce."

She shook her head. "It probably would have been too soon. Some things just need to unfold naturally and in their own good time."

"Does this mean you'll think about going on a date with me?"

She smiled. "I might even put on a dress for the occasion."

"Okay, then. Let me check my calendar and get back to you."

"Sounds good." She gestured toward the house. "Let's go inside. It's hot out here."

He followed her up the stairs and into the kitchen, where she poured them both a glass of ice water from the refrigerator. "So you've heard of Ben Morrison?"

"Yes, I have," Colin said. "Morrison was the same reporter who ripped our department to shreds in his write-up after Officer Ed Smith was found guilty of rape."

"I do remember that," she said. "It took jurors twenty-four hours to find Smith guilty. I didn't realize it was Ben who covered the story, but I did agree with the *Tribune*'s account of what happened at the time. He was questioning other officers who tried to help cover Smith's tracks. If I remember correctly, another officer went so far as to plant false evidence to help Smith. Everyone needs to be held accountable for their actions, the police included."

Colin exhaled. "So you're working with that guy?"

She set her glass on the counter. "I am."

She stared at him for a few seconds before she said, "Why do I get the feeling you're not telling me what you're really thinking?"

"You don't have time to be chasing ghosts right now, and the only thing Ben Morrison wants is for your story to give their subscriber numbers a boost. You need to focus on staying out of prison." He shook his head. "What's going to happen to Olivia if you get thrown back in jail?"

"I know you worry about me and Olivia, and I appreciate it. I really do. But Ben Morrison has made me realize I could never simply move on with my life. I need to know what happened to Sophie. I need closure. Olivia needs it, too."

He placed his hands on her shoulders. "Someone is out to do you harm. Whoever broke into Andriana's house and took the video is afraid. And if they're scared enough to break into someone's house while they're at home, then how far will they go to shut you up?"

"I talked to David Roche," Jessie said. "He's a sleazeball, but so far everything he's told me about Parker Koontz appears to be true. The good news is that I have two women who are willing to swear in court before the judge that Parker Koontz stalked and terrorized them."

Colin released his hold on her. "It'll be their word against his, a local hero of sorts."

"True, but it's something. I'm doing all I can. I have other people I plan to talk to. I did nothing wrong. It's going to be okay. I have to believe that."

"I wish there was more I could do to help," Colin said, "but my hands are full right now and—"

"Stop," she said as she put her arms around him and rested her head against his chest. "You've done enough as it is."

For a moment they simply held each other. Jessie breathed in the scent of him and wondered again why she'd pushed him away.

"Are you two friends again?"

Startled, Jessie stepped away from Colin and saw Olivia standing at the top of the stairs. "We never stopped being friends."

Olivia smiled. "Oh, I see."

Colin walked over to Olivia and gave her a pat on the top of the head. "Friends hug. It's allowed," he said.

"Enough lollygagging," Jessie told Olivia. "You have school tomorrow and a report to work on."

"Is that even a word?" Olivia asked. She looked at Colin. *"Lollygagging?"*

Colin shrugged. "I have no idea."

"Did Jessie tell you I've decided I want to be a private detective?"

"No. We were too busy hugging to talk about you."

Jessie gave him a look of exasperation.

He winked, which made her wonder why she bothered with him at all. He was a little pushy, and cocky, and way too handsome.

"Well, what do you think?" Olivia pressed.

"I think you would make a fine detective."

Olivia looked at Jessie. "I told you." And then she frowned and said, "So what's going on with the Heartless Killer case? Bella's mom wouldn't leave our side at the mall. Not even for a minute. All she talked about were the twin girls that were found recently. She said the story was on the front page of today's paper."

Olivia saw the paper on the table. A picture of the girls on the front cover.

Jessie walked across the room and hovered over Olivia as she read the story about how the girls were taken as they walked to the bus stop.

"They look exactly alike," Olivia said.

"Identical twins," Jessie said. The thought of the girls being taken and then held captive by some maniac made her sick to her stomach.

"Blonde. Blue-eyed," Olivia said as she examined the picture.

Jessie looked closer, too. Then she saw the necklace one of the twins was wearing, and she gasped.

"What is it?" Olivia asked.

"Remember what you said the other day," Jessie reminded her, "about the attention always being in the details?"

Olivia nodded.

Colin walked over to take a look.

Jessie went to her room and returned with the picture Arlo had given her the same day she'd found the shoe box under Zee Gatley's bed.

"One of the girls is wearing earrings," Olivia said as she continued her examination. "The other is wearing a necklace. The picture looks as if it was taken outside."

"Look at this." Jessie placed the picture of Zee next to the picture of the little girl.

"Zee is wearing the exact same necklace!" Olivia said.

"Who's Zee?" Colin asked.

"She's been missing for more than a week now," Jessie said. "Her father hired me to find her after the police showed little concern since she'd run away so many times before."

"She has schizophrenia," Olivia added.

Colin hovered closer, examining the necklaces.

A tiny gold swan dangled at the end of a gold chain. How in the world had Zee ended up with that necklace around her neck? Images of Arlo flashed through Jessie's mind. Arlo acting so strange. Arlo telling her she couldn't take a look around the house. Arlo with blood on his thumb.

Jessie looked at Colin.

"Tell me again how you ended up with this picture?" he asked.

"Arlo Gatley came to my office after his daughter went missing. When I went to his house in Woodland to take a look at her room, I asked him for a picture of his daughter, and this is what he gave me." She inhaled. "It's him—isn't it? He could be the man you've been looking for."

Colin pulled out his phone. "I need your client's name and address."

"Why?" Olivia asked.

"Because if the necklace Zee is wearing is the same one that's on that little girl," Jessie explained, "then Arlo could be in a lot of trouble."

"Zee's dad could be a killer?"

Jessie nodded.

"If he lives in Woodland," Colin asked, "why did he hire you?"

"He said he saw me on the news after I was able to locate Tonya Grimm. Arlo Gatley said he trusted me to find his daughter, too."

"I'm going to need to get a warrant to search his house. Do you have the file here, or is it at your office?" Colin asked.

"It's in my room. I'll get it for you." She walked back to her bedroom to retrieve the file from her bedside table. She didn't like the idea of handing over her client's information, but everything pointed to him being a suspect. Arlo had acted so secretive and bizarre at times. She thought about everything he'd told her, including his wife dying of cancer, and found herself questioning whether any of it was true. As she returned to the living room and handed Colin the file, she wondered if mental illness ran in the family.

"Wow," Olivia said. "What if you've been working side by side with the Heartless Killer all along?"

Jessie placed a hand on Olivia's shoulder. "Let's hope it's not true." She didn't want to believe Arlo was a killer. Her heart had gone out to him when he'd talked about being bullied and called names. *Innocent until proven guilty,* she thought.

Colin walked away from the two of them as he talked on the phone. When he was finished, he planted a kiss on Jessie's forehead and then took two stairs at a time toward the exit, telling them to lock the doors and stay inside.

"You look sad," Olivia said. "You liked Arlo Gatley—didn't you?"

"I did. I can't say he wasn't an odd man, but I never would have pegged him as a killer."

THIRTY-SEVEN

Zee felt dazed and out of sorts. Her stomach rumbled and growled, reminding her that she hadn't eaten in days. Her face and part of her neck was swollen from spider bites. It had taken hours to rid herself of them all. She'd begun to sweat and vomit. When it became hard to breathe, she'd thought she was dying. But Natalie had talked to her in a calming voice. The more upset Zee got, the calmer Natalie became.

Zee felt pain in her joints when she stood for too long. Worse than that was the hunger. She'd chewed on the dirty straw littering the ground, but it wasn't helping. "Are we dying?" she asked Natalie.

Natalie was in her usual spot, facing Zee, her back against the cement wall. "I don't know."

"What if he starves us to death?"

"We'll be okay. I read once that dying of starvation is a peaceful way to go."

"I don't see how."

"Do you really want to know what happens?"

"Yes, I do."

"Simply put," Natalie told her, "once the organs fail to work, the body will slip into a coma and pass away quietly."

"But I'm thirsty, and my stomach is cramping."

"That's a good sign."

"What? Cramping?"

"No. That you're still thirsty. If you were starving, you'd be too weak to sense thirst."

She's lying again. She's a big liar.

"The voices in my head think you're a liar."

Natalie shrugged. "Tell them all to fuck off."

That was one of the funniest things Zee had ever heard. "Do you hear that?" she said out loud. "Natalie says fuck off!" She laughed so hard she had to hold her sides.

Natalie laughed, too.

"What's it like to be normal?" Zee asked.

"I don't know if I believe there is a 'normal.' We're all different. I have voices inside my head, too," Natalie told her. "But I've never given them names. I always figured the voices had something to do with instincts and conscience and perhaps lessons I was taught at a young age."

"What do you mean?"

"For instance, if I feel like having an extra piece of cake, I always hear my mother's voice reminding me that the extra weight will go straight to my hips."

Zee chuckled at that. "Every one of my voices would tell me to eat the whole damn thing."

Natalie smiled.

"Are you hungry?" Zee asked.

"If you gave me a hot dog, I wouldn't turn it down. And that's saying a lot, since I don't eat meat."

"Do you think he killed your husband?"

"No," Natalie said.

As soon as the question had come out of her mouth, Zee scolded herself for being so blunt. One more bad habit she couldn't seem to stop. If she had a question, she asked it. Didn't matter what it was about. Her father told her not to worry about things like that. He told her to be herself. And to always love herself. She missed him. More than she'd ever missed him before.

"My mom died when I was very young," Zee confessed. "She had cancer."

"I'm sorry."

"I blame my dad."

"Your dad? Why?"

Zee shrugged. "I've been blaming him for so long I don't really remember why."

"People often place blame on the ones they love most."

"Why?"

"I'm not really sure, but most people are more likely to act aggressively against a friend or partner rather than a stranger. If you're blaming your father for your mother's death, then you should probably talk to him about it."

"I guess my questions would be, did Mom know she was dying? And then I would want to know if she had talked about having more kids. I want to know if she knew I was crazy and if that's what really killed her. I was only six months old when she died. Do you think she knew I was a crazy baby?"

"You're not crazy now, so my guess is that you weren't crazy then, either."

"How can you be so sure?"

"You're not on medication, and you've been lovely to talk to. In just these past few days, I'd say without hesitation that I consider you to be my friend."

"Are you always this stupid nice?"

Natalie laughed. "No. Just ask my husband. Like your father, I would say he usually gets the brunt of any anger or annoyance I might be feeling at any given moment."

"I bet you've helped a lot of people feel better about themselves."

"Well, that's *stupid* nice of you to say."

Zee's laughter was stopped short when she heard the now-familiar sound of the door above the stairs creaking open. She looked at Natalie with wide eyes. "I don't want to die."

"Stay strong. You're going to be fine."

"I don't want you to die, either."

"Is that laughter I heard?" He lit the lantern and then headed their way. "It looks to me as if you two are becoming fast friends."

Zee didn't bother standing up to see why he'd come. Beneath his bloodied shirt she saw gauze bandages. "What happened to you this time, Bozo? Every time I see you, you've either been crying like a little baby or you have a new injury."

Instead of responding, he pulled a brown paper bag from his canvas bag, held it up, and jiggled it. "I've got something for you."

She could tell the way he struggled that he was hurting. "Fool me once, shame on you," Zee said. "Fool me twice, shame on me. Or something like that." She shrugged. "In other words, I'm not falling for it."

His good arm dropped to his side, the bag along with it. He pulled a face. "You've lost all humor. How sad."

He walked up close to Natalie's cell, wrapped his fingers around the bars, and shook them hard, making the cage rattle. He then pressed his face close to the bars so that his nose stuck through one of the gaps. "Wake up. I have a surprise for both of you." He slid the brown bag, followed by two water bottles and a small black box, into Natalie's cell.

Natalie eyed him warily.

He walked a few feet away, unfolded a rickety old chair that had been leaning against the wall, and left it in the middle of the room. Then he walked over to the enclosed cell, unlocked the door, and disappeared inside. Zee had never seen him go inside before.

Natalie was on her hands and knees. She was weak, but she crawled across her cell, grabbed the goodies, and headed back to her corner.

Zee thought she looked like a skinny little rat that had been living in a dark cave for too long. Her thin hair hung in limp strings from her head. Her eyes looked bigger than usual, marbles in hollow sockets. In a few short days she seemed to have morphed into an alien creature.

Or maybe, Zee thought, she was hallucinating. She hoped not, because when she hallucinated, things got really weird, and she'd forget what was real.

Zee looked down at her own arms, glad to see she was wearing her coat. Her father had given it to her years ago after they'd watched *The Matrix* together, and she'd begged him to buy her a coat like that. She knew she'd lost some weight, which made her glad she couldn't see her arms, afraid she might look like Natalie, a skinny, pale rat. And then she waited for the voices to chime in, call her a loser or a chickenshit, but they remained quiet.

A tap, tap, tap on the bars made her look to her left. It was Natalie. She'd gone through the paper bag and was trying to tell her something. Her voice was so low and raspy it was hard to hear what she was saying.

"Peanut butter and jelly sandwiches." Her long, bony arm slid easily between the bars, and she set a sandwich on the floor inside Zee's cell. The black box the killer had put in her cell was now wrapped around her upper arm.

"Do you have your medicine?" Zee asked, intrigued.

Natalie nodded. "Come and eat. I've tasted it, and it's good. No tricks this time."

"What if it's been poisoned?"

Natalie was chewing. "If I drop dead, you'll know for sure."

Zee wondered if Natalie might be kidding as she crawled that way. She picked up the sandwich and pulled it apart, still not convinced spiders weren't going to pop out. But it looked fine, and it smelled okay, so she took a bite. Natalie was right. It wasn't bad. She ate it quickly, then grabbed the water bottle Natalie had left for her and drank it down in two long gulps.

When she finished, she noticed that Natalie was back in her corner, still eating her sandwich, nibbling on the crust like a mouse.

The rattling of chains echoed off the walls.

She looked up and saw Forrest backing slowly out of the cell, pulling someone along with him. It was a man, but he was hunchbacked, and his arms and legs were misshapen, giving him an awkward gait, one arm hung longer than the other. Like Natalie, he'd been stripped of clothing. His skin appeared nearly translucent. Clumps of white hair covered a spotted, mostly balding head. Drool fell from one side of his mouth as he was yanked to the center of the room and forced to sit in the folding chair, which squeaked under the slight weight of him.

Forrest attached the chain hanging from the man's left arm to a metal hook on the left side of the room and then did the same for the other side. He worked fairly quickly for an injured guy, but if he was the Heartless Killer, then that would mean he probably did this on a regular basis.

When he was done, Forrest straightened and looked at Natalie. "You've eaten and you have your medicine," he said. "So now you owe me. I want you to question Dog and find out why he tortured and beat his only son."

Zee's full attention was on Natalie, who simply nibbled at the edges of her bread, ignoring Forrest completely. That worried her. And rightly so, because when she looked back at the killer, she saw his face redden before he pivoted on his feet and disappeared behind the stairwell. That worried her even more, because the last time he disappeared under there, he'd pulled out a hose. The water had made a mess of things. Nearly drowned Natalie, and the straw still stank.

He returned quickly, this time holding a long leather whip.

Zee kept her eyes on him.

He lifted the whip in the air, and with a flick of his wrist, he made the leather crackle and snap.

The man in the chair flinched, but he had yet to howl, which made her think that maybe there was a wild animal still hidden within the cell.

Natalie kept on eating. *Nibble, nibble, nibble,* her eyes darting around as if she was afraid someone might take her food.

Zee kept blinking—once, twice, three times—hoping it would all go away. Maybe this had all been a long, drawn-out nightmare, and any second now she'd be back in her room shuffling her tarot cards or reading today's horoscope. But a few blinks later, she was still there. And so was the man. And Forrest, and Natalie, her new best friend.

Forrest ducked beneath the chain to get to Natalie's cell. Once again he stood close to the bars. "You're a psychotherapist, and this is your patient," Forrest told her. "Dog wants to know why he tortured his only son. Was he born sick? Or was it something else? My mother told me long ago that he was once a good man. I want to know if that's true. If you don't get him to talk, I will have to punish him, and then you, too. I will beat the very last breath from the old man if that's what it takes. Do you understand?"

Natalie didn't move.

"I know you do," he said before he returned to his place behind the decrepit man.

Zee watched all three people, her gaze darting from Natalie, to the old man, and finally back to Forrest. Waiting. Watching. The clowns had known all along where Forrest lived. They had danced and pointed, telling her which way to go when she was lost. It all made sense now. This was a circus, all right. And she was the only spectator.

"Ask him!" Forrest shouted, making Zee jump.

Nobody else moved.

The tip of the leather whip hit the old man's shoulder, splitting him open. His cry of pain came out, sounding like the screams of a dozen people.

Natalie frowned.

Finally. Something.

The snap of the whip had worked this time. Natalie buried the rest of her food beneath a pile of straw and then crawled to the door of her cell, where she could get a better look at what was going on. "Stop it," she said in a tiny voice.

Zee wasn't sure if she was telling the old man to stop screaming or telling Forrest to stop hurting him.

"Leave him alone," Natalie said, looking at Forrest now.

Forrest's eyes narrowed. "Ask him the question."

"Old man," she began.

"His name is Dog."

"Dog," she said, "why did you beat and torture your only son?"

Dog grumbled and mumbled. Zee could tell that he was really trying to answer the question, which surprised her.

The whip snapped again, slitting open Dog's other shoulder.

This time he howled.

It was the same piercing cry Zee had heard many times before. There was no other animal inside his cell. Dog was one and the same.

The expression on Natalie's thin face was a mixture of horror and rage as she cried, "Dog! Look at me!"

The silence was deafening.

And once again Forrest raised his arm, ready to strike again.

Unable to take any more, it seemed, Natalie began to shake the bars as she shouted, "What did you do to your son?"

She shook the metal bars so hard, Zee thought she might break right through.

"He took her from me," Dog said at last, his voice hoarse. The clarity of his words surprised everyone, including Forrest.

"Who did he take from you?" Natalie commanded.

"My wife."

"You were jealous of your own son?"

Forrest looked tense.

Dog began to cry, his eyes like leaky faucets, his entire body trembling.

"You didn't like the attention your wife gave your son," Natalie said, "so you tortured him?"

Dog growled. Gone was the sadness. His eyes widened, and his nostrils flared. "She only loved him! Everything she did was for him! I hated him. I wished he was never born. But when I harmed her little boy, her prized possession, she grew angry. And that anger was directed at me . . . *only* me."

Forrest looked at Natalie in confusion.

"He preferred your mother's anger and hatred over nothing at all," Natalie told him.

"Is that true?" he asked Dog.

Dog's head bobbed.

Forrest's expression changed suddenly, and Zee wasn't sure what he was thinking as he furiously worked to unchain Dog. Once that was done, he shoved him back into his cell, shut the door with a clang, and secured it tightly.

"He could have had both," Natalie said as Forrest blew out the lantern and walked away.

Forrest got as far as the steps before he turned and said, "What did you say?"

"Babies need a lot of care," Natalie told him. "If your father had been patient, he could have had both your mother's love and his son's love."

THIRTY-EIGHT

Not long after Colin had left, Jessie grabbed her purse. "Come on," she said to Olivia. "Let's go."

"Where are we going?"

"To Woodland. I want to look Arlo Gatley in the eyes when they take him away."

"Why?"

"It's something I need to do."

"What if he's dangerous?"

"If the police haven't arrived, I won't get out of the car until he's in handcuffs." Jessie didn't want to freak Olivia out, but there was no way she was going to leave Olivia home alone. "I always carry pepper spray," Jessie told her, "and we can bring Higgins along for the ride, too."

Olivia jumped up from the couch and grabbed the leash and a couple of treats for Higgins.

They had been on the highway for at least five minutes when Olivia turned to Jessie and said, "Are you all right?"

"Why do you ask?"

"You don't look well, for one thing. I'm worried about you. The cut on the side of your face looks kind of puffy and swollen."

"Don't worry. I'm taking antibiotics. I feel fine."

"I overheard some of your conversation with Colin, and I think he's right," Olivia said. "You should be concentrating on making sure you don't go back to jail. I'm scared."

Jessie's heart sank. "I'm sorry I've worried you. I don't want you to be scared, okay? Two different women have agreed to testify against Parker Koontz in court. Everything will be fine."

"Promise?"

"Yes," she said, wishing she felt as confident as she sounded. "But I also need to find Zee Gatley, okay? I have no idea if she is safe. She could be alone and scared. Now that her dad might be in trouble, she'll need my help more than ever."

"You're right," Olivia said. "She needs your help."

Jessie smiled at Olivia. "You're an amazing kid—you know that?"

"Yeah, so I've heard."

They both chuckled. The rest of the ride was quiet, Jessie lost in her own thoughts and Olivia busy texting her friend.

As soon as Jessie turned down the familiar street, she saw lights flashing and pulled over to the side of the road.

"What's going on?" Olivia asked.

"I'm too late."

An officer had his hand on top of Arlo's head, helping him into the back seat of the cruiser.

Higgins whimpered, the dog's way of letting them know he needed to go to the bathroom.

Jessie pointed ahead. "The neighbors won't mind if you take him to that empty lot over there."

Olivia put the leash on Higgins and led him away while Jessie leaned against the hood of the car and watched three police vehicles drive slowly past. Arlo Gatley had been arrested as a possible murder suspect. She could see the neighbors peeking out windows, probably grabbing their phones and letting one another know that they'd been right all along and the bogeyman was finally gone.

Olivia was headed back her way when someone called out.

Jessie looked over her shoulder and watched the woman jog toward them.

"That's Mrs. Goodman from the other day," Olivia told Jessie. "You know, the lady I talked to, the one with all the kids, the one whose house I went into, and you freaked out because you thought—"

"I got it," Jessie said, shushing her.

The woman was out of breath by the time she caught up to them. She introduced herself to Jessie and then said, "I can't believe my luck in seeing you both here." She had something in her hand, and she gave it to Olivia. It was the picture of Zee they had blown up.

"Not more than thirty minutes ago," she said looking at Olivia, "my brother stopped by, saw the photo you'd accidentally left behind, and instantly recognized the man you were asking about. My brother and this guy attended the same elementary school." She put her hands in the air. "What are the odds? First my brother stops by, and then to see you both here."

The woman had Jessie's full attention. "Do you have a name?"

She nodded. "Forrest Bloom."

Jessie made a note on her phone.

"Is your brother still friends with him?"

"Oh no. I don't think they were ever friends. According to my brother, Forrest was in class one day and gone the next. My brother said Forrest and his family used to live on a farm somewhere around here. I wish I could be more help."

"You've been a great help," Jessie said. "Would you mind if we exchanged numbers in case I think of any more questions or if I need to talk to your brother?"

"That's fine." They exchanged information, and then Jessie and Olivia headed for the car.

As soon as they were back home, Jessie grabbed her laptop.

"What are you doing now?" Olivia asked.

"I need to find out everything I can about Forrest Bloom."

"You're still going to look for Zee?"

"Why wouldn't I?" Jessie asked.

Olivia shrugged. "I don't know. I guess I thought since her father was arrested that there might not be any point." She scratched the side of her face. "If he killed all those people, then maybe he killed Zee."

"I had thought about that," Jessie said, "but logic tells me Arlo wouldn't have hired me to find his daughter if she hadn't been missing. And my heart tells me Zee needs me more than ever now that her father is in jail."

"That makes sense," Olivia said. "Do you think that Forrest guy might be able to help you find Zee?"

"At this point he's our best lead."

Olivia pushed herself from the couch, disappeared inside her bedroom, then returned with her own laptop. "What exactly are we looking for?"

"You have school tomorrow," Jessie reminded her. "You need to work on your report."

"This totally counts, since I'm using Zee's case as part of my school paper. Of course, I'll change the names to protect the innocent."

Jessie sighed as she returned her attention to the map on her computer. An hour later, she still hadn't located anyone by the name of Forrest Bloom. Instead of using pay databases to try to gather information on him, she looked through her browser and clicked on a free public database. She then accessed property appraiser records in different counties, including Yolo County, searching for Forrest Bloom's name.

His name popped up, but all hopeful anticipation was dashed when she read that the Bloom farm had been sold years ago. The problem was, none of the records stated whom the property had been sold to, which was information she could use since the new owners might be able to shed light on what had happened to the Blooms and where they had moved to.

For the rest of the night, she kept at it, checking and cross-checking, using every database she could think of until she finally hit pay dirt. Marcus Hubbard had bought a farm in Woodland from a man named Brody Bloom. She wrote down the property owner's name and telephone number. It was too late to call now. She'd have to call in the morning.

Olivia had fallen asleep on the couch next to her. Jessie took a moment to watch her sleep. She was growing up so fast. She had a lot of the same facial features as Sophie. The same nose and full lips. If her sister was alive, did she think about her daughter? Or had she simply moved on, like their mother?

THIRTY-NINE

First thing Tuesday morning, after his wife and kids pulled out of the driveway, Ben Morrison finished dressing, grabbed an apple from the bowl of fruit sitting on the counter, and jumped into his van parked in front of the house. The engine sputtered for a few seconds longer than usual before roaring to life.

The first time Ben had seen Sophie Cole on TV, he'd never thought his investigation into her disappearance would become so entangled with his own accident.

Last night he'd focused on the stolen vehicle. At the time of Ben's accident, investigators had referred to it as an open-and-shut case. Vernon Doherty had stolen the car and was driving drunk when he plowed head-on into a tree in Auburn. The morning after the crash, it was confirmed that the stolen vehicle belonged to Caleb Montana, who'd reported it missing.

The police had brought Mr. Montana in for questioning, and, of course, Ben had done his own thorough investigation, but everything had pointed to Vernon Doherty and his long list of criminal activity.

Two recent discoveries had changed all of that.

One, Sophie Cole used to steal cars. And two, she didn't have a car the night she'd stormed out of the house, but somehow she'd managed to get all the way to Auburn.

One quick search in the right database was all it had taken for Ben to discover that Caleb Montana had a son named Lucas, whose driving record at the time was less than stellar, including joyriding and underage driving; in both cases his parents had been forced to pay a hefty fine.

Which brought him to his meeting with Lucas Montana, a twenty-five-year-old rookie insurance salesman in Folsom.

Traffic was light, and it didn't take Ben long to get where he needed to go.

The young man greeted him on time, with a fresh haircut, suit, and tie—the whole nine yards. Ben took the seat Lucas gestured to in front of a neatly organized desk and pulled out the accident report from ten years ago, which included an eight-by-ten glossy of the stolen Ford Pinto—a twisted hunk of burning metal.

Smile gone, Lucas leaned forward to take a better look at both the report and the picture. When he finally looked at Ben, he said, "So I guess you're not here to buy insurance."

"Sorry, kid."

Lucas sighed as he loosened his tie. "What do you want?"

Ben gestured toward the picture. "I was in the passenger seat of that car when it went up in flames."

The kid's full attention fell to the side of Ben's face, where thick scars covered part of his jaw and most of his neck. He was used to people staring. It didn't bother him. The kid looked a little nervous, which spoke volumes.

"I'm sorry," Lucas said, elbows on his desk, palms up.

"You lived in Elk Grove with your parents at the time," Ben said. "Is that right?"

"Yes."

"And now?"

"I live with my girlfriend not too far from here, but I'm not sure why that would be any of your business."

"Just a few more questions, and I'll get out of your hair. I promise."

The kid looked more than a little jumpy but seemed to be doing his best to appear calm.

"The accident happened after midnight on Friday night," Ben said, "which in reality was Saturday morning."

"Yeah, so?"

"Your dad reported the car missing on Saturday at approximately ten in the morning."

Lucas shrugged. "Okay."

"But the car was actually stolen around, let's say, eight o'clock on Friday—wasn't it?"

"How would I know?"

"Because your dad was working the night shift, and he had carpooled with coworkers." Ben aimed a finger at the kid. "*You* took the car joyriding that night with friends in Sacramento—didn't you?"

"Joyriding?" Lucas asked. "I don't even know what that is, but so what if I did? What are you getting at?"

The kid was lying. "What I'm getting at, Lucas, is that you didn't have your license yet, but you took the car to Sacramento to party with your friends. At some point during the evening, your dad's Ford Pinto was stolen. But when you found out the next morning that your dad had returned from his trip and reported the car stolen from Elk Grove, you were off the hook—weren't you? Your parents never knew you took the car to begin with."

Lucas straightened in his chair, his hands clasped neatly in front of him. "It's been years. I don't remember where I was or what happened that particular night."

"I think you do. I'm a crime reporter with the *Sacramento Tribune*. We both know that too much time has passed, and even if you fess up now, you won't be in trouble with the law. I'm investigating a cold case that has nothing to do with you, but has everything to do with that Ford Pinto. If you tell me the truth right now, I won't publicize your name as one of the people I talked to in my write-up about this case. If you refuse, I'll mention your name, and people with questions will come calling."

A tall gray-haired man leaned his head into Lucas's office. "Everything all right?"

Lucas's face reddened.

"Everything's fine," Ben answered. "You've got an exceptional young man working for you. I think he's convinced me that I need whole life to go with my car insurance."

The man tapped his hand against the wall and smiled. "Okay, I'll leave you two alone."

"I took the car," Lucas said with a sigh. "Dad and Mom never knew."

"Did you leave the key in the car?"

He swallowed. "I don't remember. Probably. How can I be sure you won't use my name in your story?"

"I'm a man of my word." Ben stood and gathered his file, then grabbed a couple of Lucas's business cards and held them up. "I'll make sure to send some business your way."

As Ben exited the building, his heart raced. Now that he knew Lucas had borrowed his dad's car and brought it to Sacramento on the same night Sophie had disappeared, it made sense that Sophie had stormed out of the house after arguing with Jessie, happened upon a Ford Pinto with the key possibly still in the ignition, hopped in, and driven to Auburn.

He was still missing pieces to the puzzle, though. How did Vernon end up with the key to the car? Or was it all one big coincidence, and he happened to steal an already stolen car? But Leanne Baxter had stated that Ben had left the Wild West with Sophie and Vernon, that the three of them had left at the same time. Only two of them were in the car when Vernon slammed into a tree. He was right back to square one: What happened to Sophie?

Walking across the parking lot, Ben thought about his last conversation with Jessie. She didn't trust him, and she had good reason. He had yet to tell her about his talk with Sophie's old friend, Juliette. But he kept telling himself it was because he wanted to spare Jessie the pain of knowing the truth about Sophie. Sophie was bisexual. So what? The part that didn't sit well was all the rest. If Juliette was to be believed, Sophie was trouble with a capital *T*. She stole cars, then lured men into her trap and robbed them.

He needed to come clean with Jessie, tell her everything he knew. He slid his phone from his pocket and dialed her number.

FORTY

After calling Marcus Hubbard in Woodland and leaving a message asking him to call her, Jessie drove to the police station where they were holding Arlo Gatley. He'd waived his right to be booked into the station in Yolo County.

She signed in at the front desk, asked to speak with Colin Grayson, and then took a seat and waited. A few minutes later Colin appeared. "What are you doing here?"

"I want to speak to my client Arlo Gatley about his missing daughter."

"Jessie, that's not a good idea."

"I need to see him, Colin. I need to figure out what I'm going to do next. She suffers from schizophrenia. Without her father to look for her, she has no one." She sighed. "This is important to me."

He shifted his weight.

"Did you find something in Arlo's house? Is that why he was arrested?"

"We found the necklace. The father of the twins came to the station last night and confirmed that it belonged to their daughter."

Jessie anchored her hair behind her ear. She felt strangely betrayed by Arlo Gatley, an awkward man whom she'd been quick to defend against a world filled with bullies.

"Wait here," Colin said. "I'll see what I can do."

It wasn't long before he returned. She could talk to Arlo, but the meeting would be recorded. After she agreed, she was stripped of her belongings. She knew the drill. Instead of being led to the window area, she was taken to a small room with a table and two chairs. She sat quietly and waited. Colin had disappeared.

A good thirty minutes passed before Arlo was escorted into the room, his hands cuffed in front of him. He took the chair at the table across from her. His eyes were puffy and bloodshot.

He frowned. "They told me that the necklace they found in my house belonged to one of the twin girls found dead recently. Is that true?"

"Yes."

"I didn't do it," Arlo told her.

"Didn't do what?"

"Didn't do any of the things they're suggesting I might have done. I never saw those girls in my life. And I have no idea where my daughter is. I would never hurt anyone."

"I trusted you," Jessie said. "I fell for your stories about being bullied throughout your life. How does one person manage to be disliked by an entire neighborhood? You sit in your driveway for hours at a time staring at nothing. What is that about?"

"I miss my wife. There are days I can't be myself around Zee, so I wait for the emotions to pass."

Jessie stiffened. She was falling for it again. The sad face, along with the melancholy tone of his voice, made her the ultimate sucker. "You wouldn't allow me to see the rest of your house."

"I'm uncomfortable with other people in my space. I have nothing to hide. I just like my privacy—that's all there is to it."

"What about the screaming in the middle of the night? Mrs. Dixon said she used to be awakened by loud shrieks."

"Zee has suffered from hallucinations all of her life. It's taken years to get her on the right medication."

The man had an answer for everything. "You've been secretive with me from the start, refusing to let me take a look through your house and then acting disinterested when I showed you the picture of your daughter that revealed a young man taking her photo." She angled her head as she kept her gaze on his. "But you have an answer for everything—don't you, Arlo?" She glanced at the two-way mirror and then back to Arlo and said, "I've got to go."

His eyes watered. "What about Zee?"

She wondered if the tears were all part of the act. "I haven't found her yet," Jessie told him, "but I'm not going to give up."

His shoulders relaxed.

She looked him in the eyes. "I need to know if you ever heard Zee mention a boy by the name of Forrest Bloom."

Much too quickly he shook his head as if he couldn't possibly fathom his daughter with a boy.

She let out a drawn-out sigh.

"They can't keep me here—can they? I didn't do anything wrong."

Jessie exhaled. "I don't know what's going on, Arlo. My advice to you is to come clean and tell them everything you know." She stood and gestured toward the officer, letting him know she was ready to go.

"Find Zee," Arlo pleaded as she walked away.

Colin caught up to her at the front of the building as she collected her things. "If you have a minute, we'd like to ask you a few questions about your time spent with Arlo Gatley prior to today."

"There's nothing to tell."

"Humor me."

She regretted coming at all. Seeing Arlo made her question herself all over again. Innocent or guilty? She had no idea. "Which way?"

Colin led her past a maze of cubicles and down a narrow hallway.

"Talk is being thrown around that Arlo may have killed his daughter."

She didn't know what to think about that.

"You do realize, don't you, that your tendency to always root for the underdog could blind you to the truth?"

She stopped in her tracks. "And I hope you realize that your team tends to lean too quickly toward *closing* a case instead of actually solving it."

Clearly annoyed, he kept walking.

She followed.

"After receiving tips from the neighbors," Colin told her, "police have been stationed at the house. They'll start digging up the backyard in a few hours."

"Those neighbors have it out for the guy."

"Why is that?"

"Because he's different, quirky, and he has big ears."

"Come on," Colin said, disbelieving.

She snorted. "He's been bullied his entire life. His daughter has schizophrenia. People don't like people who aren't like them." And yet even as she said it, she knew she needed to get real. If Arlo had been bullied all his life, it would make even more sense that he would want revenge on mankind.

The conversation stopped when Colin opened the door to the conference room. She looked at the men in suits sitting at the table.

From the looks of it, the FBI had been invited, too.

Fuck.

———

Jessie's interview, which turned out to be more of an interrogation, lasted nearly two hours. She had just arrived back home and was about to return Ben Morrison's call when her phone rang. It was Marcus Hubbard.

"Yes, this is Jessie Cole," she confirmed when he asked. "Thanks for returning my call."

"You said it was important." His voice leaned toward unfriendly.

"I'm looking for a young man named Forrest Bloom," Jessie said. "According to public records, Brody Bloom sold his property to you. I was hoping you might be able to tell me where I might be able to find Brody's son, Forrest."

"Did something happen to Brody?"

"I don't know anything about his family," Jessie said. "I just have a few questions for Forrest Bloom."

"Is it about the farmhouse?" he asked.

"The farmhouse?" Jessie asked. "According to the appraisal report, he sold the property to you."

"Brody Bloom sold me fifty acres of farmland. They kept everything else: the house, the barn, and approximately ten acres of surrounding property."

"Forrest Bloom still lives there?" she asked.

"I have no idea. I only know his father owns everything but the fifty acres. I'm a busy man. If this doesn't concern me or my property, then we're done here."

"Yes," she said, her adrenaline racing. "Thanks for calling ba—"

The line was disconnected before she could finish.

Jessie looked at the time. It was a little past noon. If she took off right now, she could get to Woodland in twenty-five minutes, hopefully get a chance to talk to Forrest Bloom. If he wasn't home, she would leave a note to have him contact her, and still return home before Bella's mom dropped Olivia off after school.

She looked through the window over the kitchen sink and saw Higgins sleeping beneath the tree in the backyard. She'd left him with a bowl of fresh water, and the weather wasn't too hot today. Seeing the cast on his leg reminded her that she needed to take him back to the vet and see when he could get it removed.

"Focus," she reprimanded herself. She'd deal with Higgins tomorrow.

She took a breath. Today she needed to talk to Forrest Bloom. He might be the only person who could tell her where Zee might have gone. She looked at the notepad by the phone, where she'd written down Hubbard's phone number. Using her laptop, she used a mapping device to locate the farmhouse where the Blooms might still live. After writing down the address, she logged the street and city into her map app on her cell and left the house.

FORTY-ONE

Ben sat at the top of the metal bleachers overlooking the soccer field where Abigail was practicing with her team. He looked at his watch. Practice should have ended ten minutes ago. He had an appointment with the coroner, and he didn't want to be late. The coroner who had signed off on Vernon Doherty's autopsy report had since passed away. But Melissa Erickson had been trained by her predecessor and was willing to go over the report with him.

The coach called the players into a huddle, one arm around the goalie, the other around his daughter's shoulder. Eyes narrowed, Ben stood, his gaze locked on the coach as he made his way to solid ground and walked by the other parents waiting for their children to come off the field.

The coach's thumb brushed against his daughter's neck. She didn't flinch, didn't seem to notice. The coach flashed a wide smile at Abigail before the team straightened and said in unison, "Go, Pink Panthers!"

The coach was giving the girls high fives by the time Ben reached Abigail. "Come on. Time to go."

Abigail gave him the side eye. "The coach wants to talk to me."

"No time," Ben told her. "Grab your things."

The coach came between them and offered his hand. "I don't believe we've met. Henry Rogers, Emily's father."

Ben had no idea who Emily was, and he had no interest in talking to the man. Bright eyes, phony smile. Instant dislike.

"Dad," his daughter reprimanded when he didn't move to take his hand.

Ben sighed and shook the man's hand. "Gotta go. Late for a meeting." As Ben turned away, he gave his daughter a stern look, a warning she knew well, which got her moving again.

"You didn't have to be so rude," Abigail said the moment they were out of earshot.

"How long has he been your coach?"

"Ever since Mr. Jacobs had a stroke."

"You need to be careful around him."

She grabbed her things and then marched ahead to the car.

He slid open the van door.

Abigail angrily tossed her things into the back seat.

Once they were both in the van, he started the engine and waited for her to buckle her seat belt. Her face was red, and he wasn't sure if it was from running around for the past hour or if she was truly angry. "What's going on?"

"Why don't you tell me, Dad? You and Mom hardly speak anymore. You walk around in a weird daze half the time. And then you embarrass me in front of my friends and my coach. Are you and Mom getting a divorce?"

"What?" He backed out of the parking lot and then drove slowly to the exit. Abigail waved and smiled at her friends, trying to pretend that nothing was wrong.

He didn't understand his daughter lately. His wife constantly reminded him that she was at that age. Hormones were raging. She'd be smiling one minute, moody the next. "Your mother and I are fine," he tried to assure her. "We love each other, and we're not getting divorced."

"Well, that's hard to believe, since you're never home."

"Your mother and I both work long hours every day to keep a roof over your head and to pay for that uniform and those new soccer shoes on your feet."

"Mom stays late at the hospital because she's helping to save lives, but what's your excuse? You're writing stories about dead people."

He did his best to reel in his frustrations. "I'm going to let that one go, young lady." He frowned as he kept his eyes on the road. "I want you to keep your distance from Henry Rogers until I've had a chance to talk to him."

"What does that even mean? He's my coach. Why do you need to talk to him? Because he's friendly? Emily will find out, and nobody will have anything to do with me."

"He's too hands-on with you girls."

"Hands-on? Are you serious? That's disgusting. If you talk to him, I'll quit soccer and never talk to you again." She crossed her arms and sank lower into her seat.

Less than fifteen minutes later, he was pulling into a parking lot outside of a one-story brick building.

"Where are we?"

"At the county morgue. I need to talk to someone. It won't take long." He climbed out of the van and told her to do the same.

"I'd rather stay in the car."

"No can do." He gestured for her to get out.

She pulled a face, then climbed out and stomped toward the entrance.

Inside, Ben was told his daughter would have to wait in the front area while he went to the back of the building. "I'll be right back," he said.

Abigail plopped down into a plastic chair in the corner and grunted.

Ben's footsteps echoed off the walls as he made his way down the corridor. The place smelled of antiseptics. He was offered a face mask but turned it down before he was led into the autopsy room, where Melissa Erickson was expecting him. The floor was tiled, and everything else was stainless steel. The room could be compared to a big industrial kitchen.

Melissa Erickson tossed a blue paper sheet over the corpse lying on the steel table, then pulled her face mask to her chin. "You wanted to talk about an autopsy concerning Vernon Doherty—is that right?"

"Yes."

"Terrel Manderly, the coroner you asked about when you called, was my mentor."

"I see."

"I looked over the report, and I feel confident in saying that I knew Terrel well enough to tell you he would have included smoke inhalation as cause of death if it in any way contributed to Vernon Doherty's passing."

"But he didn't list it," Ben said. "What does that say to you?"

"Well, first I'd have to point out that the number one cause of death in any fire is smoke inhalation. Smoke is a mixture of heated particles and gas, which are often toxic. Once you breathe that in, there is no room for oxygen. Small particles are inhaled deep into the lungs. Vernon Doherty showed no signs of carbon monoxide in his blood, which tells me he was dead before the fire started."

"What about bruising and lacerations on other parts of his body?"

"Hmm. Even if the outside of a body is charred, the inner organs are usually fine. If the skin splits, muscle can be exposed. But lacerations, unless deep, won't usually be revealed. Broken bones, on the other hand, would show a pattern that would be distinguishable."

It was quiet for a moment before she asked, "Is there something else?"

"This might be a strange question," Ben said, "but bear with me. In your professional opinion, could Vernon Doherty have been dead before first impact?"

"Other than the driver's blood alcohol level, there are no other indications of cause of death," she said. "No heart attack or anything like that, if that's what you're alluding to?"

Ben shook his head. "Not exactly. Let's pretend for a moment that someone else was driving. Hypothetical, of course."

"Of course."

"In that case, could Vernon Doherty have been dead for up to an hour or two before the crash occurred?"

She frowned. "It's possible, but difficult to determine because of the time it took to pull the wreckage and get to Vernon's body. Rigor mortis is normally the first thing noted by an ME. Rigor normally starts in the smaller muscles in the face and neck within hours of death and then lasts up to thirty hours or so."

"And rigor mortis had set in," Ben said.

"By the time his body was examined, yes." She raised a brow. "Does that help?"

He nodded. "Thank you for taking the time to meet with me. You've been a big help." She was knowledgeable and helpful, but unfortunately, he still wasn't any closer to the truth about that night.

Jessie kept her eyes on the road as she thought about Arlo and the hopeless look she'd seen on his face at the police station. It bothered her to think she'd been so easily fooled.

She used Bluetooth to call Colin, letting him know she was headed to Woodland. There was no answer, so she left a message. After she hung up the phone, she thought about the image of the man in Zee's sunglasses.

Had Zee become infatuated with Forrest Bloom and run away with him? Or perhaps he was taking advantage of Zee's mental instability.

Intent on finding out, she got off on Exit 33, following the directions on her phone, which took her down a seemingly endless country road. She passed by an equestrian facility followed by a variety of crops, finally making a right onto a gravel driveway.

By the time she parked and shut off the engine, she realized that even if she headed home now, she wouldn't be back before Olivia returned from school. She picked up the phone and left Olivia a message, letting her know she'd be home soon after Bella's mom dropped her off.

In front of her was a faded blue farmhouse with peeling paint and a crumbling roof. She grabbed her pepper spray, climbed out, and slipped it into her back pocket.

The bottom of her shoes crunched against the pebbly rocks as she walked along, breathing in the scent of manure mixed with honeysuckle. Two wobbly wooden steps brought her to a wraparound porch. She knocked, waited, and then looked around before pressing her face next to the only sliver of glass not covered by the flowery-print curtains hanging inside. With her hands cupped around her eyes, she could see past a couple of worn couches. There was a round wooden table circled by four high-back chairs. The placed looked neat and well taken care of.

After knocking again, she walked over to one end of the porch, where she could see fields of tall grass dotted with trees. She walked back down the steps toward her car, plunked her hands on hips, and stood there for a moment. *Zee,* she thought. *Where are you?*

Looking over her shoulder at the house, she decided it would be crazy to leave without taking a better look around. With her mind made up, she turned around and followed the dirt path that led around the side of the house. Maybe someone was in the backyard. Surely Forrest Bloom would understand her concern once she explained that Zee was missing. Judging by how happy Zee had looked in the pictures, Forrest and Zee were friends, at the very least.

When she got to the backyard, she took another long look at her surroundings. The only movement was a horse in a distant field. About twenty feet away was a barn. It was wrong to trespass, but she'd come all this way, and she hated to leave knowing he might be nearby. "Hello!" she called out.

A strangled cry floated through the air.

She stopped and listened, then figured she was hearing things.

There it was again. In the distance she saw what looked like a pig-pen. Figuring an animal might be pinned or trapped within the fence, she headed that way, hoping she could help. As she passed by a crudely built wooden box, she heard the noise again.

Her skin prickled.

It took her a few seconds to realize the noise was coming from inside the rectangular box. Both sides of it were warped, but the top looked newly constructed with fresh plywood. Jessie leaned over and struggled to lift the lid before she saw that the plywood had been nailed shut. Heart pounding, she dropped to her knees. "Is someone in there?"

This time she heard the muffled screams loud and clear.

Her adrenaline roared to life. She jumped to her feet. *Oh my God.* Her only thought was to get whoever was inside out of there.

"Help me!"

Her stomach quivered as she tried again to open the lid. It was no use. *The barn.* There had to be tools inside. "I'm going to get you out of there. I'll be back!"

She turned and ran for the barn in hopes of finding a crowbar, anything at all to remove the lid. When she stepped inside, she slid her phone from her back pocket to call for help. By the time she heard movement behind her, it was too late.

FORTY-TWO

Ben and his wife were in their bedroom. The door was locked. Melony was pacing the floor in front of the bed while Ben changed out of his work clothes.

"What were you thinking?" Melony asked him. "Bringing our daughter to the morgue? Did you know she caught a glimpse of a corpse as it was wheeled through the hallway?"

He shook his head. "She didn't mention it."

"What's going on, Ben? You promised me twice that you would get help."

He sighed.

"I talked to Lori Mitchell today, and she said she called and left you a message to come see her and that you never showed up."

"Melony," he said after he pulled a T-shirt over his head, "I've got a lot going on right now. I really don't need to be lectured. I'll make another appointment. I promise."

She stopped pacing and instead crossed her arms tightly over her chest. "Abigail said that you embarrassed her in front of her friends and the new coach."

"Have you met the guy?"

"Of course I have. He's a good man, a decent husband and father. He's a busy man, just like you, but he finds the time to coach the girls."

"I might think that was a very generous way for him to spend his free time if I hadn't seen the way he touched some of the girls, including our daughter."

"What are you talking about?"

"He's a phony, Melony. His hands were everywhere, including around Abigail's shoulders. He had the team in a huddle, and I saw his thumb brushing against her bare neck. I didn't like it."

Melony stiffened. "I'm sure you're imagining things."

"I hope for Abigail's sake that you're right."

He grabbed his car keys from the top of the dresser.

"Where are you going now?"

"It's a long story."

"I have time." She released a heavy sigh. "Are you seeing someone, Ben? Because if you are, I want you to tell me right now. I don't want to hear it from Susan or Diane across the street."

Ben stared at her, shaking his head. *An affair?* He had to hold back any amusement he was feeling because judging by the look on her face, she was serious. He slipped the keys into his pants pocket, walked up to her, and put his hands on her waist. "There has never been anyone but you. Not now. Not ever. I love you."

She rested her head against his chest, and for a long moment they stood silently breathing each other in.

Ben was the first to speak. "I need to talk to Jessie Cole about her sister, Sophie."

"Why? What's going on?"

"I haven't been completely truthful with her, and it's weighing on me."

"You've been holding things inside. That's not healthy, Ben. Jessie Cole isn't the only one you need to open up to."

"You're right, but I need you to be patient with me for a little while longer. Jessie needs to know the truth about her sister. I've learned things about Sophie Cole. Things that Jessie won't want to hear. She doesn't trust me as it is, but my conscience won't allow me to keep what I know from her any longer."

"That bad, huh?"

"Yeah."

"Go, then, and get this over with so I can spend time with my husband."

He kissed her on the forehead, and then both cheeks, and finally the mouth. "Our anniversary is coming up soon. What do you think about a week in Hawaii?"

She opened her mouth to speak, but he put a finger over it. "No kids," he said. "Just the two of us."

"Money is tight and—"

"We'll make do. You deserve to be pampered."

"We'll talk later," she said. "Hurry home."

It was six o'clock by the time Ben found a parking spot and made his way to Jessie's house. He knocked, heard the dog bark, then looked up and saw Olivia looking out the window at him.

He waved, then watched her disappear. Until he heard the pitter-patter of feet coming down the stairs, he wasn't sure if she had recognized him. When she opened the door, it was clear she was upset about something.

"What's going on? Are you okay?"

"I can't find Jessie. She left a message telling me she'd be home soon, but that was hours ago. I've called everyone I can think of, but nobody knows where she is."

Higgins barked as someone walked by, so Ben stepped inside and shut the door. The phone rang. Olivia left him to run back to the main part of the house. By the time he reached the top step, she was hanging up the phone.

"Wrong number."

"Why don't you tell me exactly what's going on. Did you try calling her cell phone?"

"A dozen times. There's no answer. I think she turned her cell phone off, and she never does that."

"Did you check the office down the street?"

She nodded.

"Okay, let's back up a bit. Before you left for school, did Jessie tell you anything at all about what her plans for the day were?"

"No, not really, but I can guess. She'd been spending most of her time on the Zee Gatley case."

"Is that the missing girl?"

Olivia nodded. "She told me this morning that she'd had a breakthrough."

"What sort of breakthrough?" he asked, hoping Jessie would walk through the door at any moment.

"It's sort of complicated."

"Try me."

"When Jessie was at Zee's house, she found a shoe box full of her possessions under the bed. On Saturday morning, we were sorting through the things in the box when we saw a picture of Zee wearing some funky sunglasses. In the lens we saw a man's reflection. Jessie had the picture blown up, and we went to Zee's neighborhood and asked people if they recognized the man in the photo."

"Any luck?" he asked.

"No, not until last night when we drove back to Zee's house and ran into one of the neighbors. She told us her brother recognized the guy in the picture. He said his name was Forrest Bloom, and he grew up on a farm somewhere in Woodland."

"And you think that's where Jessie might have gone today?"

Olivia wrinkled her nose. "I just know Jessie was working on try-ing to find out where he lives now, and when I asked her about it this morning, she said that his family had sold the farm." Olivia walked to the kitchen, grabbed a notebook, and held it up for him to see. "I found this earlier. It's an address in Woodland, but I have no idea if it has anything to do with Forrest Bloom or where Jessie might have gone."

He made note of the address on his phone, then wrote his cell-phone number on the same pad of paper. "It's still early, and I'm sure Jessie is fine, but I'm going to drive to Woodland and see what I can find out, okay?"

"Really?"

He smiled. "I wrote my number there for you to call if Jessie returns."

She nodded.

"What kind of car does she drive?"

"A dark-green Jeep Grand Cherokee. Older model."

"Got it. I'll call you in an hour to check in."

She nodded again. "There is one more thing I think you should know before you go."

He waited.

"Zee's dad, Arlo Gatley, was arrested."

"Why?"

"Jessie noticed that Zee was wearing a necklace in the picture Arlo Gatley gave her of his daughter. The necklace looked exactly like the one that belonged to one of the twin girls recently found dead."

The news stunned him. "Are you sure?"

"Yes. There's just so much crazy stuff going on. First Jessie was attacked, and now she's missing. I'm scared."

"Okay," he said, trying not to let her see his concern. "Lock the door behind me. Call me if you hear from Jessie."

As he drove off, he couldn't help but worry about Jessie. Had her car broken down? Maybe her cell phone ran out of batteries, and she would be home at any moment. He tried to tell himself that there was no reason to get worked up.

But why had Jessie called hours ago to tell Olivia she'd be home soon?

He had no idea what was going on, but seeing Olivia and hearing the worry in her voice made him step hard on the gas, keeping a keen eye on the road in front of him, hoping he'd see Jessie's broken-down car on the side of the highway.

FORTY-THREE

Jessie woke to the smell of urine and rotten eggs. Her head throbbed. Her vision was blurry. When she tried to move, she realized her hands were fastened behind her back, tied to a wobbly wooden chair.

Her gaze darted around the room, but it was dark, and all she could see were shadows. Her heart raced as she took in her surroundings. Two crudely made cells and another room with a door that was secured with a thick chain and a padlock. A movement in one of the cells caught her attention.

What was that? "Who's there?" Jessie asked.

"My name is Zee Gatley. Who are you?"

"Zee?"

"Do you know me?"

Jessie's heart raced. "Your father hired me to find you."

Another shadow caught her attention. In the cage next to Zee's, a pale-skinned human on his or her hands and knees crawled to the middle of the cell, looking out as if to see what was going on. It was a woman. She looked as if she'd been starved. Her face was gaunt, her cheeks sunken.

"That's Natalie," Zee said. "And there's a man named Dog in the locked cell over there."

"Natalie Bailey?" Jessie asked.

"Yes. Are you here to save us?"

The sight of the two women made Jessie want to cry. She'd found Zee and now Natalie, too, yet she was powerless to help them. She'd fucked up. Never should have gone charging into the barn before calling 9-1-1. "I'm sorry," she finally said. "Someone's locked inside a box outside. My only thought was to get her out of there. I never should have—"

"She's still alive?" Zee asked.

"Who?" Jessie asked. "The girl in the box? Is it a child?"

"I don't know her age. I never saw her, but I know the madman found her on the side of the road and locked her up after she disobeyed his orders."

"My husband is Mike Bailey," Natalie said. "Do you know if he's alive?"

Jessie inhaled slowly, swallowed, then looked at the woman who had moved closer now. She was so very thin. Her ribs jutted out, and the skin framing her haunted eyes was a sickly grayish yellow. "He's alive," Jessie told her. "Your husband has been all over the news asking for help to find you."

Natalie began to sob, her body shaking uncontrollably.

"That chair you're sitting on isn't chained to the wall or the floor," Zee said. "If you could move closer to me, I might be able to reach through the bars and untie you."

Jessie pushed up and forward, a hopping motion. The chair moved forward at least an inch, then nearly toppled over.

"Not so fast, stupid." Laughter followed.

"Sorry," Zee said.

Jessie scooted her chair a half inch at a time toward Zee's cell. Arlo had warned her that Zee could get violent. Without meds, there was no telling what she might be capable of, but that was the least of her problems.

"Hurry," Zee said. "He could return any moment."

Natalie had crawled closer to watch. Jessie had seen stories about the woman who had been taken from her home in the middle of the night. She looked nothing like the pictures her husband had provided the media.

Jessie hobbled onward, her legs shaking. She wasn't sure she would make it, but then Zee reached out with long arms and helped pull her along, dragging and turning the chair so she could work on untying the ropes. The girl was strong. Jessie could feel her fingers pulling and tugging at the rope, determined to free her.

Footsteps above, and then a scraping noise stopped Zee midmotion. "He's coming."

The woman in the other cell dropped to the straw-covered ground and scrambled to the corner, where she curled into a ball like a pill bug.

Jessie thought Zee would run off to a far corner, too, but her fingers began to move at a quicker pace, frantically working the knots in the rope. Pulling. Tugging. Loosening.

Jessie was helpless to do anything but sit there. She pulled on her wrists until Zee yanked her hand, making it clear she wasn't to move.

She thought about Olivia being home alone, how worried she would be when Jessie failed to return before dinner. She thought about Colin. Once he heard the message she'd left him, he would find her. He'd find them all.

A door creaked open, allowing a sliver of light inside.

Footsteps sounded on the stairs, so loud they shook the rafters.

The young man standing before Jessie looked exactly like the image reflected in Zee's sunglasses. A regular-looking guy, average in height and weight. He wore denim pants and a plaid shirt, the sleeves rolled up to the elbows, as they had been in the picture she'd shown around. His hair had grown some since and hung straight and limp past his ears, one of which was missing a chunk of flesh.

It was *him*. Her attacker.

He set a tin bucket on the ground, then lit two oil lamps, smiling when he caught Jessie's gaze. It was only then that she was able to catch a glimpse of the underlying evil within.

Through it all, Zee continued to work at the ropes. Nothing was going to stop her. She wanted her freedom.

Forrest Bloom walked over to her. He slapped Zee's hands away, grabbed the chair Jessie was sitting in, and dragged it back across the room away from Zee.

"How many more people are you going to bring down here?" Zee asked. "It's getting a little crowded."

Zee's fingers were wrapped tightly around the metal bars when he walked back to her cell. He clasped his hands over hers and held tight. "Feeling claustrophobic, Zinnia?"

She yanked her hands free, then swiped them across her pants as if to rid herself of his germs.

He chuckled, then left her alone, turning his attention back to Jessie.

Jessie lifted her chin. "I called the police. They'll be here any moment now."

"No, you didn't. After I knocked you over the head, I was able to use your thumbprint and check all calls made before I shut your phone off. But not before I wrote down Olivia's name and number so I could pay her a visit later. You know—tonight or maybe tomorrow. Whenever I happen to get bored." He lifted a brow. "And believe me—sooner or later I always get bored."

The idea of this man going anywhere near Olivia made her chest tighten. "There are people who know where I am," Jessie said as she fiddled with the rope, felt it give. "This is the end for you."

"Oh, really? Who do you mean, exactly? Do you think it will be that lunatic crime reporter you've been hanging out with? Is he going to save you?" He rubbed his chin. "Hmm. The one who doesn't remember who he is or where he's from? We both know it won't be that cop friend of yours . . . the one who arrested Zee's father as a suspect in the Heartless Killer case. He's way too busy to come looking for you."

"What are you talking about?" Zee asked. "How would you know any of that? You're a liar."

He smiled at Zee. "I watched the news. I have Internet. I'm not a mental case like you."

"Is it true?" Zee asked Jessie. "Was my father arrested?"

"It's true," Jessie said. "I spoke to him this morning, told him I would find you."

Forrest Bloom clapped his hands. "And you kept your promise. Good job, Jessie Cole."

"My dad doesn't like being trapped in confined places any more than I do," Zee said before she shook the bars again, making a racket. "Let me go, you fucking monster!"

Forrest's facial expression changed in an instant. He lifted both hands and shook the metal bars right along with her. "You're the fucking monster!" he yelled. "When are you going to get that through your fucked-up brain? Where are all those people you talked about that were going to come out here and mess with me? Huh? Where are they, Zee?"

She backed away. "You're an ass."

"You're a coward," he shot back. "If you could see yourself now, you would realize all those voices in your head are just worthless thoughts in your brain. Nothing more."

"Shut up!" Natalie shouted. "Just shut up! Both of you!"

"Well, would you look at that," Forrest said. "The only daughter of the most inept social worker ever to live has some life left inside of her."

"What's your endgame? What's the purpose of all this?" Natalie asked as she pushed herself to her feet, struggling to stay upright as she walked his way. "Did you bring us all here as payback for the things your daddy did to you? Is that why we're here? Did anyone ever tell you that two wrongs don't make a right? Did you ever stop to think that you've become worse than the man who you spent your whole life despising?" She snorted. "How can that possibly make things better for you?"

Forrest turned away and walked back to the stairs.

Jessie felt the ropes loosen. She continued to work her hands, rolling her wrists, ignoring the areas where the rope had chafed her skin. *Almost there.* Just a little longer and she'd be free.

"Where are you going, Forrest?" Natalie asked. "Off to get the hose again? Or do you have more spiders to toss at us? They were delicious, by the way, kept us nourished, thank you very much. What new-and-improved torture have you worked out in that demented mind of yours?"

Forrest stopped, his foot resting on the first step. "I'm going to rip that tongue right out of your mouth."

"Oh no!" Natalie cried, her tone lined with sarcasm. "Please don't do that!"

Jessie tried to ignore the scene playing out before her. She needed to focus on getting free. Maybe Natalie knew that. Maybe she knew exactly what she was doing.

"Did you get kicked out of college because you were as dumb as your father always said you were?" Natalie asked him. "Or did one pretty girl too many turn down your unwanted advances? I mean, come on—nobody could love a boy like you. A boy his own father couldn't love."

Forrest had continued climbing the stairs as Natalie hurled every taunt imaginable at the man. Once he reached the top, his steps were loud stomps above their heads.

"I think that's enough," Zee said in a low voice. "Getting him mad is one thing, but he's going to kill you."

Jessie looked over at Natalie then, and she could see it in the woman's eyes. That was exactly what she wanted. This wasn't about escaping. She had given up. She was ready to die.

FORTY-FOUR

The moment Ben caught sight of the weather vane jutting out from the top of the barn, he pulled over to the side of the gravel road and shut off the engine. Without hesitating, he climbed out and stayed low as he crept along one edge of the road until he could see the front entrance to the farmhouse.

Parked in front of the house was Jessie's car.

His heart sank. Who the hell was Forrest Bloom, and what was Jessie doing in there? The fact that she had told Olivia she would be home soon and now wasn't answering her phone didn't bode well.

He pulled out his cell and called the police, gave them the address, telling them that an armed and dangerous man was inside, holed up with a gun and plenty of ammunition. People were hurt and they needed an ambulance. Disconnecting the call, he then slid his phone into his back pocket and continued onward. If he ended up being wrong, then so be it. He'd learned from experience that he'd rather be wrong than sorry.

He made his way to the front entry, hoping he hadn't been seen through a window. Slowly he turned the doorknob. Locked.

Standing still, he listened. Heard nothing. No sounds of appliances running, no radio or voices emitting from a television set. He backtracked down the porch stairs and made his way around the side of the house. He didn't like guns and therefore didn't carry one, but for the first time in his life he wished he'd put more thought into that decision.

As soon as he rounded the corner, he heard the grunts and squeals of hungry pigs. A dog barked in the far distance. The skinny dirt path took him the long way around the house. His senses were on full alert as he passed by a coffinlike box. Thinking he heard something, he took two steps back, leaned low, and rapped his knuckles against the plywood.

"Hello?" came a small voice.

His pulse raced. What the hell was going on?

His gaze swept over his surroundings before he sank to his knees. "Hang tight," he said. "I'm going to get you out of there." He felt around the lid until he found a spot where new wood met with old. He jammed his fingers into the tight space and pulled, gently at first.

"Help me." The voice sounded weak and raspy, causing a rush of adrenaline to sweep over him and give him extra strength. Blood rushed upward through his body to his neck and face as he grunted and pulled and yanked the lid free. The metal lock was still latched, but the rotted wood beneath failed to hold.

The young girl inside the box was naked and so fragile-looking it broke his heart to see her lying there. She was somebody's daughter, and he thought of Abigail. Dark shadows circled her eyes. As gently as possible, he scooped her bony frame from her makeshift grave and carried her in his arms as he ran back around the house and down the driveway to his car. He placed her inside, grabbed his water bottle from the front, and gave it to her, then rummaged through a pile of Goodwill donations Melony had asked him to drop off weeks ago. He found an extralarge T-shirt and slid it over her head. She didn't blink or move or say a word.

He told her that the police would be there soon and to hang on just a little while longer.

Her body shook, but she said nothing.

He didn't want to leave her, but the thought of Jessie inside that house with a lunatic was too much to bear. He couldn't risk waiting for backup. "There are other people in there I have to help, okay?"

No response. The blank look in her eyes made him clench his jaw. He shut the side door and then ran around to the back to grab the tire iron.

Tears wet his face as he ran back to the house and up the stairs to the porch. Stopping at the front door, he launched a booted foot close to the door frame. Splintered wood rained down around him as he kicked his way through.

———

Jessie struggled to loosen the ropes around her wrist when she heard the *thump thump thump* of Forrest Bloom's feet as he came down the stairs to the basement.

The monster was back.

Time was running out.

She yanked her arm as hard as she could, surprised when one of her hands slipped free of the ropes. Her breathing hitched. She needed to play it cool, didn't want him to know what she'd done.

All was quiet as he came forward.

Chills crawled up her spine as she realized he only had eyes for Natalie. He was furious with Natalie for taunting him. It wasn't until he passed by that she saw what he held behind his back—a butcher knife, the steel blade glittering in the semidark room.

"He has a knife," Jessie warned.

But that only stirred Natalie to insult him further. "What's the matter, Forrest? Don't tell me that after all this time we've spent together, I finally managed to piss you off. The truth sucks—doesn't it?"

"You're just like your slut mother," he said with a sneer. "The bitch knew my father was abusing me, and it turned her on—didn't it? I watched her shake his hand, her eyes heated with desire as she looked at him. He could have taken her right then and there atop the kitchen table if he'd wanted to. Your mother was panting for it. But she was a used-up hag by then—wasn't she? Your own father didn't want her, and neither did mine." He snorted.

"The difference between me and you," Natalie said, her voice calm, "is that I know the truth about myself and my mother. My truth can't be distorted by the words of a demented man who still cowers beneath his father's larger-than-life shadow. You're weak, Forrest. You couldn't help yourself, let alone your poor, dear mother, and now everyone must pay."

At the same moment he raised his hand, Jessie lunged for him, bringing the chair still fastened to her other wrist with her. She used her free hand to grab a fistful of his hair and then pulled back hard.

"Rip his head off!" Zee shouted, rooting her onward.

The knife dropped to the floor.

Enraged, he whipped around, picked Jessie up along with the chair, and tossed her to the side. Her head smacked against the wall. Pain sliced through her skull, and her other hand came loose as she hit the ground.

She crawled toward the knife, but he snatched it from the ground and turned back to Natalie, who remained pressed against the metal bars.

"Run!" Jessie shouted to Natalie.

But Natalie didn't move a muscle, not even when he brought the blade down hard and swift, through the bars and straight into her chest.

"No!" Zee jumped up and down, her hands clasped around the metal bars as she shook them, shouting obscenities.

Natalie's fingers held tightly to the knife's handle as she stumbled backward, a smile on her face.

There was nothing Jessie could do for her now, and she looked away. Chaos surrounded her. Upset about Natalie, Zee was making a racket. An eerie howling came from the enclosed cell, and a loud crash sounded upstairs. She wondered if Forrest had heard the noise as he walked past her. He stopped at the bottom of the stairs and picked up the bucket he'd set there when he first came down.

What was he up to?

"I usually interview the people I bring down here to my private study," he told Jessie, speaking loudly enough to be heard over Zee's anguished cries.

Jessie crawled toward the chair, hoping to use it as a weapon.

"But I learned enough about you when I sliced open your pretty face," he said as he headed her way.

The dizzying pain in Jessie's head slowed her.

"Leave us alone!" Zee cried.

Taking slow, casual steps toward Jessie, Forrest said, "I wish I could replay the look on your face when you saw the blood on your hands. A private eye who's afraid of blood. Who would have guessed?"

"I hate you! I hate you!" Zee chanted.

Jessie reached the chair just as he caught up to her. She grabbed the wooden leg and pulled, but it was too late. He stood over her, a sickening smile on his face as he poured the contents of the bucket over her head.

Blood, thick and dark red, oozed its way through her hair and down both sides of her face. She squeezed her eyes shut as rivers of the stuff coated her nose and mouth, making it difficult to breathe.

He took his time, making sure to drench every part of her, including her clothes.

Unable to hold her breath, she coughed, her hands shaking as she swept a thick coat of blood from her eyelids. This was not the stuff made for movies. No ketchup or corn syrup and red dye, but instead metallic and coppery in scent.

Every muscle stiffened.

She tried to move, willed herself to do so, but her body failed her. Finally her eyes snapped open. Through the blood dripping down her face, she stared at Forrest Bloom as an eerie howling erupted in the enclosed cell behind him, dampening his glee.

Beneath her blood-soaked body, her pulse raced.

The eerie sounds of a dying animal caused more confusion.

What was going on? It was as if the devil himself had come to life.

Again she concentrated on moving, cursing herself for being so fucking weak. The notion that the mere sight of blood, whether it was a small drop or an entire bucket, could shut her down was illogical. She needed to get out of there.

As the howling increased in volume, the rattling of the metal bars ceased. Calmly, barely loud enough to be heard over the howling, Zee said, "It's pig's blood, not human blood. You can do this."

Forrest pounded on the wall of the enclosed cell, trying to quiet whoever was making all the noise. He pulled a metal loop of keys from his pocket and slipped a large key into the slot in the padlock. Chains rattled. At the very moment the cell door came open, Jessie saw a man appear on the stairway above.

———

Ben couldn't make any sense out of what he was seeing or hearing as he came forward, taking slow, careful steps down the stairs and into a dark underground room lit only by kerosene lamps. A long mournful cry of a dying wolf was followed by laughter. A woman sat motionless in the middle of the room, drenched in blood. Another woman lay faceup in a cage, her eyes wide, her hands clasped around the knife in her chest. The other cage was also occupied. But the young woman inside that one was alive and well, talking to the one covered in blood, trying desperately to get her moving.

And within a room he couldn't yet see inside of came another eerie howl, like nothing he'd ever heard in his life. It wasn't until he got closer that he recognized Jessie as the person covered in blood.

Continuing on at a slow pace, he heard a voice.

"I'm tired of your filth and your constant racket, Dog. Today is a fine day to die."

Ben stopped at the entrance of the enclosed cell and tried to make sense of what he was seeing. A tall, lanky boy he assumed to be Forrest Bloom was tossing darts at an old bearded man confined in chains. Every time a dart struck, the man he called Dog would howl. And the boy would laugh.

Ben inhaled as familiar images of broken bodies and bloodied corpses flashed in rapid succession through his mind. He squeezed his eyes closed, and when he opened them again, he saw a dart strike the old man's forehead, right between the eyes. The howl that erupted from the man's gaping mouth was a bloodcurdling cry filled with pain and sorrow.

The scene before him was madness, and he could feel the tingling of rage flushing him with heat as he drew in slow, steady breaths. Images continued to flash through his mind: the woman who'd been stabbed, Jessie covered in blood, and the girl in the box. It all needed to stop. It needed to stop right now.

The howling continued as he stepped inside the tiny room.

When the man's captor realized he wasn't alone, he turned around and merely smirked at Ben as he raised his hand to throw another dart.

Ben swung the tire iron, catching him on the shoulder.

The young man stumbled backward, his back against the wall as Ben tossed the tire iron to the side, stepped forward and wrapped all ten fingers around Forrest Bloom's neck.

"You can't stop me, old man," Forrest cried out in a raspy voice. "Nobody can stop me. Dog! Take care of him, or I'll put you in the snake pit."

The old man didn't move. He simply shook his head as he leaned tiredly against the wall, one eye still open, watching, perhaps waiting for his captor to take his last breath.

Ben felt a tightening in his chest as he continued to squeeze. The bloody images wouldn't stop, flickering like a filmstrip in his mind's eye, again ending with the sickly pale girl he'd found in the box. His muscles quivered as the beat of his heart thundered within his ears.

Forrest struggled to get free, his legs flailing and his fingers clawing at Ben's as he tried to get loose. Ben felt the muscles and tendons in his forearms tighten as he crushed Forrest Bloom's windpipe until finally he felt the full weight of the madman's body in his grasp.

And there it was. A wispy sort of gasp escaped Forrest's mouth before his body went slack.

Only then did the old man's shoulders relax. His head fell gently to the right, and a trickle of blood slid from the place between his eyes where the dart protruded. The old man was dead—of that Ben was sure. Only then did he let go.

Forrest Bloom crumpled into a heap at his feet.

Ben stepped over the body, pulled the dart from the old man's forehead, and tossed it to the ground before he felt for a pulse. Just as he'd thought, there was none. He gently closed the old man's eyes and then bent over and grabbed the keys from around the killer's neck.

Ben walked around Jessie, stepping through sticky blood, his shoes making a suctioning noise as he made his way to the first cell and unlocked the door. A loud whooshing sounded in both ears, like ten-foot waves crashing against the shore.

The dark-haired girl thanked him as she swept past. She went straight to the open door of the cell he'd just left and peeked inside.

Ben wasn't sure what she was doing, but he had an inkling she wanted to make sure her captor was dead.

By the time he unlocked the other cell and knew for certain the woman lying inside was dead, the girl was pulling a hose out from behind the stairs. He had no idea how long she'd been down there or what, if anything, had happened to her, but the normalcy with which she moved about was impressive. She turned on the water and then pulled off her long-sleeve coat and used it as a wet rag to wash the thick coat of blood from Jessie's face and neck.

Ben looked around, unable to comprehend all that he was seeing.

Sirens sounded in the distance, and it was then that he took a breath of rotten air and said, "Let's get out of here."

The girl dropped the hose, and together they helped Jessie up the stairs and outside, where he watched the dark-haired girl put her face to the sun and smile.

FORTY-FIVE

The sun had begun to rise the next morning when Jessie shot up in bed, her arms waving about as if to ward off whatever might be coming at her.

Somebody grabbed her arm, stopping her from flailing around.

"It's okay," he said. "You're safe."

It took her a second to realize she was home in bed. "Colin?"

"It's me. I'm here."

The dizziness passed, and she saw him clearly. She caught her breath and said, "It's good to see you."

"I'm always glad to see you."

She smiled.

"I wanted to make sure you were okay," he told her. "I've got to get back to work soon, but if it's okay with you, I thought I'd stop by later with some Chinese food for you and Olivia."

"Yeah, I'd like that."

"It'll be crazy busy for the next few weeks."

"Understandable." She inhaled. "Is Olivia home?"

"No. Andriana took her to school. She's doing good, though. She was with you at the hospital last night before we brought you home."

She put a hand to her temple. "I hardly remember."

"The doctor gave you something to help you relax." He shook his head. "I'm sorry about everything, Jessie. Mostly I'm sorry I wasn't there for you."

"It's not your fault. I rushed in when I should have been more careful."

"By the time I heard your message and found out what was going on, you were being brought to the hospital."

"It's been a crazy time for both of us. You've been busy. We both have." She pushed the covers off her, slid her legs over the side of the mattress, then got to her feet and wrapped her arms around him, holding him tight.

"It's okay," he whispered as he rubbed her back. "Everything's going to be okay."

Frightening images came to mind: Natalie lying in a pool of blood, Zee rattling the bars, trying to get out of her cage, the high-pitched wails as Forrest Bloom tortured the old man, and the silhouette of a man standing on the stairs.

Ben Morrison.

The look on his face when he'd seen Forrest Bloom torturing the old man was a look she'd never forget. As blood dripped off her face, she'd seen his eyes grow cold and hard, his jaw rigid as he wrapped his meaty fingers around the madman's throat, pressing hard, still squeezing long after the life had left the other man's body.

She stepped out of Colin's embrace and headed into the living room where Higgins greeted her, his tail wagging. "Good dog," she said, scratching the top of his head. The TV was on. One of the local news stations showed the long gravel driveway leading to the Bloom farmhouse lined with police cruisers and media vans.

Colin came to stand beside her. "You've been to hell and back. Maybe you should sit down."

He was right. Her knees felt wobbly. She took a seat on the couch.

"People have been calling in to talk about how Forrest Bloom was tortured by his father," Colin told her. "After his mother died, he returned to the farm to get revenge on his father. They're saying he kept his old man chained in the basement."

The man Forrest had called Dog, Jessie realized, was his father. Pictures of Ben Morrison flashed across the screen, and then a picture of a young girl with blonde hair and blue eyes. She was being interviewed from her hospital room. Her name was Erin Hayes. Ben Morrison had rescued her from the coffinlike box found on the property.

"I heard her screaming," Jessie said, her heart racing again. That was the voice she'd heard before she'd run to the barn. Erin was alive. She'd made it. Her eyes watered. "What about Ben Morrison strangling Forrest? Is he in trouble?"

Colin shook his head. "There won't be any repercussions. It was determined that Ben Morrison's actions were in the best interest of everyone involved. He wasn't carrying a gun, and he managed to get you and Zee out of there safely." He took a seat beside her. "You're lucky to be alive."

"What about Natalie Bailey?" she asked.

"She didn't make it."

Jessie's heart sank. "I could have saved her." She shook her head.

"Don't blame yourself, Jessie. It's not your fault. If it weren't for you, who knows how many more people would have fallen victim to the Heartless Killer? If not for you, Zee Gatley would still be locked up, and Erin Hayes never would have survived another twenty-four hours."

"Any word on where Zee Gatley is staying?"

He nodded. "Her father was released late last night. Arlo and Zee are back home."

"I'm glad."

"In a day or so, when you're up to it, we'll need you to come down to the station and answer a few questions."

She nodded. "You should go. I'll be fine."

After he left, she headed for the bathroom, turned on the water in the shower, and then went to the sink to brush her teeth, her reflection staring back at her.

Her hair was as tangled and matted as her thoughts.

A girl in a box.

A man named Dog.

A house of torture.

Fuck.

She couldn't get the sound of rattling cages out of her mind.

Butcher knives and a young woman with schizophrenia rooting her on. That was fucked up. She was never going to be the same.

Blood. Knife. Guts.

Numb, body and mind.

Get a grip.

"I live in one fucked-up world," she said to her reflection, using her toothbrush as a pointer.

She rinsed. Spit. "You could have stopped him."

As she stared at the mirror, studying the line of stitches on her left side under her chin, where the killer's blade would forever leave a mark, she decided if she was going to continue in this line of work, she needed to be vigilant, starting with taking a self-defense class. She would run and lift weights and figure out a way to overcome her aversion to blood.

Straightening, she narrowed her eyes and said, "You've got work to do."

FORTY-SIX

Two weeks after Jessie escaped the bowels of hell, she found herself sitting in front of the TV, drawn in by a news reporter's account of what they knew about the Heartless Killer up to this point.

The reporter started off by saying that psychiatrists across the country were still discussing the case, theorizing and seeking rationalizations for his actions. For the most part they agreed that Forrest Bloom wasn't merely a bad seed. After interviewing teachers, neighbors, and people who'd known him growing up, he didn't appear to have held any deep-seated hatred for his mother. The autopsy report showed no signs of brain damage.

Although most psychiatrists agreed that not all abused children grow up to be killers, they were quick to point out that every psychopathic killer known to mankind had been mistreated early in life. From what detectives had gathered so far, Forrest Bloom had been severely abused by his father since the time he could walk, prompting one female groupie to express her deepest sympathies for the killer and beg authorities for a lock of his hair.

Thanks to Mike Bailey, journals and reports written by Sue Sterling were found in storage. Although it seemed the ball had been dropped somewhere along the way by Child Services after Sue Sterling's passing, it was also determined that by the time she visited the home in 1999, the worst of the damage had been done. All in all, investigators were still sifting through Bloom's life on the farm, and would be for quite some time.

Jessie picked up the remote and shut the TV off.

Colin had filled her in on the rest. She knew investigators had talked to witnesses and people who had known Forrest Bloom over the course of his lifetime. As expected, the killer had been extremely isolated for most of his life. His relationship with his mother appeared to have been a normal one. During his years at UC Irvine, not too many people remembered him. With the exception of one professor and a roommate of two years, both of whom had described Forrest as quiet and socially awkward.

Forrest Bloom's grades put him in the top 5 percent of his class. He had no criminal record, not even a traffic violation. He never held a job, and until he met Zinnia Gatley, it seemed he'd never shown any interest in the opposite sex.

Authorities found three journals in Forrest Bloom's house. The killer had devoted an entire journal to descriptions of the abuse he'd endured at his father's hands. Forrest Bloom was subjected to both physical and psychological abuse at a very young age. It was no wonder he went on to inflict pain on others.

The other two journals included a total of twenty-one names listed in order of date captured. The list of names did not include his father, the man he called Dog. Beneath each name were details about the victims: age, approximate weight and height, occupation, hobbies, favorite foods, hopes, dreams, and fears.

Of the twenty-two victims, there were sixteen females and six males, ranging from the age of five to sixty-four, Dog being the oldest.

Another trait noted by Colin and others was Forrest Bloom's extreme cleanliness. His bed was made, the floors swept clean, and not a dirty dish or towel could be found. The only macabre items found within the house were three bleached white skulls lined up neatly on the pantry shelf. Who the skulls belonged to had yet to be determined.

Jessie stared at the blank TV screen, wishing she could spend a day doing absolutely nothing, but she had work to do. Her day in court had been moved up. In less than forty-eight hours, she would be sitting in the courtroom before a judge. And things were looking iffy at best. Friends and family were determined to defend Koontz at every turn. Other than Adelind Rain and Fiona Hampton, nobody had anything to share about Koontz's Peeping Tom tendencies.

By five o'clock that same afternoon, Jessie was working in the living room while Olivia did her homework at the kitchen table. Colin had called earlier to say he'd pick up a pizza on his way over, but as was the norm, he couldn't stay long. Andriana paced the living room, her cell phone pressed against her ear. When she disconnected the call, she said, "You're never going to believe this."

Jessie looked at her and waited.

"Parker Koontz is responding to certain commands."

Jessie raised an eyebrow. "I don't understand."

"I have a friend, a nurse who works on the same floor where Parker Koontz has been staying. She's been keeping an eye on him, and she told me that this morning he opened his eyes. Not only that, he moves his fingers in response to commands. She'll call me later if anything changes."

"If he comes out of the coma," Olivia said from across the room, "then you would be off the hook, right?"

"It's not that simple," Jessie told her, trying not to sound defeated.

Andriana sighed. "If only I'd looked at the video you took at the park before it was stolen. It keeps me up at night."

"You need to let it go," Jessie said. "Neither of us would have thought someone would bother to steal the GoPro."

"You can still look at the video," Olivia said without looking up from her homework.

Jessie and Andriana looked at each other before Jessie peered over her shoulder at her niece. "What do you mean, Olivia?"

Olivia set her pencil down, stood, and walked over to where they were sitting. She put her hand out, palm faceup, and said, "Give me your phone."

Jessie did as she asked.

"You asked me to order the GoPro for you after I told you about the one Bella uses, remember?"

"I remember. So?"

"So I ordered the newest model, the one that automatically hooks to your Bluetooth, and I set up an account for you, remember?"

"It rings a bell," Jessie said.

Olivia snorted as she clicked away. "All you have to do is go to your GoPro Plus account, then to the Hero Session, find the app, and there you go." She pushed another button and then looked at Jessie. "Do you want to view the video on your mobile or your laptop?"

"You have got to be kidding me," Andriana said.

By the time Colin showed up with the pizza, they were watching the video on Jessie's laptop, fast-forwarding to the part where Jessie followed Parker Koontz through the rose garden at Capitol Park.

Colin set the pizza box on the kitchen counter and then came to hover over Jessie to see what was going on. "You're all so quiet. Looks like serious business going on here."

"It's the video Jessie took when she was following the Peeping Tom," Olivia told him. She then went on to explain how the video was automatically uploaded via Bluetooth on Jessie's phone.

"Well, look at that. He definitely fired before you pulled out your gun," Andriana said.

"Can you rewind the video?" Colin asked.

She rewound the tape, then waited.

"Farther back," he said, his voice strained.

They all watched closely as she did it again.

"There! Hit 'Pause,'" he said.

Again, Jessie did as he asked. "What is it? What do you see?"

Colin pointed at the upper-right-hand corner of the computer screen. "See that man, the guy right there? The entire time you're walking, he's looking directly at you. Right as we hear a shot fired, he cuts off abruptly to the left and disappears."

She reversed the video again. They all watched him. "I see him," Jessie said, "but what does it mean?"

"It's him." Colin exhaled. "That's David Roche."

"Koontz's partner," Andriana said.

Jessie watched again. He was right. It was definitely him. "I went to his office to talk to him. He was so arrogant and full of himself, but I never thought he might somehow be involved in all this."

"Why would David Roche be watching Koontz," Andriana said, "unless he knew something was about to go down? Do you think there's a possibility he planted the blanks in Koontz's gun?"

A restless feeling settled over Jessie as she began to realize what this could mean. If David Roche was somehow involved, this could be the Holy Grail of evidence needed to prove she'd acted in self-defense.

"Why would Koontz fire at Jessie in the first place?" Colin wanted to know.

Nobody had the answer to that.

Andriana rubbed her temple. "If David Roche somehow deceived his partner, he's not going to be happy to learn that Parker Koontz is waking from his coma."

Colin frowned. "What are you talking about?"

"Andriana's friend works at the hospital where Koontz is staying," Jessie explained. "He's showing signs of recovering."

Colin smiled at Andriana and then grabbed Jessie's hand and pulled her from her chair so he could wrap his arms around her.

She laughed. "Are you happy about the video or Koontz's possible recovery?"

"Both. Everything. We might be able to keep you out of jail, after all."

FORTY-SEVEN

Two days later, after a long day of courtroom drama, rousing revelations, and celebrations, Jessie returned home to Olivia and Higgins, who had stayed up to say good night. As she watched her niece head off to bed, Higgins on her heels, Jessie found it hard to believe he was the same dog from only weeks ago. His cast had been removed, and he'd become more playful and less fearful of people. He'd also become dependent on Jessie whenever Olivia wasn't around, following her like a second shadow. She wondered how they'd ever gotten along without him.

Jessie plopped down on the couch, picked up the remote, and turned on the TV. For the second time in the past three weeks, she was the main story. On the screen, a reporter on Channel Ten news looked into the camera lens and talked about what went down in the courtroom behind closed doors.

"Parker Koontz, a well-known attorney in Midtown, awoke from a coma yesterday," the reporter said, "and was well enough to tell investigators that his partner, David Roche, convinced him to shoot Jessie Cole after he was told she would ruin the firm's reputation when the public learned of his Peeping Tom tendencies."

The report continued. "Events around the Cole-versus-Koontz case escalated when the receptionist at the law firm told the court that the firm was in financial trouble, and David Roche had set up a Key Man Insurance Policy, which compensates businesses for financial losses that often occur in the result of the death of a key player in a business. Many law firms have such insurance."

The reporter went on to talk about how David Roche had replaced real bullets with blanks, knowing that Jessie Cole would most likely return fire to protect herself and others. They went on to show clips of the video Jessie had taken, circling the area with a red pen where David Roche was clearly visible. Both men were charged. David Roche was taken into custody, and Parker Koontz would soon be transported to the prison infirmary.

Jessie shut off the television and headed for bed. It was late, and she still had trouble sleeping since the Heartless Killer incident. For the next few hours, she tossed and turned. Finally giving up, she lay awake, her mind churning. During the first week after Arlo Gatley's release, she'd talked to him more than once. During their last conversation, she'd been glad to hear that he was making a concerted effort to meet the neighbors. Whether out of guilt or shame for judging Arlo based on his looks and mannerisms and thinking the worst of him, or sheer compassion, the neighbors had come out in full force, plying him and Zee with home-cooked meals and invitations to barbeques. Mrs. Dixon, a long-time widow and Arlo's next-door neighbor, had invited him to dinner. He'd been surprised to admit that he'd enjoyed being in her company.

Despite solving the mystery of Parker Koontz, and her tremendous relief in knowing that the Heartless Killer had finally been stopped, she couldn't stop thinking about Ben Morrison.

A week after he'd saved her life, and others, he'd called her and asked to meet with her, telling her it was imperative that they talk. She'd met him at the office. After hearing what he had to say about Sophie, she'd been angry that he'd waited so long to tell her what he'd heard. At the time, she had a court case looming, so she'd pushed it out of her mind.

But now, as she lay in the dark, she thought about Sophie's friend Juliette Farris. After Sophie had disappeared, Jessie had met with Juliette on more than one occasion. She remembered Juliette coming across as quiet and sort of standoffish. Long before Mom ran off, Jessie had realized Sophie was a troublemaker. There was the time Sophie stole a pack of gum from the grocery store, and then was suspended from school after forging their mother's name, excusing herself from school due to illness. There were other things, too, but a car thief? Luring strange men away so she and Juliette could steal their money?

Sophie had a wild side, and she'd liked to let loose every once in a while, but Jessie also knew the Sophie who cried easily at movies and spent more than one weekend baking cookies to raise money for families worse off. All Jessie had to do was shut her eyes to see Sophie spending endless, sleepless nights watching over Olivia when she was sick with croup.

Ben Morrison, Leanne Baxter, and Juliette Farris had nothing to gain by making up lies about her sister.

And yet every time she talked to Ben, it seemed there was one more link between him and Sophie. And it always pointed to the last day Sophie was seen alive.

Her stomach tightened.

No matter how Jessie twisted the sequence of events around in her mind, Ben and Sophie's connection seemed to begin at the Wild West and end at the scene of the accident—an accident that had changed the course of Ben Morrison's life.

Ben had said they should focus on Sophie's last day.

Jessie began to tick off everything she could remember.

When Jessie had returned home early from work, Sophie was wearing a red dress. Her dark hair had been curled, and the way she'd done her makeup had made her look much older. She'd been antsy to get out of the house. They had argued. Jessie had lectured Sophie about being irresponsible. She had a daughter to look after. Jessie recalled telling Sophie that she needed to have a life, too.

But Sophie had always been selfish, and she'd marched around the house gathering her purse and sweater. The last thing Jessie had said to her was, "If you walk out that door, don't you ever come back."

Jessie swallowed the lump in her throat.

She thought about the stolen car Ben had talked about. Everyone had assumed Vernon Doherty had stolen the car, which made sense at the time because authorities assumed, rightfully so, that there had been only two people in the car.

But things had changed. According to Ben, the owner of the car's son had confessed to having taken his father's car without permission to a friend's house in Sacramento, not far from Jessie's house.

Did Sophie steal the car?

The last time anyone saw Sophie was when she'd left the Wild West with two men: Vernon Doherty and Ben Morrison.

If Leanne Baxter's account of what happened was to be believed, Sophie broke a bottle in the parking lot and used it to get Vernon Doherty to back off. Did she hurt him? Possibly even kill him?

Continuing with her line of thought and the sequence of events that day, she recalled what Ben had said about Vernon Doherty's autopsy. The report revealed that he was most likely dead before the car caught on fire because there had been no smoke in his lungs or carbon monoxide in his blood. There were two possibilities, as far as Jessie could tell.

Doherty could have died on impact, or he could have been dead at the Wild West before he was placed in the car. If that were the case, then that would mean Sophie could have been driving the vehicle that night.

Jessie's insides twisted as something occurred to her.

Her heart raced as she climbed out of bed, grabbed her computer, and took it to the family room to search the Internet for information on Ben Morrison's accident.

As she skimmed through one article after another, she already knew that if everything happened the way she thought it did, then Sophie's last day could only have ended two different ways.

Sophie either escaped without injury and walked away, or she was thrown from the vehicle.

The first scenario would mean Sophie could still be alive. The second scenario would lead Jessie to believe her sister had perished but her body was removed . . . or never found.

She clicked faster now. She stopped scrolling when she came to an image of the overturned vehicle. It was still in flames when the picture had been taken. It wasn't the car or the wreck that grabbed Jessie's attention, but the deep gorge beyond.

Jessie's hand went slowly to her mouth as she whispered, "Sophie."

Even if everything she'd learned about her sister was true, nobody could convince her that Sophie would have abandoned Olivia.

And that was when it dawned on her with such clarity she could no longer sit still. She made note of the name of the road where the accident had occurred and then went back to her room and pulled on hiking boots and a coat.

Next she went to the kitchen, grabbed a flashlight from the drawer, then left a note for Olivia in case she woke up while Jessie was gone.

FORTY-EIGHT

For two hours Ben had been sitting at his desk, looking over the accident report from his crash. Years ago he'd had every photo taken of the Ford Pinto—before and after the accident—blown up to eight-by-tens.

After the wreck was towed up the hill, it was placed on a flatbed. The windshield was broken—a large, gaping hole. *If* Sophie had been driving, and *if* she had not been wearing a seat belt, she could have easily been propelled forward into the night, before the car burned and rolled.

He thought of his last trip to the place where the accident occurred. In his mind's eye, he saw the ravine made up of a mixed species of woodland, dead trees, shrubs, and an uninterrupted patch of thorny blackberry bush that would be difficult if not impossible to traverse.

Why hadn't he seen it before?

Because he'd never once thought anyone else was in the car with him. His heart quickened as he looked at the time. Moving quietly through his bedroom, he made his way into the walk-in closet, where he dressed quickly. Ten minutes later, his wife found him in the garage piling tools into the back of the van.

"It's late, Ben. What are you doing?"

He kept working. "It's about Sophie Cole. I think I know what might have happened to her on the night she disappeared."

"She's been missing for ten years. It can't wait until morning?"

He slid the side door shut, then came around the van to where his wife stood and placed both hands on her shoulders. "This is important to me."

"Why?"

"I don't have time to explain. But I promise I'll tell you everything tomorrow."

"Does this have anything to do with you, Ben?"

He dropped his hands from her shoulders and raked his fingers through his hair. "This has everything to do with me."

"So, no matter what you find out there, this isn't the end—is it, Ben?"

"What do you mean?"

"For ten years you've been telling me that the past is the past and you were fine with not knowing who you used to be, but that's not true any longer. Is it?"

He said nothing.

"I'm worried about you—about us—because you haven't been yourself. You've become secretive and obsessive. You wanted better ratings for your newspaper, and after finding yourself face-to-face with a serial killer, that's exactly what you got. But I can see it in your eyes—it's not enough." She sighed. "If everything you've been doing lately, disappearing into the night at odd hours and failing to call home, is the beginning of some fantastical journey into your past, I'm not sure how much more I can handle."

This time he placed the palm of his hand on her cheek and said, "I love you, Melony—more than ever, and I promise to do whatever I must to make our marriage work because I don't ever want to lose you. But I also find myself yearning to know who I once was. Bits and pieces of my memory are beginning to return. You said yourself that the doctors knew that was not only a possibility but a probability. Tell me how to bury it all, and I will do everything in my power to do exactly that."

She frowned, and he gently brushed his lips against her forehead. "Go," she said. "Do what you have to do. We'll figure this all out tomorrow."

By the time he climbed behind the wheel and opened the garage door, Melony had disappeared back into the house.

It took Jessie much longer than she thought it would to find the area where the car had crashed into a tree and then rolled down the embankment before hitting another tree. Her Jeep was pointed down the hill and into the ravine beyond, two headlights shedding beams of bright light, giving her a path to follow.

She stood there for a moment, staring, wondering if she'd gone completely mad. Being out here at this time of night seemed like a fool's errand. The sun would rise soon, but it hadn't yet, and the creatures that used the dark as cover could see her, but she couldn't see them. She could hear them, though. A chirp. A strange intermittent cawing. A rustling and skittering of tiny feet. The croak of a frog in the distance.

A light breeze rustled the branches of trees, and for the first time in forever, she felt as if her sister was talking to her. She listened closely, her gaze focused on the terrain. Sophie was here.

Jessie pulled the hood of her coat over her head and slipped on the only pair of gloves she could find before leaving the house. They were thin with a flower print. Garden gloves. They would have to do. She didn't bother using the flashlight. The headlights were enough.

Taking one step at a time, she made her way down the hill to the tree that had stopped the car from rolling into the abyss.

The abyss.

The thought that Sophie might have been thrown from the wreck-age and left to die among brambles and overgrown brush made her insides churn. If she was down there somewhere, hidden in the over-grown brush and weeds, would there be anything left? Would wild animals have carried her off?

The sound of a car approaching pulled her from her thoughts. She looked back to the road and saw a vehicle approaching. The tree she was standing next to wasn't wide enough to hide behind, so she quickly but carefully stepped over the edge, where the hill met the ravine, and held tight to a shrub so she wouldn't slide too far. She hoped the car would pass by. It could be hikers getting an early start, or maybe people lived farther down the road. She wasn't sure.

But the car stopped and the engine was shut off. A door opened and then closed, and then opened and closed again. Whoever it was walked to the edge of the embankment. She couldn't look into the bright lights, but she could make out a silhouette. It was Ben. He stood perfectly still. He held something at his side—a tool—maybe a shovel or a rake. No. It was a sickle.

"Jessie?" he called.

The moment she heard his voice, she saw his face clearly in her mind as he squeezed the life from Forrest Bloom. Twitching jaw, puls-ing veins, nostrils flared as he tightened his grasp around another man's neck, easily taking his life. No one else had seen the look on his face. No one else had seen what he was capable of. And after the dead man crumpled to the ground at his feet, Ben had looked her way. In that instant their gazes had locked as if in a strange secret knowing of what lurked within him.

For the first time since she'd met Ben Morrison, she realized he wasn't the only one who wanted to know who or what he'd been before the accident, before his memories stripped his past from him, before he married and had kids and became a family man.

He was trudging down the hill now, moving much faster than her snail-like pace. As she had done, he stopped at the tree with its bent trunk and arthritic branches.

He was close. Too close.

The thinnest sliver of sun reached out to reveal her hiding place. He left his sickle leaning against the tree and came to the edge where he could plainly see her and she could see him.

Had he killed Sophie? The thought hit her without warning.

Bent over slightly, he offered his hand to help bring her up from her precarious holding. But she didn't take the lifeline he offered. Instead she released her grasp on a handful of brittle branches and found herself sliding, unable to get a foothold. She grasped for underbrush, felt the weeds and dead branches slide between her thinly gloved hands as she fell farther and farther until she was rolling into thorny brambles that clawed at her face, forcing her to shut her eyes, afraid she might be blinded.

She hit something solid, the smack to her body taking her breath away. A dead tree had blocked her descent and kept her from rolling farther into the ravine.

For a few seconds, she merely lay there breathing. Another moment passed before she tested her arms and legs to see if anything was broken. *Still in one piece,* she thought.

She sat up, the tangled vines hanging tight, tearing her lightweight jacket when she pushed herself to her feet. And it was then, out of the corner of her eye, that she saw a scrap of red fabric.

And she knew even before she took a closer look that after all this time, she'd found Sophie.

Walking that way, stepping through thorns and brush, she stopped just a few feet away from Sophie's final resting place. Her sister lay faceup in the deepest part of the thicket, protected by a blanket of thorny vines, her red dress faded by time, her skeleton intact. Jessie's next breath caught in her throat. For a moment she stood there unable to come to terms with what she was seeing. Her insides twisted and turned.

After all this time, she'd found her sister.

"Oh, Sophie." Tears slid down both sides of her face as she looked up toward the morning sky, now brushed lightly with orange and pink.

"Jessie," she heard Ben shout in the distance.

She wasn't sure how long she stood over her sister's bones before Ben found her. Disbelief and despair had settled over her shoulders, weighing them down. Loneliness pricked her skin. She wanted to scream out at the top of her lungs, release some of the emotions she was feeling. Instead she stood quietly, trying to accept the moment fully.

"You're okay," Ben said, his relief palpable, before his gaze followed the direction she was looking.

"Yeah," she said. "I'm okay."

"You found Sophie."

A long moment passed before Jessie found the energy to look away from her sister and focus her attention on him. "What made you come here tonight?"

"I couldn't sleep, so I did what I've done nearly every night since the accident. I went over the files and reports. But this time it was different. This time I knew that there was a possibility that Vernon wasn't driving. If he wasn't driving, then who was?" He shook his head. "Investigators at the time had no reason to think anyone else had been in the car, let alone search the ravine."

"What now?" she asked.

His brow furrowed. "What do you mean?"

She said nothing.

"When I reached for you, did you let go on purpose?"

She wasn't ready to answer him because she didn't know the answer.

"You're afraid of me—aren't you?"

"I don't know you," she said in her defense, still unsure. Still cautious. His expression was unreadable, and she wondered if he was angry. Frustrated? Confused? She had no idea.

Sirens sounded.

"Did you call the police?" she asked.

"Why wouldn't I? I didn't know if you'd broken your neck on the way down. I was thinking the worst and hoping for the best."

Maybe he truly was a blank slate. Maybe she could trust him, after all. He'd saved her life. Without his help, she never would have found Sophie. She smiled at him, a subtle twist of the corner of her mouth.

He released a ponderous sigh, obviously not happy to know she'd chosen to risk her life rather than trust him enough to take hold of his hand.

"What?" he asked when he saw the smile playing on her lips.

"Looks like we've solved another case. Twice in a matter of weeks," she added. "They're going to think we're some sort of bizarre investigative team."

"Bizarre?" he questioned. "The Cautious and the Circumspect."

"Or maybe the Young and the Restless," she murmured sadly, her gaze back on her sister.

"I guess that would make you the 'Restless,'" he said, but their few seconds of camaraderie were over and done with.

She looked toward the flashing lights above and stiffened. She didn't want people to think the worst of Sophie. What good would it do for the public and, more important, for Olivia to know the truth about her mother? "I'm hoping nobody ever finds out about Leanne Baxter's account of what happened on Sophie's last day. People would talk, and we both know it would all be meaningless. Unless you regain your memory, we'll never really know what happened outside the Wild West. It would all be speculation, and I wouldn't want Olivia to think less of Sophie . . . her mother."

"Leanne who?" he asked.

Again Jessie met his gaze, and for whatever reason she knew then that he'd come there to get answers for himself, but also for her and Olivia.

He took a step back and then turned to her and said, "Are you coming, or are you going to stay here with Sophie while I show them the way so we can get her up the hill?"

"I'll stay."

He nodded.

"She had a lot of good qualities, too," she told him.

"I'm sure she did," Ben said, waiting.

"Sophie had the most amazing singing voice. The sort of voice that brought tears to anyone who was lucky enough to hear her sing. And she could do wonderful impressions of famous people. She wasn't always easy to live with, but she sure could make me laugh."

"I wish I could have met her."

"Apparently you did."

It was his turn to smile. "I'll be right back," she heard him say as she turned back toward her sister, ignoring the sting of prickly thorns as she walked closer, removing the thickest brambles until she was at Sophie's side. She kneeled down and took Sophie's brittle fingers in hers as she remembered all the things they used to do together. Making clothes from scraps of fabric for their dolls, running around the back-yard hunting for Easter eggs, putting on lipstick and their mother's heels and playing dress-up. They rode bikes and pushed each other on the swing set. They loved playing Monopoly. They laughed often, and mostly they loved each other.

None of it had been a figment of her imagination.

Her mother, father, Jessie, and Sophie.

The memories were real, and for a moment in time, they had all been happy.

ACKNOWLEDGMENTS

It's good to have Amy Tannenbaum in my corner. Thank you, Amy, for sharing your wealth of knowledge and for offering to help me at every turn.

Thank you, Charlotte Herscher, for continuing to challenge me as a storyteller while also helping to bring clarity and emotion to every book.

Brian McDougle is the first real-life detective extraordinaire I've had the good fortune to meet online. He's funny, smart, and always willing to share his expertise. Thanks for your help, Brian.

Robin O'Dell. Copyeditor and fine-tuning miracle worker. Thank you so much for such a thorough read.

My fictional heroines, Lizzy Gardner, Faith McMann, and now Jessie Cole, aren't the only ones who need a team of people to get things done. Many thanks to Liz Pearsons, Sarah Shaw, and the entire Amazon Publishing team for your ongoing enthusiasm and support.

ABOUT THE AUTHOR

Photo © 2014 Morgan Ragan

T.R. Ragan has sold more than two million books since her debut novel appeared in 2011. A former legal secretary for a large corporation, she is now a *New York Times, Wall Street Journal,* and *USA Today* bestselling author. T.R. is author of the Faith McMann Trilogy and six Lizzy Gardner novels (*Abducted, Dead Weight, A Dark Mind, Obsessed, Almost Dead,* and *Evil Never Dies*). In addition to thrillers, she writes medieval time-travel tales, contemporary romance, and romantic suspense as Theresa Ragan. An avid traveler, her wanderings have led her to China, Thailand, and Nepal. Theresa and her husband, Joe, have four children and live in Sacramento, California. To learn more, visit her website at www.theresaragan.com.